ERIC MARGOLIS

The Golden State

First edition

This book was professionally typeset on Reedsy.
Find out more at reedsy.com

This book is dedicated to my grandparents and their parents.

Nothing unreal is allowed to survive.

Franz Kafka on his deathbed, asking that all
of his stories be set on fire.

Contents

Foreword

This novel intends to be upsetting at times and hopes to be thought-provoking at others. It does not pretend to submit any thesis on Americanness or Jewishness or Jewish-Americanness. You may invent any thesis you wish. Some but not all of the events are based on true history.

I am alone on the grassy shore—
does no one else care for the beauty of dirt?
Am I alone in my urge to catalog
half-glittering, fully-broken things?
I come from a quiet hollow of diaspora,
I live on the shores of cultural dissolution.
My name echoes Baltimore courts and
pearl traders on the shores of Arabia.
My work catalogs futile angst, angry
desires, remarkable feats.

Eric Margolis
New York City
2019

Prologue: Ariana

How to Change Your Name

1924, New York City

You want to change your name? If you want to change your name, wipe that kitschy smile off your stupid face. You cannot be happy. What is this, a musical? You must struggle to speak proper English beyond niceties and prattle like "How do you do?" and "One pound of flour, please." You must rot with loneliness. You must wish you had not come to the city and met so many crows squawking in a dead language that only ghosts can understand. You must despise the female gossip at the market and the nods from tallit-wrapped men on your way there. And you must hate New York. You must hate the gray-smog city that is not your home and you must dream of a place that is beautiful and where you will be free. A place like California.

You must be like Ariana Fuchs. She was unhappy. Even the curls of black hair that sprung out from her headscarf were unhappy. Unhappy loneliness rusted the edges of her words and rotted their cores, so when she spoke, she felt like a monkey trying to communicate with men, a baboon yodeling at the country club.

Now that is tsores. Gebrenteh tsores.

Unhappiness. And without it your name will never change.

You must also have an ugly name. Changing a name is difficult and requires much determining, so if your name is not considerably ugly you do not stand a chance. If your name is Bradshaw do not even think about it. If your name is Adams or Williams, not worth it. If your name is Elliot or McCarthy or even O'Connor I would recommend against it, although some O'Connors are unhappy.

Take *Fuchs.* You do not think this is an ugly name? This is not a good name, even in the Old World. It means fox, or someone sly or cunning, or a vile man with beet-red hair. It reeks of German, although her husband was born in what is today Soviet Estonia. You must look at the name in the English letters and have convincing that there is something squirming like a snake or leech or poisonous centipede. You must look at the Latin letters and see something overcompensating and desperate in the length or the brevity, the consecutive vowels or the clashing consonants. You must see history stamped into that name! When you pay the water bill and see the printed letters you must shudder with rage. This name, a name that is taken down on a 1908 census by a seventy-seven year old graybeard on a mule in Kopu, Estonia, and added to a list by the sheriff and his deputy. This name that is your husband's name when he is chopping wood in the forest during the Russian festival, and he sees smoke rising over his village, his precious village wherein lived every man whose sage whiskers he kissed and every woman who gave his family eggs. He must chop the wood and rend the bark and drink his own tears like they are wine.

An ugly name becomes uglier if you have an object that reminds you of the ugly history stamped into all ugly names. Like a small purse or a tattered book, or like the Spanish leather bracelet that your father kept in a box along with the Talmud he received on his thirteenth birthday. This history can be controversial, because it involves not only Hashem (adonai ehad) but also Jesús y el Espirito Santo of the Spanish Gentiles who had it made, and glittering Inti and shadowed Urcaguary, from whose Incan mountains the gold was mined. It is better when history leaks from this Spanish bracelet strung with a gold coin that has carved into it a gray spear and the black letters "CALIFORNIA", and it is best when this bracelet is known to have saved your family from many pogroms. Then you cannot forget your ugly history, and you will be all the wiser for it.

For history spills from an ugly name. History is water, blood, and wine. Life demands it, but if you find it all around you it is certain that you have perished.

Drink history and suck on its shadows. The Russians know you are a Jew because they watched from the shadows when your mother walked into a bakery to buy apple cake for Yom Teruah. Every day they are knocking on your windows and throwing stones at them to see if you are still alive. The Russians with the axes, the Greeks with their clubs, the Slavs with their stones, demolishing your world. They hang your mother in the street and strip her naked and whip her body so that flesh hangs down in tzitzit. Your father puts the bracelet on your wrist, and it glows faintly like a star and you and your brother run to Reb Shmuel who puts you in a train car to Vilna with the chickens. They squawk all through the night and your hearing will never be the same. You vomit many times and your brother clutches the bracelet and your wrist as if his life depends on it, and it does.

But only fools believe that history is trauma. This is not zikkaron. Save the yizkor for when your name is changed and your brain consists of tube televisions and air conditioning units. You must remember, but you must also understand. Understand that the sticks and stones of the Slavs and the leaden pipes of the Greeks were symbols of protest against the slavery of capital, and that the Czarists put the blame on to the Psychoanalysts and Jewish bankers, away from themselves, the leeches that slurped Odessa and the sweeping plain dry. Sense the slurping of history and the regurgitating in the vomit, on the train car, on the bare fields, in the winter rain.

But whether or not you vomited on the train car, on the bare fields, in the winter rain, if you want to change your name you must have an irrepressible will to live *more*. You must love to make life greater than what it is. Use art, use romance, use science, use God. Jump off cliffs and climb mountains, dance, dance, dance, and dance! All of the vomiting that comes with history may take the joy out of you for years, but in the long run, you must be irrepressible. A little girl in Odessa, you danced. A young woman in Vilna, no longer. You did not dance there and nor in New York. But after fifty years of never dancing, your son Leonard will take you out in Los Angeles, and after dancing there you never stop.

Vilde khaye! Rebittsen! Yefayfieyeh! The joy! You dance all night! You dance your son to sleepy eyes and a softly rising chest as if he is again an infant. You have control over your body. Your limbs and bones belong to you and you alone. Let freedom titter like a golden bird caged within you, and master the corporeal realm that surges with expressing, your expressing, you, sister, beautiful you.

When you go to change your name, this bird eggs you on. A name escaped from history. How freeing it will be! This bird's tittering rejects your husband's protests. He says you annoy him when you are angry? Be angrier! You are not angry enough! Destroy history! Change your name! How freeing it will be! How beautiful! How much like California!

Your husband does not want to change his name, but that is not the spirit of living more. It is not that you do not love him. You love his loyalty and his tenderness, his faith and the way he bears the factory smoke and iron loads of Canal Street, and the way he tells your children stories about Estonian castles and villages of snow. You love your husband, but you know that he is wrong. When you wish to change your husband's family name and he is of disagreement, some inner pintl comes in handy.

Last but not least, you must utilize the formally established process for the changing of names. Yes, yes, you must not forget the process. There must be government bureaus. There must be papers, a broker. You must ask your rebbe where to go and he must advise against it, saying a name-change is for spite alone and not worthwhile. So you must walk two hours in Manhattan in search of a building on a map to find it closed on Sunday.

Closed on Sunday? The goyim are bananas. Because now you must be waiting for Easter to pass but in the meantime, practice your English. You must be understood. You must not sound like a mongoose cantillating. "I am here to change my name. How do I change my name?" Practice the words! They are the difference between life and death. Practice them, you khamer! "I am here to change my name. How do I change my name?" Lign in drerd un bakn beygl! Practice while you hang laundry, while you cook dinner, while you pray and while you are making love on Tuesday once a month. "I am here to change my name. How do I change my name?"

Go to the designated building and perform your English for an old Welshman with ruddy cheeks. By a miracle he understands you. The problem is that you can't understand *him.* But he repeats himself enough times and you realize he can do bopkis. If this is not heartbreaking, I do not know what is. He can do beans for you! Albany can mail you the paperwork and you can mail Albany and Albany can mail you back and it can take six months. You cannot wait six months. You must feel the violent pangs of despair begin a pogrom in your heart and your America. You must realize that you cannot survive in America as a Fuchs, and you cannot go back to Ukraine, you cannot be like your cousin who was not fertile in America, so she went back to Ukraine to have five children, because it is 1924 and Ukraine does not exist anymore. Maybe you should die.

You idiot! Ignoramus! Kadokhes! Fopdoodle! You should not die! All you must do is walk outside and meet the man who changes everything. But this man is not a man. He is a cowboy.

Walk outside where the cowboy waits. He is tough and leathery and chews tobacco. He wears boots and a hat and draws near to you, glittering like a snake. He tells you he can change your name because he has an "in" at Albany and was traveling there himself. He tells you he can be doing the documenting, so you will not need to read English that you cannot read. You cannot imagine better luck. All he wants is an ounce of gold.

Do not do it! I beg of you, do not do it. No one will believe an unlikely story like this one, so it may as well be untrue. But it is not untrue. You have an ounce of gold on your person, an old and beautiful ounce on a bracelet and inscribed with the word "CALIFORNIA." You hesitate for a moment, because you used to dream about moving to the land of mysterious black letters, where you might find guardian amulets of Spanish gold, and give one to each of your children. This moment of hesitating is infinite times too short. You think you cannot pass up this chance. But you can! Oh, do not do it, sister! Do not change your name!

You do.

You hand over the bracelet, and the man tips his hat at you, smiles, and wanders off.

On May 8th, 1924, just three days later, your surname becomes "Stern."

And my bloody story begins.

1

The Delaware Water Gap, Part One

"Fuck!" Becca cried. "Fuck!" She couldn't stop saying it. "Fuck!" She said it twenty times. "Fuck fuck!" Fifty. "Fuck fuck fuck fuck!" She pounded the dashboard and pumped the accelerator. "FUCK!" Rain blasted over, under, around us, and the poor Volkswagen hummed, growled, and coughed. I could tell we were stuck—the water was too deep. If we had only gotten past the dip in the road before the bridge we might've made it. Instead, we were stuck at the Delaware River, three thousand miles from home and drowning in the leftovers of Hurricane Katrina.

Is that too crude? Is this how I should really begin? Is this really how it ends? Not with a bang or with a whimper, but a fuck?

Let's try again.

Once upon a time, on August 31, 2005, my sister and I almost died in the Delaware River. We'd been listening to the news, so we thought we knew everything there was to know about Katrina. Cuba was underwater, New Orleans was apocalyptic, Mississippi a bloody, stormy sea. But it's one thing to hear about Katrina and another to meet her up close and personal, and the sky turns black and dumps oceans on you and your car gets stuck in a flash flood at the Delaware Water Gap. Becca was freaking out. I tried to stay cool.

"So," I said loudly, "what are our options?"

She gave me the hell-glance. I call it the hell-glance because it's worse than a death-glare. It happens in about half a second, but the fury in her eyes could torture a thousand sinners for a thousand years. Her pupils blew up to fill her eyes and she grew a quick pair of horns.

"We have no options!" she screeched. "We're trapped! Matt, we're dead!"

It was a grim analysis. I didn't feel dead, not yet. Our car was stuck on the road in four inches of floodwater. If the water got any higher, it would carry us off into the river to serve as skinny offerings to the Storm Gods. We could jump out. We'd be standing on the highway, water thrashing down around us, no idea where to go, on the wrong coast in the wrong time zone and at least a hundred miles from our destination. But we *might* survive, so it was a chance worth taking.

The water rose and the car could swim off at any moment. We needed to go.

I flung the door open. A belch of rain and wind slapped me and slammed the door in my face. I tried again with the same result.

"What are you doing?" Becca cried.

"We need to get out of the car, or we'll definitely die."

Becca's eyes widened. She seemed to see the logic in it. She glanced towards the trunk, at our suitcases—*her* suitcase, for that matter, which surely had some prized possession worth remembrance. I thought about mine but couldn't remember what was in it.

"Come out my side so we can stay together." Becca grabbed my arm and pulled me and I scrambled over on to her lap. Before I could calculate the proper angle for evacuation, she kicked open the door so hard I wouldn't be surprised if it came off its hinges. The door hung ajar and in a sudden jerk the car began to slide in the water. I tasted something sour and cold and the wind was tearing at my eyes. Holding on to each other we jumped out of the car.

We landed in dirty water to my knees. "For the trees," Becca shouted but I couldn't see any trees. She grabbed my wrist and we slushed our bodies off the road as water spattered and doused us. I thought about how in all his years of travel, something like this probably happened to Grampa Andy, but he made it out okay, for the most part, at least until he got old. I was young. I couldn't afford to die.

We charged for the tree line that only Becca could see. My body waterlogged and I felt like I was dragging another person along with me. Becca squeezed my hand and a flash of lightning split the sky in a violet scar. Wind hit us like a brick and I gasped as it knocked my breath away. I realized I was lying on my back in the cold water, no longer attached to my sister.

"Becca!" Swirling claws of rain swiped at the sky, scrambling up, where, where?—Becca was kneeling in the water, her arms tangled around a branch. I grabbed her. "Are you okay?"

Blasting rain bellowed out her meager response. Then she said: "Matt—what can we do? Where can we even go?"

I looked around. I couldn't see shit. It was all gray, all storm. "Away from the river," I said. "That's all I know."

She pulled in a deep breath and took my hand again.

A violent gust of wind whipped another branch at us and we dove out of the way and in our frantic leaping, shielding our faces from the flurry of twigs like angry bees, I found my body sinking in water much deeper than before. I reached for Becca and pulled her closer as my legs pumped and cycled through water. "What's happening?" I cried.

In the sky, gray monsters duked it out with swords of flaming white. "We're in the river!" Becca shouted, treading hard, pulling me with her. She heaved for an invisible shore as arrows of twigs spiked at our heads. "We must've gotten turned around!"

I kicked but the turbulence above and below sapped all of my energy. There's no way Becca could keep this up. Falling rain leapt and dived like flying falling fish and filled my eyes and ears and there was only water, water, water. I held my breath and prepared to go under, prepared to die.

All the while, a tiny window in my mind floated images and memories like a magic movie screen. George Yoshida and the desert fence, Salvador Mancuso and the boiling earth, Janet Perkins and the devil's breath. What had started off as a road trip seized control of my life and brought me to the limit.

Or maybe this is all wrong. Maybe I need to go back a little further.

2

Chestnut Creek

On June 5, 2005, Grampa Andy died. The news didn't come in until two days later and they were unable to recover his body from the wreckage. I remember Becca being pretty upset back when Grampa Leo died, but I don't think I understood the meaning of death then. So this was my first significant experience with death.

Death is a strange motherfucker. Some people walk into its arms, like a mother and child reunion. Others run from it until the bitter end, tripping over roots and getting swallowed up by the formless void. Others are ambivalent. Life? Death? They're codependent, a cycle. One and the same. I figure Grampa Andy was in this final category. There's no way he believed in God. His faith was probably one of those intellectual, mystic mix-ups with a tablespoon of Kumbaya. That's not to say he wasn't serious about the result—Grampa Andy was the type of man that had a philosophy and stuck to it. I doubt he feared death at all. Otherwise, he wouldn't have gone sky-diving sixty-two times, hang-gliding a dozen more. He always said he gave himself an extra dozen years by quitting BASE jumping when he was forty. His secrets to good health?

"I follow Ben Franklin and Chinese medicine," he once said to Becca and me on a ski lift. "Never wake up after 6:00. That gives you time in your day to exercise and eat healthy. Besides that, ginseng, jumping jacks, and a good, clear sense of hierarchy should be enough to get you and me to eighty-three."

He didn't make it quite that far, but when you're as adventurous as he was, seventy-five isn't half-bad.

Grampa Andy isn't my real grandfather. He's my mom's uncle. But he became more or less grandfather 2.0 after Grampa Leo died seven years ago. Grampa Andy was the grandpa every kid wishes he had. He took us skiing and rafting and to national parks. He gave us coins and candy from all over the world. He made kickass tacos because he lived in Mexico City for a dozen years. Meanwhile, I had barely left the state of California. And he was the one who got me and Becca started on our road trip in the first place.

I was out at track and Becca was at lacrosse, which she attended when she wasn't too busy planning the anarchist revolution, and when we came home Mom had this grave look on her face. For a second I thought my SAT scores had come in so I tried to bolt, but she called after me.

"Something happened," she said.

"Okay," I said, hopping impatiently in the doorway. Becca was unpacking her bag, one item at a time. She's a methodical one. Packed and unpacked her backpack every day. She made herself lunch too, even though seniors are allowed to go out in town. She liked her backpack. She was attached to *things* in a way that I could never understand. Not like knick-knacks you buy at Disney World-things—the girl lives low-waste—but *things* in a deeper sense. Objects and ideas have meanings to her beyond the thing in itself—they're metaphors, symbols, metonyms, zeugmas, onomatopoeias, the whole nine yards. This trait is hard to explain because I don't get it myself. Rather, I don't get my sister at all.

"Uncle Andy passed away two days ago. We just heard."

At first it didn't register. Grampa Andy dying seemed generally unlikely. There's no way he'd die of a heart attack, or of cancer, or in his sleep, all the usual ways grandparents die. It would have to be a car crash or a terrorist attack. Maybe he was murdered. Got into a fist-fight in Mongolia, and due to the unfortunate circumstance that his opponent was an ex-KGB Russian ninja motherfucker, ended up headless in a ditch.

"Two days ago? How did he die?" Becca asked.

"It was a train crash," Mom said. "In Kazakhstan, his train derailed. He was headed skiing."

Well, it wasn't a mafia fistfight, but I could live with it. At least his last moments had some excitement. I could picture it: Grampa Andy, in his brown leather jacket and skinny silver tie, staring out the train window. Green mountains capped with snow survey him from a distance as he surveys back. A moment of recognition. Then the train begins to quake. He stands. A flash. A screech! The steel caterpillar and all its limbs leap and Grampa Andy's feet leave the ground and his tie shoots out like a chameleon's tongue. His eyes widen with profound curiosity: *What happens now?* But before he can finish the proverbial train of thought the train itself smashes and implodes to smoking rubble.

It was an appealing story. The adventure-crazed traveler goes out on his ultimate and maddest journey into the belly of Asia, towards the glistening slopes of the Ural mountains, only to die unfulfilled and glorious.

Becca and I were silent. We had spent a lot of time with him over the last few years.

"Will there be a funeral?" Becca asked.

"I hope so."

"You hope so?"

"Well, you know Andy. It's not like him to want a funeral, so we'll have to check his will. I'm sure he wanted a cremation, but since they can't find his body..."

"They can't find his body?" I asked. This news upset me. My feelings about the whole incident began to shift. At first I felt glad that he could go out with a bang. But his vanished body made me feel a little queasy. He was eradicated from the Earth, without even a corpse to show for his existence.

"Apparently it was quite a crash," Mom said. She walked over to me and put her arm around my shoulders. "I know you were close. This is really terrible to hear."

"Why can't they find his body?"

"We don't know. There must be a lot of debris—"

My hands started to jitter and I pulled away from Mom. "Why? No, that's stupid. What, was he literally obliterated in the crash or something?"

Mom looked at me and shook her head. "We don't know."

Fuck that, I thought, and left. I leapt up the steps two at a time and went to my room and shut the door.

I felt like punching something. I knew Grampa Andy had made promises to me, though I couldn't remember any of them—probably to go skiing somewhere, rafting somewhere. He was my ticket out of this life, out of banality. He was the only person who didn't care that my grades weren't as good as Becca's. I was angry that the promises had shattered, and even angrier that I couldn't remember what they were. I was upset that his life had ended the way it had. I hated myself for thinking it was good to die like that. Who wants to die in the agony of a splintering train? No, better to die in bed surrounded by loved ones. And all those feelings came before the significance of death began to settle down on me like snow. What does it mean to die? To vanish from the earth? The body and the self dissolve and survive only through memories carried by the living. But the living too will one day die, and their memories in turn dissolve. Certain artifacts like photographs can weather many lives, but they're shells without accompanying memories of the living, and memory is so unreliable! I needed to keep my memories of him, stuff them in my pockets. I needed to spread Grampa Andy around. Shake his dust all over the world. I was already forgetting what he looked like. A sharp nose. Sharp as a pocket-knife. But when I tried to imagine a nose as sharp as a pocket-knife, the picture wasn't quite right.

I sat on my bed, thinking. I went on my computer. Glanced past the news. I thought about making a MySpace post for Grampa Andy, something I had seen other people in my school do for their grandparents when they died. Write a nice memorial post, add a few photos. Consolation would flood in through comments and in school the next few days. But making it public seemed wrong. It would take the events out of my own hands and throw them into cyberspace, and who knows what happens out there? But I had to tell *someone.* I settled for messaging Christine and Chelsea on AIM.

"I need to tell u something..." I typed and sent it twice. While I waited for a reply I looked out the window. Where did the details of the world go? I could only see the vaguest outline of my neighborhood: a street, some trees, houses. It didn't look like anything in particular. Had I gone blind? Had my life always looked this way? Our neighborhood was just houses and trees and people doing their jobs so they could add pools to their backyards. I stared at the bug trapped in the window screen, a tiny gnat, twitching translucent wings against the black crosshatch. As I watched it, its body began to swell, engorge, feed on the wire. I watched it grow until it was a monstrous bug as big as the earth, and then I felt safe, and like I didn't need to cry.

I got replies. Christine was first: "What is it??" Chelsea second: "Wat, r u ok". I announced solemnly to them that my grandfather had died.

I suppose I ought to explain who Christine and Chelsea are. Christine and I had been "together" for some four months now, but it wasn't official, and I had the silliest crush on Chelsea, so I was hitting her up too, though she ignored me a lot. But Christine, my first love! I'm thankful to Christine for a lot. She was my first kiss outside of one of those middle-school dares, and we planned to lose our virginity to each other sometime this summer. We were both too weird about it so we hadn't gotten the words out, "Let's fuck." But we'd done pretty much everything else.

The point: Christine is the bomb. Her dad wanted her to be a doctor about as much as mine wanted me to be a lawyer. That's how we started talking, Jew jokes and Asian jokes, quipped about ourselves to the other, although I didn't really consider myself Jewish, just my parents are. It turned out that Christine was a badass, and with Grampa Andy as the prototype, I always take an interest in a proven badass. She taught me how to skateboard, how to roll a blunt (even though neither of us like weed that much, she rolls for her friends, and don't tell me that isn't badass). I taught her how to ski and lie to your parents. We had a hell of a time doing anything and everything together last winter break. We were pretty weird. Sometimes we skated over to the dump, looking at all the creepy and sad shit people throw away. I made lists to share with Becca and get her all riled up about capitalism. Christine is the first person who looked me in the eyes, and the time she said she cared about me at the beach when it was cold I cried uncontrollably. We just needed to get over the whole sex thing.

Christine was faster to respond than Chelsea, so I messaged her. I could never juggle two conversations at once, slinging messages left and right like a lot of my classmates.

Christine suggested I ask my parents if she could come over for dinner, but something about the idea made me feel uncomfortable. Maybe it was too soon. Then I realized the person I really should've told—Will. But Will and I would see each other tomorrow anyways. He played guitar and wrote music, and I was helping him record his songs.

I'm not sure what Becca was up to. Becca had just broken up with her boyfriend, a big hairy hilarious Jew named Aaron, one of those end of high school breakups. I wondered if she would turn to him about Grampa Andy. I was under the impression that they hadn't ended things badly.

I went downstairs. "Mom, where's Becca?" Mom was at her laptop.

"Is she not in her room?"

"Uh, I don't know."

"Well then."

Back upstairs, to Becca's room. I knocked. No answer. I opened the door. She wasn't there.

Weird, I thought. She couldn't have gone out to see friends because I saw the car in the driveway, so she had to be nearby. I zipped downstairs and went outside.

The day was strangely chilly, the sky a gray cloth. Slick, damp breeze. Becca wasn't in our backyard, some grass with three tall pine trees and a hammock. She must've walked somewhere. But where?

As far as I know she didn't have any friends in the neighborhood. I could think of just one place that she could've gone. It came to me in a cloudy memory—the place she went when Grampa Leo died.

I walked down the street, itching with déjà vu. Seven years ago I had led a college kid down this way—an older neighborhood kid who was helping Mom look for Becca. Becca had run off for a whole twenty-four hours after Grampa Leo died. Mom was scared shitless. Little did she know it was all a big game. Becca was running away to 'Japan' so she could go be with Kaori, our half-Japanese cousin that we met when we went to visit Uncle Larry the previous summer. I could remember everything—an eleven-year old Becca insisting to me that Kaori had saved her from a ghost at a magic shrine, me believing her, promising to not tell Mom and Dad where she was going, the well in our neighbor's backyard, now a fantastic underground tunnel bound for Japan, full of ghosts and demons. I kept the promise, at first, until the college kid, named Jonathan Stein, who I now know had been kicked out of college for too many suicide attempts, convinced me to bring him to Becca. We climbed down into the well. I was happy to betray Becca's trust because I was all upset that she had run off without me. I walked Jonathan down this street. It looked the same, here and there, then and now, exactly the same, even though that couldn't possibly be true. Then and now I crossed my neighbor's yard, past a grove of trees, branches heavy with crabapples, into a mini wilderness of brush that descended into a ravine. Then and now, at the bottom I saw the stone outline of an old well, a circle of stone surrounded by tall weeds and spiny bushes. Becca was sitting on the well, on top of the rocks. She noticed me and looked away.

I took a peek inside the well. It was all filled up with dirt. Weird. Back then, the well descended some twenty feet deep into a cavern. The tunnel at the bottom of the well that Becca thought went all the way to Japan—surely it didn't go more than fifty yards, but I could've sworn it *existed.* I remember looking for Grampa Leo's ghost and seeing so many horrifying faces, beautiful and grotesque, laughing and groaning, screaming and whispering, but never his face, only faces that I'd never seen before and never saw again. But there was neither tunnel nor well. Only the crumpled outline of something long ago collapsed. Had the well been real? The tunnel? I sat down beside Becca. She looked at me with foggy hazel eyes and a dull expression.

"You remember this place?" she asked.

"Kinda," I said. "I remember that you used to come over here. It came back to me—when you ran away from home after Grampa Leo died. You're not running away to Japan, are you?"

She didn't laugh. That was a bad sign. "Not this time," she said.

"You're upset."

She made a face at me. "Shame on me for feeling something. We spent so much time with him. I had a feeling he'd die in such a stupid way. It's wrong."

"You're right. I was just surprised you ran off here."

She sighed. "Give me a break, Matt. I wanted a breather."

"No, you're right. With Grampa Andy acting as our dad, we should be mourning."

"Oh shut up, Dad's around. It's his job."

I didn't think I was entirely wrong. I spent more time with Grampa Andy in the last six years than with my own dad in all sixteen.

"Hey," I said. "Didn't there used to be an actual well here? I swear, when I came to try and find you I remember climbing down a ladder into the well..."

Becca glanced at me and looked back at her own knees. She shrugged. She must've forgotten.

"I wonder if he left us anything in his will," I said.

Becca gave me an exasperated look. I know, I'm not up to her moral standards, but Becca is a remarkably moral person.

We sat on the stones for a while. Becca was probably remembering Grampa Andy, his face, his words, his deeds, while I all I could do was think about how the hell I got it into my head that there had been a well and underground tunnel here when all I could see now was dirt and some dandelions.

"Do you ever have dreams?"

Becca suddenly asked me.

"Dreams?" I said. "Nope. Never had one."

"Fuck you," she said. "Not ordinary dreams. Strange dreams." She tugged at her hair, like she was trying to wake up from one now. "Dreams that feel just as real—or even more real—than regular life. Dreams that you remember perfectly in the morning."

Breaking news: my sister is a lunatic. "Have you?" I asked.

"Yes," she said. She looked up at me. "You can go now."

"It's called lucid dreaming, genius." I stood up and shrugged. "Just trying to spend time with my big sister."

"We can hang out this summer," she said. "I was thinking about a road trip. There's so much that I want to see, and I better do it before I go to school in California for four more years."

"That'd be fun," I said. "Where?"

"Maybe Seattle. Maybe Utah." Oh sister, just wait till we end up in Ohio.

I stood. "I look forward to the day when we can spend such time together. I shall henceforth take my leave."

She snorted and I left her to her grieving. Becca is always full of deep and complicated feelings I'm incapable of understanding. I knew whatever she was feeling was different from whatever I was feeling, and an overwhelming desire to know how she felt suddenly struck me. But I was stuck in me. What a ridiculous and frustrating limitation. Me, me, it has to be all about *me*. And what was *I* feeling, anyways? I was feeling the world change. Without Grampa Andy, the Earth darkened, emptied, became dangerous. It lost one of its liveliest souls. I was also feeling something like pain, but it wasn't despair. As I walked back home, I started to think about how Grampa Andy might continue to live through me. I had to do something. I had to change something about my stupid life to follow in his lead. I remembered one time when he said something like, "They always say look before you leap. Think before you act. I disagree. Now, I'm not saying jump off a cliff without looking over the edge, but I see no reason action and thought can't happen at the same time. That's not so much to save time as to get you deeper into things, into the thick of them. Think too much and you'll never get anywhere. Don't finish every thought to its conclusion, don't keep things closed. If you start doing and thinking and thinking and doing, you just might find yourself in unexpected, beautiful places."

I don't remember him saying *all* of that, but if I had to sum up his life philosophy, I'd say that quote does the job. And it was up to me to follow his wisdom. No more waiting for Mom's permission. No more sticking around in this plastic town. No more deference to Becca's pointless politics. No more reading newspapers and encyclopedias, keeping track of all the world's murders and suicides. No more dreaming—seize the day! As if I had any dreams in the first place, besides wondering whether the anarchist revolution would come along with some new Nintendo games.

Just a few days later, I went to Grampa Andy's funeral, and discovered that a lot of what I knew about him was wrong. So here, on the threshold, the brink, a mild June evening, before the funeral, before the road trip, before Cowboy Jim and Kaori and everything else, I will allow myself to meander home with a childish vision of my great-uncle shining in my mind. It's not that Grampa Andy turned out to be a bad guy. The story was just a hell of a lot more complicated than expected.

Let's fast-forward one week. One week, in which I broke down in front of Christine because she just wouldn't stop talking about how much I *really loved* Grampa Andy; in which Becca and I skipped a few days of school and then showed up frantically trying to catch up; in which Will and I had the unfortunate experience of catching Becca sliding into third base with Aaron on the hammock; a week in which the mysterious mild fog yielded to California sunshine.

3

Berkeley

My mom and her siblings (read: my mom) decided to have a funeral for Grampa Andy, a Christian funeral of all funerals, and I was in an ugly mood. Still, someone secured the money for it, and even a bodiless coffin. Over 150 guests came to a cemetery near UC Berkeley, where he had served as Professor of History for thirty years.

It was a pretty place, yellow light and cool breeze washing against the trees. I liked how the gravestones weren't arranged in a grid, instead sprouting up naturally like mushrooms. Mom and Becca and I stood at the front of the mass of people. Two men brought out the empty coffin. Standing nearby was Grandmother, dressed in tar-black silk. Mom held her one hand and Uncle Michael, who had come in from Chicago, the other; it had been too short notice for Uncle Larry to fly in from Japan, and, apparently, too short notice for Dad to get back from LA. Grampa Andy had married twice and both wives attended with a few kids, though the children were from other husbands. (That being said, one of the ex-wives has six kids and the other has four, so I didn't rule out the possibility that one or two were Grampa Andy's—regardless, I'm sure he treated them all as well as he treated me and Becca.)

Besides our extended family, there were dozens of gray-haired friends and colleagues I'd never seen before, a caravan of Mexico City business executives and their families, and the entire history department from Berkeley, making a motley crew of ages, colors, and dispositions. A tall, bald man with piercing blue eyes towered above the rest and stood directly in front, although no one seemed to know who he was.

The empty coffin came up. It was set down in the ditch. White shine on the wood.

We marched past the coffin. I couldn't help but to wonder—what if this whole funeral was premature? His body was never found, after all. What if he was still alive? But that's the sort of thing that happens in mystery novels and on TV, so I let the idea go. After all, Grampa Andy hated what he called storybook crap. In the past week, I had gotten over it, more or less—after all, someday I'll die, too. I'll die, my relatives will disobey my last will and testament and make a show of an empty coffin. They'll let my friends tap-dance through elaborate displays of grief in an effort to console the lonely woman left behind. And a Christian priest sanctifies the grave! I had never seen anything so unholy.

Except for one thing. The thing that I had failed him. That I hadn't done enough. I could accept that he was dead, yes, but I could not accept that this would be the end of our relationship. I was still hellbent on doing *something*, albeit still unsure what that thing would be.

The lonely woman of the day was my lone non-Jewish grandparent, Karen Wessel Stern. Mom tells me that she was born and grew up gentry, an old California family related to Leland Stanford by marriage. It's pretty useful 25% blood to have, as far as partial inheritances go—it links me in with the guts of America, the glory and the gore. As for why a California lady went and married a movie-making Jew scrambling up the ranks of Hollywood, no idea. And her brother, the deceased. Always brilliant, sent to boarding school and then to Harvard. I was listening to some relative standing in front of the crowd, telling the story of Grampa Andy's life. He was doing it terribly. He focused on the accomplishments as the plot-points. The Harvard rowing team, academic accolades, enrollment at UCSF medical school. He at least had the courtesy to mention Grampa Andy's love of travel. It was a love that started in America, even if it didn't end there. From a young age, Andy Wessel bathed in the chill of the Pacific, refreshed his thirst in the falls of the Sierras, made his first trek north to Alaska. After getting his first big paycheck developing drugs for a pharma company, he splurged it all on a grand European tour. If I were to tell the story with the same facts, I would start with the adventure and weave in the accomplishments. Listening to his cousin's biography you'd think Andy Wessel was some normie medical-devices-exec-turned-academic who from time to time would wake up pleasantly surprised to find himself in Liberia. I had to resist the urge to run up to the podium and wrest the microphone out of cousin William's chubby hands.

After thick-hands Will, Uncle Michael gave a speech on Andy Wessel's special type of kindness, followed by some reminiscing on 1940s Oakland from a childhood friend. One of the grey-bearded Mexican businessmen, fingers coated in sparkling rings, came to the podium and said, "Este es un hombre que era tan hermoso como el polvo de estrellas." I liked those speeches better because they didn't try so hard to make a narrative. They left things more open for me. But none of them changed my view of my great uncle.

After the speeches, we walked past the coffin to pay final respects. I stopped at the coffin, faced it directly, and gave a simple, solemn nod.

This isn't over. Not yet.

We followed the mourner's march of cars back to my grandmother's house in Oakland. She lived in the Victorian house of her parents, a miniature castle with white adornments that looked like frills on the house's blue dress. She had moved back from LA after Grampa Leo died, and at Mom's insistence, boarded two sort-of-relatives that Mom scavenged from the dusty corners of the Earth: Juliette Rogers, a second-cousin and contemporary artist, and Brian Chang, one of Grampa Andy's PhD students, holed up and writing several volumes on the history of Oakland.

No one in my family spoke a word on the drive. By the time we arrived I was itching to get some fresh air, so I took a lap around the neighborhood. Every house in the neighborhood was an old Victorian. Some were fixed up like Grandmother's, but some had clearly suffered for decades. I didn't realize houses could look sad. Streaks of dirt on the arched roofs, thin strings of wood splintering off the bannisters. The color palette of pink, blue, and orange made me feel like I had ended up in Willy Wonka's experimental enclave, before he put the candy in. The gardens and grass alternated between ratty and lush.

Returning to the baby blue and well-kept rosebushes of Grandmother's house, I went inside.

I found Grandmother talking to Becca in the narrow but long kitchen. "There you are, darling," she said, and kissed me on the cheek. I did that awkward thing where I put my cheek on hers, reluctant to kiss anything.

"Hi Grandmother," I said. "I'm sorry. I loved him. We had so much fun together."

"Didn't we all? I think he enjoyed himself more than any man alive." A sad smile rested on her lips. "And yet I believe always had a purpose."

"What do you mean?"

"Well, darling, he traveled to learn. He sought thrills to remember just how fragile life is. He always had intellectual projects. He did a lot of his traveling in the last few years with a passion not unlike that of a man on a mission. I can't help but to wonder if he was somehow anticipating his own death."

That confused me because I always thought Andy's lifestyle was easygoing, shooting the breeze, experiencing the best of the world. "I'll miss him," I said. Eyeing a tray of cheese and crackers, I added, "I think I want some food. I'll be back."

I went to the kitchen table and nibbled cheese and crackers by myself. Grandmother's comment was small—tiny, really—but it had implications on how I was to interpret Grampa Andy's life. If I were to go on carrying his spirit, it would do him disservice and myself dissatisfaction to have interpreted his life incorrectly. Was there a mission there? In *everything* he did? That's a much more difficult way to live a life.

I got caught up in "How is school?" conversations with Uncle Michael, cousin Kathy, and a few others. They were the type of interactions I would normally grit my teeth through, but I was so distracted by my own thoughts that I heard myself speak correct responses and even outright lies to whoever happened to be talking to me. I excused myself to the bathroom. I only had to pee but I sat down on that porcelain toilet for a solid ten minutes. What was I supposed to think about him? What could I do for him? I went to ask Becca how she had interpreted Grampa Andy's way of living. Maybe she had caught something I missed. After all, she was a psychopathic anarchist who believed in the elimination of personal property, organized religion, and industrial technology. I found her in the den, a low-ceilinged room with a stocked bar, leather couch with a bearskin, and unfinished wooden desk. But she was with someone else—the tall bald man I had noticed at the funeral, eyes crystal blue, made furiously bright by the glints of orange lamplight. For a moment I thought I was looking into the eyes of the devil, but then he smiled—almost. His mouth curled upwards, to be sure, but I can't imagine that *smile* is the right word for it.

"I was about to send your sister in search of you; our conversation has been considerably delayed." His mouth barely moved as he spoke. His voice was velvet, soft and motionless.

"Um." I swallowed. "Who are you?"

"I apologize for not introducing myself..." he trailed off and extended his hand. I shook cold and bony fingers. His face and nose were long, eyes slanted. The skin on his face looked hard and he wore a close-fitting black suit. "My name is Roger Emersen. I was your great uncle's lover."

Boom. Suck on that, Matthew Rosen.

"Sorry?" I asked.

"Andy Wessel was the love of my life," Emersen said. "And I was the love of his."

My jaw must've dropped because Becca literally punched me in the gut. I reeled at the unexpected pain.

"What's your problem, asshole?" she hissed.

"I'm sorry. I'm so sorry." A wave of shame swept over me. What *was* my problem? What's wrong with Grampa Andy being gay?

The gleam in Roger Emersen's eyes seemed to intensify. I felt like I had taken a hit straight out of Christine's older brother Joe's *feng wan* (Chinese for "crazy bowl" because no one knew what was in that shit). I felt like I was staring at the sun, like my eyes were about to evaporate. Roger Emersen was a naked god glistening in a billion stars and he laid a finger on my beating heart. He spoke.

"There was no way for you to know." He made a gesture. "Andy Wessel lived many lives. *Qui vivra verra.* Life for you children has only begun."

"He has the rest of Grampa Andy's will," Becca explained. "There's a part just for us."

I sat down in a chair, trying to collect my thoughts. The first bomb had dropped. Grampa Andy, to the knowledge of seemingly no one, had loved men. What did it matter? It didn't mean anything. It shouldn't. And yet it did.

But Roger Emersen wasn't going to wait for me to collect my thoughts.

"I asked Rebecca this question, Matthew, so let me ask you," he said. "Have you ever heard of Rubin Yakovlev? The uncle of your mother's father?"

"No," I said. "Well, just a little. I never met him."

"He died long before you were born," Emersen said. "In 1980." His words were soft, fast, precise, uninterruptible. "The man was a lunatic, dangerously unstable. After he passed away, Andy began to take great interest in the wild man's deeds. Because when Andy discovered a motive, a target, he sought it until his arrow struck the mark. It was his greatest strength and his greatest flaw."

Sure, I could buy that.

"Andy decided he would aid your Hebrew uncle on an unfinished quest he pursued for more than fifty years. Andy is a historian, you know—he couldn't help it. And—" Emersen suddenly halted, glancing around. His eyes sparked and then darkened. "We don't have enough time here. Come to Muir Woods in three days, at noon. I will meet you at the entrance."

"Muir Woods?" I stuttered.

Emersen looked to his left, at the redwood desk. Hung up over the fireplace was a big topographic map of Muir Woods.

"I'll take you to the largest tree in America," Emersen said. "Do not forget it." He walked into the doorway. I realized then just how tall he was. His bald, gleaming head nearly touched the doorpost. "I don't think you will. You are children of the covenant, after all—memory is your gift. And Andy has left the pair of you some dough." He rubbed his forefinger and thumb together. "*Gelt.* You wouldn't want to miss it, would you?"

4

Muir Woods

Roger Emersen was wrong. I took the liberty to look it up on the Internet, and the largest tree in America is actually the General Sherman tree, located in the Sequoia National Forest in southern California. It's about the same height as the tallest tree in Muir Woods but has a much larger circumference at the base. So, he was wrong about that.

Believe it or not, I hadn't been to Muir Woods before. But don't accuse me of California heresy—of course I'd seen big redwoods, up in Mendocino, down in the Sequoias. I've also been to Yosemite twice, which I've heard was Muir's favorite place in California anyhow.

Becca and I drove up. I wasn't exactly anxious to meet Roger Emersen again, but I wanted to know more about this "quest." It could be the very thing I had been hoping to learn about Grampa Andy, the perfect puzzle-piece to complete the story of his life, so I wouldn't have to stew in regret at the pointless, childish, idiotic ways I had talked to him, interacted with him, never listened to him, because they kept popping up in my head and I hated them, and I hated me. Meanwhile, in the car Becca lectured me about not being a closeted chicken-slinging evangelical redneck and it took every ounce of my willpower not to slap her in the face. I had been taken aback, that was all.

The day was warm and sparkled with brightness, a far cry from the chilly day when we first heard that Grampa Andy had died. We waited for Roger Emersen at the entrance for a few minutes before we saw him walking towards us, wearing long pants despite the heat, blue eyes hidden by gold-rimmed aviators. He paid our entry and said nothing until we entered the forest.

Huge redwoods were everywhere. They clustered around the dirt path, which we followed, a few steps behind him. The sun's beacon flooded gaps between leaves, shooting a million white lasers. They beamed on the trail and bleached leaves to white. The veined redwoods towered in darkness. The contrast between light and dark was dazzling, even painful to the eyes. As we walked, Roger Emersen did not look at either of us, but finally started to talk.

"Let me begin with saying that Andy asked me a little over a year ago to convey this story to you when he died," Roger Emersen said. "I have known about it for a while now, since Andy and myself shared everything together, but it's not a story I have any interest in. This was simply Andy's request to me: to tell, to enlighten, to illuminate."

"Well, that sounds good to me," I said.

"Good," he said. "I mentioned a mission your grandfather had?"

"Yep."

"I believe I used the word quest. I wondered retrospectively if the words I had chosen were too strong—if they had too many letters or were too sonically rich. *Goal* does the job just fine. It was something he wanted to do."

"What did Grampa Andy want to do?"

"Not Andy," Emersen said. "It was Rubin Yakovlev. Yakovlev spent his life in search of a bracelet."

"A bracelet?"

I glanced at Becca, who had stamped all over her face not confusion, not shock, not even bewilderment—instead, absolute horror.

"Not an ordinary bracelet," Emersen said. "An amulet with strange powers. Some would call it magic. It had been in the Yakovlev family for generations, and Yakovlev's sister, your great-grandmother, sold it after they immigrated to America, to Yakovlev's fury. He then spent his life searching for the bracelet, tracking it all across America, as it appeared to be a bracelet with properties beyond the familial, beyond the historical. It seemed to belong to everyone and no one: to come with the rain and to vanish with the wind. It was not a family object, certainly not a Jewish object. The bracelet was *pantothales*, as the ancient Greeks would say. Because of this special quality, Andy was drawn into the search after Yakovlev's death, when he discovered a notebook filled with clues. He saw the eternal quality of the bracelet interact with fleeting moments of history—different people who came across the bracelet, and loved it, hated it, sold it or stole it—perhaps he saw a history book there." Emersen frowned. "He claimed he wasn't interested in turning the story of the bracelet into research, and yet it wasn't too far off from his research in the first place. But for Yakovlev, the bracelet was everything. Monstrous, godly, horrifying, beautiful. A bracelet with a Spanish coin from the old California colony."

Wind rushed through the leaves. Our steps crackled on twigs. For a moment I had to focus on the sounds—whooshy-wind, crunchy-twigs, zip-zippy mosquitos—slow down, Emersen, slow down! I didn't know what to think, or what to say. It was completely unbelievable and untenable. It connected to nothing I knew about my family, but then again, according to Emersen it wasn't even *about* my family. Definitely not about Grampa Andy, and really only a little bit about Rubin Yakovlev. Luckily for blank-brained me, Becca swooped in with the perfect question.

"Why?" she demanded.

Emersen paused but didn't turn, still facing straight down the dirt path. "Because the earth goes round the sun and the living die. Why what? Be specific."

"Why was Rubin Yakovlev so obsessed with the bracelet? Was it important to him?"

"I told you: Yakovlev was insane. He believed that the bracelet saved them from riots in Ukraine when they were children. It was a family heirloom, deemed by the local Hebrew authorities as able to protect the community. Yakovlev's parents were still killed by the mob, although he and his sister escaped and snuck into America before World War I broke out. The story goes, they survived, only thanks to the bracelet's power."

Why hadn't he started out with that? The way he framed things was all twisted—I could already tell that his story was littered with lies, or at least untruths, and that I'd need to do a lot of sorting through the facts to get Grampa Andy's role in all this straight.

"So our great-great uncle Rubin tried to find the bracelet, which ended up appearing all over the country?" Becca asked.

"All over, indeed," Emersen said. "It seemed to be everywhere at once. Yakovlev would find a family who'd seen it in Mississippi, only to learn that the bracelet had been shipped up to Chicago. Once Andy got his hands on Yakovlev's notes, he organized them into a notebook and started to search for clues himself. Between the two of them, there is a whole notebook of clues, sorted by place name, that I have in my car, ready and waiting for the two of you."

"He wanted us to have the notebook?"

Emersen suddenly stopped. He pointed ahead.

"There it is. 260 feet tall. 12 foot diameter. Almost as tall as the Statue of Liberty."

"But not quite?" I asked.

"Not quite."

It was impossible to see how high the tree went. It soared up through the canopy, out of sight. The nameless behemoth was marked with a post inscribing its statistics: 258 feet tall, 12.3 foot diameter, 3000 tons.

"*Zoi*," Emersen whispered. He took off his sunglasses and looked up.

Becca and I glanced at one another, letting the man have his moment. It was a tremendous sight, a startling mass heaving up up up, and up, and so old, too. But I was too shaken up by Emersen's story. I tapped my foot impatiently and waited for him to speak.

At last, Emersen turned to me and Becca. "Andy didn't ask that I tell you here. He asked me simply to tell you about your uncle's goal to find this bracelet, and to give you all that you might need to find it, if you desired to. To this end he has left you the notebook, and also his car, the Volkswagen, and some money on top."

"*Did* he ask us to find the bracelet?" Becca asked.

Emersen head moved almost imperceptibly. "He did not explicitly say those words."

"But he seems to want us to."

"That is one interpretation."

Whether or not he said the words, I thought the intention was clear. I tried to catch Becca's eye, but she was looking at the giant tree. A magic bracelet? A crazy great-great uncle? A lifelong quest? Grampa Andy's dying wish? About *our* family, not his? Yeah. Bullshit's never been this dank. Maybe Emersen should put down the pipe from time to time.

"Andy was not a man to waste his time," Emersen said. "So I do believe there is something significant about the bracelet. Yakovlev, in his madness, thought the bracelet was of immense importance: he thought it was essential to your family, and maybe your race, and maybe, just maybe America, and maybe, just maybe, if only it could be, the entire world. Andy, I don't know what he thought." For the first time Emersen's voice faltered, and I sensed honesty and confusion in his slick voice. "He—he believed in Yakovlev's mission. He wouldn't waste your time with a pointless errand." Emersen looked at the dirt ground. "He believed in something about this bracelet, and he left to you in his death the tools to find it. You can read into that what you will."

His words started processing, even though I wanted to throw them all straight into a blazing fire. Car. Bracelet. Family history. The scope of the tale was too big. It was like staring at a mountain from a foot away.

"Impossible," Becca whispered.

Emersen turned away.

"You should know," he said. "I believe in a secret to life. There is a truth that whispers in the wind and laughs in the foam of the waves; a universal spirit that guides all things. The bracelet is a part of this truth, but if you try to conspire with the truth, you also conspire with a danger. If you decide to chase the bracelet, I have two pieces of advice. The first is to not make the mistake of thinking that the bracelet is a personal artifact. It has nothing to do with you or your family. Thinking that it belongs to you will only lead you into narcissism, and sin. The second is to follow the omens that nature gives you, the omens of the universal guiding spirit, and to never take them for granted." He shrugged. "That's everything I have to say."

There is no way that Grampa Andy loved this man.

That's all I could think about on the way back to the car. I had to clench my mouth tight to hold back a tirade of brutal roasts. But the moment we left Muir Woods, we saw something.

"Look," Emersen said.

He pointed up at the sun. It glinted through a circle of white clouds. There it was, hanging in the sky, believe it or not: a ringlet of clouds, sun glare a sparkling Spanish coin dangling from airy threads. The bracelet.

5

Pine Woods High

Not that I bought into any of Emersen's bullshit, not at first. I was mad about it. Even as I gobbled up the notebook in a single night. 150 pages of Rubin Yakovlev's notes, and 75 more from Grampa Andy. I hadn't read that much since I tried to read the entire Tanakh at age ten, but the only thing I remember from that is that if you jack off or menstruate (God forbid!) you need to leave town and take a ritual bath. And if your husband cheats on you, you get to spit in his shoe.

It took time to wrap our heads around the situation. The notebook, written in either Grampa Andy's handwriting or some CIA-level forgery shit, verified what Roger Emersen told us. Becca seemed to believe the story, though nothing could be more out of character. She hates the past. She's said it to me about a hundred times, usually in the context of claiming that the Democratic Party is regressive. "Fuck the past. I don't care that LBJ did something good for poor people once." And there's nothing more past than a hundred-year-vanished-bracelet.

But rather than rejecting it, she pointed to the hundreds of pages of notes, saying all this *writing* couldn't have just come out of nowhere. It wasn't *just* a story—there was physical evidence! Proof!

My response to that? *So what?* Still ain't real. No fucking way. I don't believe in universal spirits, and I don't particularly care that the bracelet saved great-great Grandpapa Vladimir Yakovlechivichoff, long dead and buried in the ground.

Still—I was glad to have an excuse to keep thinking about Grampa Andy, at least temporarily. Could he really have devoted himself to finding the bracelet? I couldn't stop thinking about how I fucked things up. I should've done so much to thank him, to connect with him, to learn from him. But I didn't. I was a stupid brat, and spent his money on GameBoy games and never used the compass he bought me, or the pocket knife. From my memory I calculated: 16 ski trips, 6 rafting trips, 27 state park visits, 55+ breakfasts at the local diner, 1 snorkeling trip. That's less than 500 hours together, out of 17,093 hours of my life! And how many sentences were exchanged? How many words?

How many times did I even *look* at him?

So, despite myself, I read the notebook. I read it again. It was all I had.

The first few pages, written by Grampa Andy, clarified two points. 1: It was known in the Yakovlev family that this bracelet had saved them from not one, not two, not three, but *four* different pogroms, despite the supposed kvetching of the rabbi over the Yakovlevs owning a pagan amulet. 2: Rubin Yakovlev, inspired by the incoming 1943 news of Jews in ovens, decided he must recover the bracelet (sold by his sister in 1924) to protect the family, were another disaster to befall the Jews. So regardless of what Emersen said, the bracelet certainly had grounding in family. It wasn't just a mystic mythic *ta-DUM!*-amajig. It *was* my family's, or it used to be. Looking for the bracelet wouldn't be like looking for the white whale.

What it *would* be, however, is a fool's errand. The bracelet had been 'missing' for almost a hundred years—no wonder Rubin Yakovlev or Grampa Andy never got their hands on it.

That didn't mean the idea didn't tempt me. A search for it would make things fall into place for me and Becca. We had a car, now, and more than just a car, we had a road. The places in the notebook even made a convenient route since suspected locations of the bracelet ranged from Sacramento to Cheyenne to Chicago. I started to think: maybe this was my chance to live the way Grampa Andy did. To keep him around through not just my thoughts, but my actions. I started to think that maybe this was my only chance to make something greater out of his death. As the two of us thought about it and chatted in Becca's doorway, the story gradually became more and more real. Thinking back, it was almost like we were talking ourselves into a whole new world, where Grampa Andy was not just a historian but a hero, out to solve the mystery that would save America, and we could finish what he couldn't.

And I couldn't seem to forget the moment, that moment when I followed Roger Emersen's gaze to the sky and saw the bracelet and gold coin floating there like a sign from God. I suspected I was having dreams about it, but I couldn't remember them in the morning and I tried to remind myself that a dream, no matter how meaningful, is still only a dream.

That's what I was thinking about in Room 214 at Pine Woods High. Throw the bullshit out the window? Or wallow in it? I was in Pre-Calculus, staring at the back of Chelsea's head. She had me hypnotized, her hair's dark waves rippling at the slightest shift. She bent over her desk and I saw the shadows of a waterfall. She turned to use her eraser, and midnight storm clouds flurried past. There were two days of school left, and the girl paid perfect attention. I had never met a sexier nerd—and by that I don't mean Chelsea's physical attraction. I mean that I had never met anyone who could make me sweat by devotion to academics alone. She was one of those WASP girls whose family members were all geniuses and academics, who lived out in the country on a farm with sheep and avocado trees and other California shit. She's destined to be a poet or artist. You get the sense that she could never fail even if she tried. She wore big round glasses over large blue eyes, and her wavy hair fell thick and long and her skin was flawless. I got used to losing myself in her hair during class. That day I was close up—leaning over my desk like an aggressive-note taker, in glimmering-waterfall-midnight-stormcloud mode. I tried to imagine being at her house, up in the pale-green hills that smell like wine, but for some reason I couldn't. Instead, I remembered the first time I went over to Christine's house for dinner, during my Ayn Rand phase, when I skimmed *Atlas Shrugged* and decided libertarian politics were for nerds. Picture us at the dinner table.

(The curtain opens to reveal a suburban setting. Steaming meat buns and other

assorted dishes are on the table. Hua-Jin, Helen, Joe and Christine Li, and Matthew Rosen sit on wicker chairs by a window framed with azaleas.)

AUTHORITATIVE VOICE

Tā dí mǔ qīn yǐ wéi tā shì yī wèi hǎo hái zǐ, dàn shì tā dí fù qīn bù tóng yì.

HUA JIN

Tā xiàng zhū yī yàng luàn chī, nǎo zǐ yě bù zěn me yàng.

MATTHEW ROSEN

(Turns to face the camera with a million dollar smile.) That there is Mandarin Chinese, of which I understand exactly four words. Charlemagne said that if you know another language you have another soul, so I've got about one billionth of a Mandarin soul. An argument's broken out over Christine's skateboarding habit. I think that she's trying to use me as defense—pointing out that I don't do any useful extracurriculars, and that Hua-Jin and Helen don't criticize *me*.

CHRISTINE

(Grabbing the sleeve of our dashing hero.) I mean, Matt, you help me with my physics homework all the time, don't you?

MATT

I mean I guess so. *(Again turns to camera, cheeks red.)* That's only half true. I get my physics homework answers from Chelsea. Does that make me duplicitous? *(Leaning over and somehow whispering so that only Christine can hear.)* Can't we leave? I'm not hungry.

CHRISTINE

(Whispering) Yes. *(Not whispering.)* Hǎo bā, wǒ mén xiàn zài zǒu lā. *(Matt and Christine go and make out, and the topic of dinner table conversation becomes amiable.)*

"Matt, what are you doing?"

I jerked my head up. "What? What?"

"Weren't you paying attention?" Chelsea placed three fingers with red nails on my desk. "She talked about guns *again*."

"Guns?" I asked. "Which ones this time?"

"She didn't specify." She sighed. Chelsea had this way of sighing in response to the ills of society. "I think she heard too many of us giggling about the SIG Sauer Firearm from before." She tapped my desk with her fingers. "But Matt, you can't stop paying attention now, of all times." She handed me a pencil that had rolled to the edge of my desk. "We have a test tomorrow."

"Is that tomorrow?" I asked, shoving stuff into my backpack.

"The test is Thursday, and Thursday is tomorrow. So yes, it's tomorrow."

We stood to begin our customary walk to physics. "Thanks for reminding me. I've been lost in thought all day," I admitted.

"About Miss Li?"

I rubbed my arm. I didn't like that one bit. Chelsea had caught wind about me and Christine and loved teasing me about it. "No," I said. "I'm trying to decide if I want to go on a road trip with my sister."

"A road trip?"

"To Chicago."

"No way. That must take forever."

"Well, if you drove straight it would only take about 30 hours, but there would be a lot of stops to make."

"Sightseeing?"

"More than sightseeing."

I had caught her attention and was loving it. She moved closer, brushing my shoulder. "Are you going to explain yourself or not?"

As we settled down in Physics, I recapped the improbable story to her. It was useful to hear it out loud—it helped me keep track of the convoluted tale and get into the hypothetical mood. I, Matthew Rosen, might seek my family's missing heirloom. Along with my sister Rebecca, I could cross spacious skies and amber waves of grain, following the clues left to us by Rubin Yakovlev and Anders Wessel. Starting in Sacramento, we can travel east. And when we find the bracelet, we shall return it to my mother and her siblings, and they will determine what to do with it. At the end, Becca and I step out of the old Volkswagen, enriched by experience, family history, and having seen the grand ole US of A, and send Grampa Andy's spirit off harmoniously into the dark.

That was the thinking. My explanation to Chelsea, full of the irrational overconfidence that kicked in whenever I talked to her ("That's incredible," Chelsea said. "You *need* to find out. How could you not? It's an incredible story. I want to hear all about your trip.") convinced me that the road trip was more than just a fun idea. Childish? No doubt. But come on, when a cute girl tells you you *got to* do something...

There were legitimate reasons to go on the road trip. I realized I knew nothing about my family—my great-grandparents living through pogroms was news to me. I also knew nothing about my country besides California. I'd gotten glimpses: A field-trip to D.C. Becca visiting colleges in Chicago. But what about the farms? The fallen factories of Appalachian coal country? The cotton fields of Mississippi? And the *people*? Evangelicals, Scots and Nords, Jamaicans and Indians, east coast enclaves of real Ashkenazi Jews—they're all a part of my country, and all a mystery to me. My determination kicked into high gear, bullshit or not, and Becca even promised to bag on her "packed" summer agenda of anti-Iraq and anti-Israel protests.

One day, Becca dropped a curious bomb on the whole road-trip-bracelet-quest-scenario.

"How would you feel if we met Kaori in New York City?"

"What?"

"You know, our cousin. I keep in touch with her. We're like pen-pals. She wants to come to New York, and if we're going to do a road trip and look for the bracelet, then at the end we could meet her there. Whadya think?"

I hadn't seen Kaori since we went to Japan when I was about eight. The more the merrier. "Sure," I said. "Let's find the bracelet before New York, and we can show it to her."

"Matt—", Becca started, and then she stopped. She looked confused and did that thing where she bites her forefinger.

"What? It would be cool to show it to her, wouldn't it?"

Becca nodded and took a deep breath.

"Are you sure you've never had any dreams?" she asked.

No, Becca, no. I asked her if she was experimenting with magic mushrooms or something, but she acted all offended and walked away. We decided to leave for the road trip on Wednesday, July 15th, giving me a few weeks to make some money and us plenty of time to meet Kaori in New York four weeks later.

So when school ended, I was pumped. I suppose you could say I was feeling self-important. On the last day, Joe Li threw a rager. Not the high school rager that you see in the movies, but the type you can only go to in the Bay Area. The classic ingredients are there: parents out of town, a pool, some beer. But with a crowd featuring some three dozen Asians, a dozen Jews and—count it—three ordinary goyim, all of whom were *also* headed to UC Berkeley, I can tell you it wasn't *Animal House*. There was Super Smash Bros projected on the garage wall, two-hundred dumplings, and quite possibly an equal number of edibles.

Needless to say Christine and I got so high that neither of us could move by 10:00. We were sitting on the couch in the living room, which Joe's friends were using to watch TV: three episodes of "Friends," two-thirds of *Forrest Gump*, half of *Yojimbo*, and one episode of SNL from 1989. Christine laughed uncontrollably while I lay on her shoulder and she patted me on the forehead from time to time. The weed really started kicking us in the brains about ten minutes into *Yojimbo*, when we happened to make eye contact.

"Matt," Christine said. "You don't seem like you."

"*Wakatte iru yo. Kore ga nen da yo,*" I snarled in response. Then I realized it wasn't me. It was the old man on the TV. I blinked in surprise.

If she had said that thirty minutes ago, we would've erupted into a hacking bout of laughter and gotten stares from Joe's friends. Instead, her comment triggered something. I felt like the terrified old man on the screen, struck by a biting sensation of fear, and I looked around. *Violence*, the dead air seemed to murmur. *Violence.*

"Christine," I said. "I have something to tell you."

I saw a glitter in her eye, and I had the fleeting thought that perhaps we were meant for more than being stoned together on a couch, and that I should confess my love to her and we should lose our virginities to each other, this very night, and go official too, because if we like each other then why the hell not?

"Let's wait," she said. "You don't seem like you right now. But you'll be back later." Forehead pat.

"*Yamete kure!*" I cried. "*Mo takusan da!*"

I wrenched around to face the samurai, who was desperately trying to calm me down. The voice was the TV again, not my own. *Maybe I'm not like me,* I thought. Then my brain did this thing where it hopped on two tracks at once, and I started thinking about how I couldn't not be like me when I still was so much solidly myself, while at the same time thinking about how weird it was that I could have such thoughts while also thinking about having those thoughts at the same time. Kids, don't do drugs.

I tried to focus on Yojimbo. Even though I vibed with the old dude and was so in the zone I understood the plot without reading the subtitles, I got a headache pretty fast. The other kids watching were big guys with glasses and black sweatshirts sitting near the TV, pizza in their laps, providing frequent commentary. An unsavory mixture of pizza-smelling thoughts swirled in my mind: Christine, sex, the bracelet, Grampa Andy, being so high that you can think in two layers. My heart was pounding. No, no! The high of marijuana is a low! The cools of cannabis are the hots of hell! After that night, I vowed to never have edibles again.

Christine and I somehow mustered up the willpower to move from the couch to the pool. The party had died out and there were only a few people outside. I moved my legs through the cool water, pushing around swirls of bubbles and spreading my toes. A chill clung to me, tiny droplets on my thighs.

"Do I still not seem like me?" I asked Christine.

She was staring at her reflection in the pool. From where I was sitting, it looked oblong, discolored, oversaturated. Her cheeks looked swollen, red and blue. It had to be true. I wasn't me, and for the worse. Maybe I was gone for forever! But she replied: "You're back."

"Thank God," I said, and from there it all rushed out. I wish I could remember what I said. I just know it was a jumble of thoughts—that I liked her so much but couldn't shake this weird crush on Chelsea, that I was going on a road trip with my sister to find a lost family heirloom that I didn't believe in, that I couldn't stop thinking about Grampa Andy and was having nightmares featuring Rubin Yakovlev, a demonic Russian Sherlock Holmes with tentacles and bulging eyeballs, and I haven't had nightmares since I was eight and had just figured out that death was a thing. Even though she was probably too fucked up to register every word, what she did say struck me to the point of sticking for weeks.

She said: "Going away is a chance to sort out things by being away from them. When you come back, we can decide whether or not we want to be together."

Bear with me for a moment because those lines have *layers*.

Christine can be talkative, but when she says less, she means more. I've always had the impression that Christine understood me better than most people, and it shines through with a statement like that. I registered her response initially in terms of our relationship, so I responded, "Do you still want to have sex?" Sure, it's important to realize that Chelsea is a silly crush and Christine's been the one sticking with me all along. But the next day, after school let out and Will and I were in his basement setting up his gear, I remembered our poolside exchange and took things in a different light.

"Going away is a chance to sort things out." What Christine meant—and this is what I hadn't considered before—is that I had shit to sort out in the first place. Imagine that! Me, a sixteen-year-old, realizes that, indeed, he has shit to sort out. Think about it: 1) I was having nightmares, 2) After getting good grades freshman year things weren't looking nearly so hot in year two, certainly not Berkeley caliber, 3) Bush was blasting apart the Middle East at record speeds while casually destroying the environment, too, 4) Luckily for me, my Dad was a lawyer and we lived in a town so pointlessly decadent that the world could burn and it wouldn't affect us in the slightest,

5) I scored the occasional party-invite but basically had no friends outside of Will and Christine; my reputation was basically Jewish pothead, 6) I was a good runner and had spent two summers working at the Oakland zoo, but besides that I didn't have any discernable talents or marketable skills, unless you consider operating amateur recording equipment a skill. For the first time I realized that I had to sort my shit out. Was Christine criticizing me? No, she liked me the way I was. But somehow that girl knew that I had never even bothered to recognize the unsorted shit that I needed to at minimum alphabetize, but ideally really sort thing by careful thing if I ever wanted to get anywhere meaningful in life.

Wanna hear the kicker? That blazed night at Christine's wasn't even the most significant thing that happened to me during that week. (If you're curious, she did agree that we should have sex. Time and place TBA. As my man Mario would say, *wahoo—!*) But no, it was the next afternoon at Will's place that took the cake.

Will is a musician. He plays the guitar well, and the drums okay, and he has a great voice. He's an alto—it's a high-pitched, girly voice, in a good way. You could call it a sexy voice. A little whiny, with a sparkling shiver. He'd been writing songs since eighth grade and wanted to make an album, and I told him I would help. Over the past three months I read a bunch of internet blogs about amps and mics and MIDIs and Cubase and successfully became Will's producer as the lone prospective applicant. Will and I have been friends since fifth grade. He showed me a lot of good music: Nirvana, Foo Fighters, Radiohead, Arcade Fire, The Strokes, and his newest obsession, Grizzly Bear. I always made fun of his music taste for being so white, since anyone who knows anything knows that Black people made American music but for whatever reason Will didn't like rap. Still, he lived for music, and it felt good to help him live his dream and make an album.

Neither Will nor I were good at school the way our siblings were (he had an older sister at Stanford) or that our parents hoped we'd be, so we both felt a drowsy sense of relief that the year had ended. When you're going into 11th grade, summer no longer feels as free as it used to. The horrors of college applications loom. So down in the familiar chill of his unfinished basement, feeling both anxious and relieved, we kicked into recording routine. I plugged the amp into the wall and the USB into his dad's laptop.

Something was off with Will. I could tell his voice wasn't in tune, and we had to restart the recording about fifteen times before even making it through the first section. It was a complicated song. Will called it "It All Burns Out," his magnum opus. It had six parts that stunted through different rock tropes, singing the first-person tale of a Kurt Cobain or Jimi Hendrix or John Lennon who died in '79 and now watches over the demise of rock music from the dead, because, as Will said, "Rock music died with Kurt Cobain. It's kaput. Gornish," which I corrected to *gornisht*, like how Dad's dad refers to what Kerry would have done for Israel. An hour in, after I had gotten fidgety and bored, Will called it off.

"Screw this," he said. "Let's go outside."

The fresh air felt good. The day was bright and hot, but a cool breeze with a hint of salt in it blew strong and steady. We walked up his street and into a wooded grove where Will and his sister before him went to smoke, although there was no weed this time, especially for me. We sat on two flat stones. But rather than talking shit about classes or assholes on the track team, we fell into a seemingly never-ending silence.

I wanted to ask him if something was wrong, but I'm shit at those sorts of things. I had to wait for him to talk. I glanced at him from time to time. He bit his lip. Fixed his hair. Mentioned the new Mother 3. Finally, when I was starting to get annoyed, he told me.

"We're moving," he said.

"What?" I said.

"We're moving. My mom got a new job."

"Wait, what? Where?"

"In Florida."

"*Florida?!*" I turned to him, furious. He couldn't go to *Florida*, of all places. Florida was full of maniacs!

"Florida. Tampa Bay, Florida."

"You've *got* to be kidding me. But your sister. She goes to Stanford."

"That's why. We can't afford tuition. Mom's gotta take the job."

"Doesn't your dad help—"

"He's not even in the picture."

"But don't they have financial aid—"

"Not nearly enough."

"But what about you, you're in the middle of—"

"Matt, what do you want me to say? It's already been decided." He crossed his arms. "It's been decided for almost a month."

"*A month!?*"

"Sorry I didn't tell you, Matt. Sorry I didn't feel like telling you."

"Yeah, why the fuck didn't you tell me?"

"I didn't feel like it."

"But when are you leaving?"

"We're moving in July. The house is gonna be sold."

"But—I won't—well, did I tell you about the road trip? I might not be here in July, and—" He gave me a confused glance, so I ran him through the flash-fiction version of the story. At the end of it he nodded.

"That sounds really awesome, Matt. We'll just have to say bye before you go."

I shook my head. "That sucks. That's actually the fucking worst."

He didn't respond. He had found a twig and was drawing circles in the dirt, each inside the previous one. When he narrowed to a button-sized circle at the center, he tossed the stick into the brush behind us.

Beads of sweat dropped down my arms. I said, as steadily as I could, "We need to finish your album before you go."

He shook his head. "It's not going anywhere. I'm not good enough."

I was all riled up, so in ordinary circumstances I would've gone on an impressive tirade: *No,* you are an incredible musician, don't be ridiculous, the album is going great, what's the point if you're just giving up now, haven't we been happy with the songs so far? But at that moment I couldn't speak: I had seen something.

When Will had been drawing in the dirt with the stick, in the middle of the circles his stick had hit a metal coin. I reached over and peeled it up out of the soil. I wiped it off with my shirt.

It was a quarter, but with a strange error. George Washington's face gazed in his typical triumph on the front side, but on the back, the coin was split half and half between two states. The left half showed the statue of liberty topped with the text "NEW Y", and the other half displayed "ORNIA", the severed wing of the eagle, the smooth descent of a mountain, and in smaller text, "YOSEMITE VALLEY." The two halves were divided by a dark scorch like a lightning bolt. A coin split between New York and California.

I knew then that there was no escaping this road trip.

6

The Golden Gate Bridge

Will's unfortunate announcement was the start of a sharp decline in lifestyle quality for yours truly. At first, Becca and I just got caught up in organizing our road trip. For the first two weeks of summer I barely left the house. I devoured the notebook Grampa Andy had left us, while Becca made arrangements with Uncle Michael in Chicago and Kaori in New York. I wanted to get closer to Grampa Andy and his quest—what it meant to him, why he was doing it—but it was a frustrating task. The pages were crisp, old sheets of copious notes scrawled out by Rubin Yakovlev, dotted with concise, authoritative paragraphs by Grampa Andy, and flooded in a deluge of annotations in either Yiddish or Hebrew.

בטוב

אפשר

טשיקאווע

And so on. I paid special attention to Grampa Andy's paragraphs, reading the notes with a focus typically reserved for the great artists of antiquity, chipping away at marble to reveal the ideal man within.

There were two suspects for the start of the bracelet's trail: Chicago and El Paso. Yakovlev wrote about a 1936 murder in El Paso, supposedly over the bracelet, which seemed to be the earliest reference, until Grampa Andy pulled up something even earlier: a newspaper clipping from Chicago, 1928, on a kid named Dick Rivers, who hit a home run every time he stepped to plate, and claimed a lucky bracelet was the key to his success.

I quickly realized that my methodology didn't make sense. I needed the most *recent* place the bracelet had been spotted. Grampa Andy had leads on the bracelet being somewhere in California in the 90s, but after a pit-stop in a St. Louis laundromat in 1999, the trail seemed to have run dry. I decided the best that we could do was to go to Chicago and eventually New York, visiting sites that Rubin Yakovlev or Grampa Andy had mentioned but never investigated along the way. A list and a plan started coming together. Sacramento, Reno, Salt Lake City, Omaha. Becca researched the logistics of the road trip, finding motels, buying maps, making a packing list, and even taking the Volkswagen to get fixed up. Then, about ten days into summer break, Dad got wind of the plan.

It's not that we didn't tell our parents—we told them about the bracelet and that we wanted to go on a road trip. Mom denied the bracelet's existence entirely. She said a bunch of times that Grampa Andy was inventing a silly game for us to play, and I don't think Dad realized that Becca and I were actually gonna do it. He wasn't happy. He had assumed I had gotten an internship or a job, and that Becca had gotten both. Apparently Mom had been "quite vague" in communicating our summer plans to him, and he expected better from us.

The timing was shitty. The day before, Dad had caught me and Christine sneaking out two handles of Patron to bring to some party, so he grounded me for a week. After finding out about the road trip, he delivered an over-the-top assurance that we would never receive another cent from him in our lives if we drove to New York. The next day, my grades came in.

That was the kicker. Before my report card, all his howling about "never giving us another goddamn cent in our lives" was him bluffing us into getting jobs. But there's nothing like a C in Physics to make shit real.

He grounded me a second week. The road trip was off. I hadn't seen Will since he told me he was moving and I still hadn't lost my virginity and I was living the exact opposite way that Grampa Andy had wanted me to. I didn't know what to do except call the Oakland Zoo, where I worked last summer, and go in for the orientation, even though it's impossible to forget how to clean up animal shit. This year I would work in Great Apes. Young Matt's dream.

That was ten days into the grounding, and almost 20 days into my summer. I'd lied and told Dad that I had another orientation so I could hang out with Jake Hyman and some of his friends, but I'd forgotten that Jake thought I was a dweeb and used me to prove to his other friends that he's a Real Cool Cat. Jake and I were best friends as kids, but all he wanted to do nowadays was hustle fake IDs and try to hit on college girls. He was tall enough for it. He wanted to be Important Silicon Valley Man™, an entrepreneur, and I guess fake IDs is as good of a start as anything. They only invited me so I would pay for the weed. So the Jake Squad ditched me after about one hour and forty bucks, and the whole outing was a stupid waste of time.

So I went to Baker Beach by myself. I stared up at the Golden Gate Bridge, furiously angsty, steeled in my conviction that the Golden Gate Bridge was the worst piece of architecture in the continental United States.

For one, the Golden Gate Bridge (henceforth GGB) gives a false impression of California. The elegant design and eternal steel. The sunsets of red flames and golden mist. It's a fitting image for the glorious extremity of the insurmountable-yet-ingloriously-surmounted American landscape of 1937, but in today's postmodern, consumerist world (I did my English project on *White Noise*), I couldn't help but to wish the bridge could refresh accordingly, turn corny and trashy and hung with billboards and advertisements. Something more representative of river-slurping almond farms, overdosed hippies, Hollywood limousines, and the big www.com splotch of smog slouching in the sky.

For two, it's just begging people to jump off of it. There's no suicide hotspot in the world like GGB. I don't know anyone who did it, but I know people who know people who did. I bet the numbers are terrifying. Because jumping off GGB is the most romantic death in the world. No responsible Bay Area resident hasn't at least considered it. Leaping from sunset steel to silver fog, murmuring blue ocean, through sailing feather clouds—how can the chronically depressed resist? The bridge is a murderous false icon.

I glanced at the parking lot. People were leaving the beach. The well-dressed couples and families with small children had left around dinner, and now as the sun simmered away, the older couples, long-bearded men and gray-haired women in floppy hats, dog-walkers, and the younger couples, blond-bearded guys and girls in ripped jeans and sandals, packed up at last. A screaming gull flew overhead, and a flock left their roost in the bay.

I thought about Will. We had never fought before, but some stubborn wall had sprung up between us. Suddenly we had nothing to say to each other.

I kicked the sand. Everything was pushing down, squeezing me. I hadn't been upset about losing the opportunity to go on the road trip because I figured Dad would change his mind, but now I didn't think I even wanted to do it anymore. I mean, if you think about it, the story is ridiculous, implausible in the first place, and I didn't particularly care about Rufus Yakocic and the shtetl Fuchses of yore. During the spare hours of my grounding I had read the notebook too many times, and I ended up drowning in an ocean of words. A sort of Jewish, very ugly, very poorly written *Moby-Dick.* Finding the family bracelet would be a hopeless task. Rubin Yakovlev had spent his entire life searching, but I wasn't any closer to finding it than he had been in 1950. By 1945, the groundwork had been established: the bracelet traveled fast, and people loved it and bought it and stole it and craved it and sold it or lost it or gave it away within a few years, months, weeks or even days. Most often, a mysterious figure known as "the cowboy" was the one who facilitated the transaction. In 1950, Rubin Yakovlev was sure it was in Chicago; much later, Grampa Andy wrote that Cheyenne was more likely. Rubin Yakovlev had wasted his entire life, and Grampa Andy ten years of his own. It almost made me sad to think that Grampa Andy cared so much about his in-laws. This entire notebook, the countless trips—he really loved us, he really did. His love was enormous, oppressive, overwhelming, and now I'm not just squeezed and submerged but flattened too, rolled out like Jack Kerouac's endless scroll that I'd been reading while I was grounded, dancing and wriggling on the bodies of Mexican prostitutes. Did he think that as a historian he could restore some sort of Yiddish-Ukrainian heritage for us, for me? He was wrong to try. There's nothing there. Whatever Yiddish-Ukrainian heritage my grandfather had dissolved when he married into a California family. Jewishness passes through the mother—so my mom, and therefore me—we're not technically Jewish! Judaism *can't* mean something to me. If the bracelet is out there it wouldn't connect with me because there's no Fuchs in the family left, and even less Yakovlev.

At that moment I felt a hand on my shoulder.

I jumped up and shouted. Becca shrieked at me.

"What the fuck is wrong with you?"

I kicked the sand. "Jesus. Sorry, Becca. You scared the shit out of me. What are you doing here?"

She jerked her head towards the parking lot. I saw the gray outline of the Volkswagen. "Picking you up."

"I told Mom to come."

"I came instead. Wanna go, or should I drive home and tell her to come get you?"

I sighed. I followed her across the beach, kicking up sand as I went, spreading shit around.

"You're going into the DMV tomorrow," she said, starting the ignition. I was flicking at the window, trying to scrape away a little piece of dirt, but it wouldn't budge.

"Did you hear me?" she asked, car leaving the lot.

"What?" I asked.

"Tomorrow I'm taking you to the DMV," she said.

"Why?"

"You need your driver's license."

I groaned. "Not now, Becca. I'll do it in August."

"You need your driver's license now."

"Why? Dad can drop me off at the zoo—"

"Oh yeah," she said. "About that—you'll want to call and quit."

"Dad will be thrilled," I said.

"*Because*," she said, "we need to leave on the road trip by next week, or we'll never make it to New York and back before the end of summer."

I stopped flicking the window.

"You need to get your driver's license so we can split the driving, and reorganize your notes because you know more about the bracelet than I do—"

She was pissing me off. I spoke loud and at the window. "What are you talking about? Dad said we can't go. We're not doing the road trip, we threw it out the window weeks ago."

"Don't worry about it," Becca said. "I've sorted it out with them. Mom convinced Dad about the whole thing. All I had to do was promise Mom that that we wouldn't look for the bracelet. I just pretended like we had both lost interest completely and that we're just sightseeing and meeting Kaori in New York, which should be great anyways. Plus Kaori already got her plane ticket. They're even giving us money for motels, which means we can use Grampa Andy's money on gas and food! Matt, we're fucking going—"

"I don't want to go," I said.

"—and as for other costs, we both have some money saved. I already have maps and stuff, and the car is—"

"I don't want to go, Becca. I don't want to go."

We sped down the dusky highway. Cars' headlights on the other side sparked. Our own headlights were shadows in comparison.

"Why not?" she asked. "You wanted to do it before. For Grampa Andy. Right?"

I wanted to throw the whole fucking car off the highway into the bramble. I slammed the dashboard.

"*I don't want to.* Is that good enough for you?"

Out of the corner of my eye I saw her bite her lip and exercise restraint. That only made me angrier because it meant that she thought I was acting immature. I had to prove her wrong, so I restrained my reaction to her restraint.

"If you are so dense that you require an explanation," I said, clenching my fists, "there's no fucking point. There's no bracelet, or if there is, it could be virtually anywhere in North America—"

Becca shook her head. "You're wrong, Matt. It's out there. It's waiting for us. I know it."

"Thank god we have *your feelings* instead of the physical evidence that proves we'll never find it. Neither Mom or Dad want us to go. And you know what? The biggest reason of all is that I don't think I could survive being alone with you for that long. I think I'd have to kill you in order to not go completely insane." I looked at her. "Is that a good enough reason?"

Becca was nodding. She looked like she might laugh. I wanted to punch her. Fortunately for her—and me too, considering we were cruising down the highway at 70 miles per hour—she said the right thing.

"That's good enough for me."

I fell silent.

7

Leonard

The Day You Were Hit By A Car On Sunset Boulevard

1979, Pasadena, California

3 Waverly Dr.
October 19

Dear Dr. Hartenstein,

I am writing regarding a follow-up appointment for my uncle, Rubin Ahav Yakovlev, aged 75, with regard to his extreme instances of psychotic behavior, schizophrenia, & multiple personality disorder. (Of course, all information must be kept absolutely private at all costs. You know the risks involved. There are certain facts that I cannot record in this letter.)

I am certain that it is in the best interest of our family to proceed with institutionalization, pending of course, your recommendation & approval. I would like to provide background concerning the origin of his disturbed mind that I have gleaned from him via productive conversation over the last several days, & corroborated via reference to a certain notebook, which we may safely consider to be my uncle's diary for all intents & purposes. I hope that it may prove enlightening for your own research, diagnosis, etc., since these stories may demonstrate the relationship between migrant status, certain other historical phenomena, & madness—which I will endeavor to spell out over the course of this letter.

As you know, Rubin Yakovlev, henceforth *the subject*, was born in what is today the southeastern, Oriental regions of the Ukraine, and made refugee by Russian pogroms. After reaching manhood in the U.S., he went west to Kansas on a land scheme and barely survived the Great Depression, only to go completely bankrupt in a drought after fifteen years of hard labor. It was around then that he arrived back in New York, a broken man. After some time, he got back on his feet, went to Forestry School, and began his career as a surveyor for the National Park Service. By that time—1939, to be precise—we have full reason to believe that his psychotic tendencies had already begun to manifest.

The initial trigger occurred during this return home. The subject was staying with his sister, Mrs. Ariana Stern, at her home in Brooklyn, NY, in 1939. They enjoyed small talk over dinner, remembering the "old country." The subject refused soup & leaned over the table, asking with notable aggression why his sister did not wear the bracelet, a relic of their Eastern origins, repeating the question numerous times & eventually growing enraged when Mrs. Stern admitted she was unaware of the location of the bracelet. It may be theorized that in this precise moment, the subject became unhinged.

His sister would soon impart to him that the bracelet of his childhood had been sold. This news rendered the subject able to fall asleep & dream, despite previously having been an insomniac for many years.

We may speculate that Mrs. Stern, in uttering the truth, pulled a sort of lever in the mind of the subject. The subject could not let his ancestors' sacrifice evaporate in the great American desert. The subject could not let his heritage be sold for a few months of smiles from affable Gentile folk & invitations to barbecues. We may conjecture that dream-powering energy turned like gears in a clock tower, like air rushing through the pipes of an organ; this "lever" was pulled, wondrous mechanics were engaged in the mind of the subject, & that night he had a dream, never again to experience a rational moment in his long, delirious life.

This delirium set him off on his never-ending quest. He searched for this certain leather bracelet, while he surveyed forests for the U.S. government. In each state, the subject hurried through six months' worth of surveying in two and got to "business." He collected contacts & notes, names, police stations, auction houses, jewelers, post offices, etc. With little luck, the subject grew isolated & dogmatic, which duly leads us to a hot day in August, '44.

On the day in question, the subject encountered Jetta H. Kanosh, wielding a shotgun at 2— West — Road, El Paso, a two-room house converted from a trailer & sunken into the cracked ground. The subject had been pursuing Mr. Kanosh. According to the subject, Mr. Kanosh had killed a man named James Wesley Hardin Jr, whose father, James Wesley Hardin Sr, had purchased the leather bracelet in question from the subject's sister. The subject claims that he prayed for revelation, putting on his phylacteries & reciting the Kaddish, a traditional Jewish prayer. After his prayer, the subject had a vivid dream: a leather bracelet with a winking glitter hanging on a wooden peg, among moose antlers, possum skins, & cured human scalps; a door swinging shut, with rifle-fire resounding like rain & blind eyes the color of sea-fog.

Mr. Kanosh, at length, lowered the shotgun. When standing among the crooked floorboards of the cob-webbed, sunken trailer, the subject's hallucinations became manifold: he alleges to have seen James Wesley Harden Sr, cowboy, outlaw, & Indian scalp collector, capture with his group of militants numerous Indian villages in the Nevada desert for the purpose of white settlement, and the mother of Jetta Kanosh, torn from her home, babe in arms. He alleges to have heard the sheen of a knife and sound of tearing flesh as Kanosh murders James Wesley Hardin Jr and slips the bracelet on his wrist, a prize. He even alleges to have sniffed bloody brains & vomit in the silky desert grass, to have tasted anesthetic & chlorine, as Dr. John Wesley Hardin III, MD, founds "Planning Your Family", an assimilation scheme championed by the Indian Health Service, disguising chemical sterilizers as birth control, presented to Native women in more than thirteen states. Brutal processes of revenge, and now the subject found himself within them.

The subject insists that these instances are intimately connected, all brought about by a single moving force of will. He considers them to represent a "chain reaction of revenge," in which Jetta Kanosh murdered James Wesley Hardin Jr. because Jetta Kanosh's Paiute village was destroyed by James Wesley Hardin Sr., & that James Wesley Hardin III medically sterilized Paiute women, pioneered by a single, daring, violent force. Of course, these motivations in these actions disconnected by geography and generation are implausible. Here we can clearly see the subject assign layers of meaning on to happenstance.

In their respectively western & emigre accents, Mr. Kanosh asked Mr. Yakovlev how he found him, & Mr. Yakovlev asked in return about the location of the bracelet.

Mr. Kanosh stated that he entrusted the bracelet to his daughter. Meanwhile, Mr. Yakovlev made up a fictional response: that his sister possessed a receipt from the bracelet's sale to Hardin Sr., enabling the subject to track down Hardin Jr. to El Paso; murder reports led the subject to the police and a detective who worked on the case but never located the prime suspect, Jetta Kanosh; the subject found Mr. Kanosh by inquiring after Kanosh's relatives at the Paiute reservation on Pyramid Lake, Nevada. A wholly rational observer may see this as a realistic series of events, but in truthfulness, they never occurred; as you may recall, the subject alleged that the address of Mr. Kanosh came to him in a dream. Mr. Kanosh's answer, too, turned out to be a lie: the subject reportedly tracked down Jetta Kanosh's daughter, who reportedly had never heard of the bracelet in her life. Mr. Kanosh 'mysteriously' passed away shortly thereafter.

A strange story, is it not, Dr. Hartenstein? Some facts and historical truths, events that were indisputable in their moments, seem to lose themselves to the currents of time. Mr. Yakovlev's fabricated lie was much more realistic than the impossibility that his dream revealed the location of the bracelet, which not even the police could discover. Therefore, we may consider the fabricated lie to be truth, even though it was truly a lie of appreciably imaginative fabrication.

According to my uncle's notebook, that fateful day was the beginning, not the end of his quest. And in certain ways it was. Certainly from that day he would continue his roaming ways. But we now have knowledge that on that fateful day, there was an additional change. At a certain point, lies must be crushed. At a certain point, only the truth can be allowed to survive. I believe we have reached that moment, if not on the page, at the least in our hearts & minds.

In earnest, we ask that you proceed with his institutionalization. He has been set loose on his family and this country for long enough.

Kind regards, & to the Mrs.,
LEONARD STERN
PARAMOUNT PICTURES

* * *

Leo put down the letter, fingers leaden with exhaustion.

It was still dark out. Nearly sunrise. This was atypical for Leo. He usually slept in, sometimes past nine to the silent frustration of his wife. His excuse was that he didn't need to be at the studio until 10:00, but traffic meant that even waking up at 9:00 cut things close, with his need for a morning shower and shave. Why does he sweat like a frog? Why is he as hairy as an ape? Night-gowns and suits will never be gartels and mantels for such a hairy man. It's more than early puberty and a stressful job.

Karen's body was meaningless form and mass beside him. He crept out of bed and took a long, cold shower. He shaved, and watched his own face and its many lines, scribbled on as if his skin were parchment. He remembered that he should visit his hospitalized mother. It was lung cancer.

He slept late because he never got into bed before 2:00, and even then he often found himself staring at the mounted clock until he could make out the thin line of the hour hand in complete blackness.

The hour hand never moved when he watched it. It moved too slowly to decipher the motion. He simply stared at it until his eyes burned with effort, and all the sudden the hand would be pointing at the four. After that, he usually fell asleep.

Leo arose a few hours later and wrote the letter to Dr. Hartenstein. Then, when he stepped outside to get the newspaper, he happened to exit his house at the exact incipience of sunrise.

The flaming orb crawling into the sky struck him as a horrible omen. No: a natural wonder. For a moment, he comprehended various articles of scientific literature he had read before. He saw the inferno, the center of the solar system, exploding atoms and supercharged gas erupting from a churning nuclear core of a million degrees. He felt thankful that Earth was a safe ninety-three million miles away. Eight whole light minutes, he reminded himself, but in those terms, the sun seemed entirely too close. Less than the time it takes to drink a cup of coffee. If the sun moved any closer, the whole earth might boil. Quickly, the sun became blinding to witness. The light was violence, bombing the heavens. The might of G-d annihilates; there is no vessel for His love; if you submit, your body will shatter. Resist, and remain a godless, ordered world.

Hydrogen.

Photons.

Morning: Surely, this is good.

The sun repainted the dusky sky with airy blue. The entire sky recolored in the time it takes Leo to brush his teeth.

Leo returned inside and stared at the empty kitchen table. Years ago, his son Lawrence would've been sitting there, no matter the hour of the morning, playing with construction paper and crayons.

"Morning," Leo would say. "What're you drawing there?"

Lawrence would raise his messy head of dark hair. "Good morning daddy." He looks down. "It's a drawing. It's private."

But no Lawrence today. No Lawrence for years. After Columbia, the boy had run away to Europe. Now he claimed he was going to Japan. The Orient! Some dim dark, red-colored corner of the world that Leo could barely imagine. And his other two boys were at Columbia now. And his daughter, Berkeley. Los Angeles had emptied out.

To work. Leo slipped upstairs and put on a suit in a hurry; the tie was crooked, and he'd need to retie it later. No matter. He drove off to work, sweat beginning to stain his white shirt, before Karen even stirred.

Once he left the house, he drove at a halting pace. Something about the sight of sunrise had put him in a philosophical mood. What was he doing? Producing movies. Why not retire? He was only 57. How did he get here? He recalled the first time he earned a listing in the credits as *Executive Producer,* some fifteen years ago. The picture with Harry Belfonte was blowing up box offices, so he suggested getting Elvis Presley for an exotic comedy adventure with the sexy Ursula Andress. Aikman loved it.

Aikman loved the idea for the same reason Leo despised himself: he was a born imitator. When he looked in the mirror, sometimes he saw a monkey, with his thick hair and slightly hunched shoulders. After all, a monkey mimics men. He could write Hollywood blockbusters, dress with style, marry a California woman, move from Boyle Heights to Westwood Village. (And leave the Poles behind? The Negroes? Now, that was a decision made long ago, and one he could not afford to regret. In the 60s there had been riots, and that should serve as reason enough.)

But it required more than mimicry. It required ruthlessness. Leo felt as if he stood atop the dead bodies of his rivals, threatened with legal recourse and sometimes the shadows of physical violence, trapped in dead-end jobs, cast off to other studios. A lion of the cinema takes no prisoners.

And while he could remember his reason for moving from the sort of urban neighborhood he had grown up in to a white-fenced white hamlet with neither baker nor shoemaker, he strained to remember why he moved to Los Angeles to begin with. To live in the world of stars and swimming pools, and not in the rotted husk of New York City? To change his world? It was a metamorphosis, he told himself, but a good one, he added, remembering Kafka. How could he forget Kafka?

Six blocks down Sunset, right before getting on the highway, Leo remembered that he ought to send the letter to Dr. Hartenstein. He did a u-turn and pulled off the main street to the post office in West Hollywood. Uncle Rubin had written a few weeks ago from Scranton, Pennsylvania that he was coming to Los Angeles. Leo had ample reason to believe that his uncle suffered from schizophrenia and split personality disorder and had committed multiple heinous crimes. A vat of emotion churned furiously within—anger at what had transpired, fear of taking away his mother's brother from her side, bafflement at considering the consequences. The story of that bracelet was a never-ending, preposterous, and bloody story, and Leo shivered at the thought of his uncle's furious blue eyes.

He remembered when Uncle Rubin drove him from Brooklyn to Los Angeles, nearly thirty years ago. At the time it was a matter of convenience, as Rubin Yakovlev always drove around the country in the course of his surveys. But on the trip, Leo's cranky *Feter* had insisted on all sorts of absurd detours. Leo followed in good humor, at first. They visited a gun-toting farmer's stand in Kentucky. They stopped at a goldsmith in Chicago, where Leo sorted through six hundred sales records. They hiked all the way up to Lincoln's beard at the recently completed Mount Rushmore, in the middle of a thunderstorm. Leo remembers the endless mounds like dark bodies shuddering under wind and rain, and the preposterous futility of it all. Leo remembered his uncle's eyes, a sky blue back then, and his endless dreams, dream after dream after dream. He knew his uncle's dreams, he knew every one. But Leo couldn't remember his own. Not since he was nine and scared of the dark. Leo remembered the moment of realization when he understood the idiocy of his uncle's quest. Leo felt pity, and even anger that the old fool was still searching, still suffering, after all these years—it's blasphemous, Leo thought, to waste one's life away like that in America.

As Leo put the letter in the post box and waited at the light to cross the street, he recalled that road trip. It wasn't long ago, in the grand scheme of things, his youth. He ought to remember it better. But a Los Angeles smog hung over his memories, distorting their hue like damaged film. Leo knew one thing: he planned to leave his old self behind in the East and form a new one in the West. He had determined to follow the American character to where it flourished: on sunny Pacific shores, among the palms. His old Brooklyn self—high school quarterback, Kaddish leader, lover of Shoshanah and Marlene, schlepper of *Der Amerikaner,* youngest of three—blew off the Atlantic coast when he made that trip with his mad uncle. Leo went to cross the street.

Then a lazy, southern drawl of a voice made Leo's face bright red and his guts squirm. "Hey kike. What exactly do you think you're doin' in Los Angeles?"

Anti-semites! Leo turned and saw a middle-aged man in a broad cowboy hat and tall boots. The cowboy grinned a white-toothed smile. Then a blinding flash eclipsed the world into a savage darkness.

The dark began at the crown of Leo's head, like a bruise. The root of pain. It flexed, trembled, and bludgeoned his skull with a hammer. The pain refined, and again, filled reservoirs and emptied out nine more times, so much pain that it erased the world. Leo lost track of his body. He didn't know who he was. He knew nothing. The darkness everywhere, and everything.

Shema yisrael. Leo gasped in the dark. *Adonai elohainu.* The pain consumed souls, devoured the sun, obliterated even gravity and soon nothing would remain. *Adonai ehad.*

The darkness slithered away and slipped to earth in rising and falling rushes of trickling grains. The sand poured down around him. Dry rain, desert storm. It smelled like stone and a frying sun. By the time the rain stopped and all was silent, Leo realized he was in the desert. He looked at the sky and saw that there was neither sun nor stars.

Brutal heat and endless sand. And then, to Leo's shock and awe, he saw the Israelites marching in the distance. They were a parade of staff-bearing elders and toddling children alike. Leo could even see the Holy Ark, marked by its gold trappings. Were you wrong to disdain them? The wind picked up. Leo stumbled towards them in the sand. *My people!* The whole parade, the whole populace bore a mark; or rather they formed a mark, a circlet, a scorched insignia, a desert stamp of YHWH.

It read:

WE ARE THE VICTIMS

The burning sand scarred Leo's pale feet, blackening them as he rushed across the desert, every step sinking sinking into the shifting dunes. As he sprints towards the clan with all his might, each individual separates into chronological lineage: Abraham, Jacob, Moses, Ishmael, Eliyahu, Solomon, Maimonedes, Rabbi Akivah, Baruch Spinoza, Theodor Herzl, Leo's father... those who he has failed to live up to rose in a glittering line before his eyes, and the last in the line, the closest to him and rapidly approaching, was the very devil.

It reared on the sand like a stallion, screaming in an unknown language, and charged. Leo tried to run but it was too late. The fiend had him by the throat and then there was a softening of the grip and the sand hardened beneath his feet and he realized it was his Uncle Rubin.

"Sholom, Eli," he said.

"Ku-c-r Yubin!" Leo choked, mouth full of sand. "Shpet! Shit! Hat happened? Ham I dekh? Har you dekh?"

"You have been hit by a car, but you are not dead, and I am not dead," Uncle Rubin said, gesticulating, stunted by a thick Yiddish accent.

The words brought relief. He still had time. Leo looked up at his towering uncle with a smile to show that he was not concerned.

"But both of us *vill* die," Uncle Rubin continued. "Ve vill be killed by de same forces of darkness dat have attempted to kill you now, Eli."

But Leo was no longer looking at his uncle. He tapped his foot on the packed sand familiar to a California foot, and raised his voice."Uncle Rubin, you know, you're the reason I ended up here. Don't you know that? Some cowboy thought that you were me, and then—"

"Dat cowboy is evil." Uncle Rubin grabbed Leo's hand. "Our family has done battle vith him forever, even ven he vas not a cowboy. He is Ishmael, he is Esau. He is not us. He vill dog us to de end of days—"

"You old fool!" Leo growled. "Even now, rattling on about that cowboy!"

"Do you know vat he did to your cousin Rivka?" Uncle Rubin asked, tears streaming down his cheeks. "Ven de Nazis came to Vilnius..."

"I don't care what he did to Rivka! Just stop it with the goddamn cowboy and the goddamn bracelet!"

"Dat bracelet; yes, dat bracelet dat has varded off de darkness dat plagues de vorld. Dat darkness dat turns men and vomen into monsters and makes collapsing of societies! Your mother sold the bracelet trying to have us assimilate but did not realize dat assimilating meant assimilating into de darkness. It is de sole source of order, systems, reason in dis poor universe, and I am de arbiter, Eli. I am de sword of Elohim! Ve must fight de darkness. Ve must fight vith our swords and decide for our own who vill live and who vill die."

"Stop rambling, Uncle Rubin. There's no darkness. We're in the sun. We're in the *goddamned desert!*"

Uncle Rubin shook his gray head and closed his deep-set eyes. "Tell me no lies. You fear de light even as you fear de dark."

Leo stamped his foot. "You're trying to trick me. When you came at me before you didn't look like yourself. Who are you? What are you trying to do? You're not my uncle—"

Leo could not see him anymore. The sunless sky was too bright and every grain of sand a beacon. The sky pulled closer to the Earth, growing heavy and full of chains that link into a massive ring. Crumbling thunder shuddered, and with a desert-shattering screech a pure, golden orb fell from the hairy sky, sparking with absolute brilliance, scalding his mind to hot milk and his body to a cloud.

He awoke.

The right half of his body felt like cracked stone. Petrified. Not his own. The piercing white of fluorescents made his eyes water. He smelled antiseptic. Pain rose and fell in a dull throb across his chest.

"Leo!" a voice exclaimed. "There you are."

Leo could not see who it was.

"Happened to be passing by when Karen called, so I made sure to hop in. She'll be here soon as traffic permits." Peering into Leo's frame of vision was Andy Wessel.

Irritation stirred in Leo's gut but he couldn't move a muscle to express it. Why was Andy Wessel, of all people, here now? He gets murdered by a Nazi and of all people, goddamn Andy Wessel gets there first?

"You all right there, Leo?" Andy asked. His sunglasses were up on his hat, a hideous, broad-brimmed cowboy style. A frown of genuine concern wrapped all the way across his face. Andy had huge expressions that took up his mouth and eyes and entire face—trying to be charming, trying to be charismatic, but Leo was not a fool.

"Who are you supposed to be, Billy the Kid?" Leo grunted.

Relief broke into Andy's frown and a big smile took its place. "You were lucky, Leo. Got hit by a car, right in the middle of Sunset Boulevard." Just as quickly the frown came back. "You were only out for an hour. Glancing blow."

Leo remembered crossing the street, turning. The strange cowboy.

Andy sighed. "The universe operates in such strange ways. I know you're a staunch atheist, Leo, so forgive me when I say this. But with all the weird things happening out there in the world—getting run over by a car on Sunset Boulevard for Christ's sake—it's hard for me to believe that there *couldn't* be a God. Seems backwards, but it's true—God's the only possible way the universe could be so illogical."

A headache thudded at Leo's temple. "The other man," he grumbled. "Did he die as well?"

"What other man?"

"What do you mean, what other man? There was another man, standing in the street, right behind me. Tall, and his hat was even worse than yours."

Andy shook his head, tracing the rim of his brown hat. "That's the first I've heard of him."

Leo grunted. "He must've already been carted off. He probably died on impact."

A long silence followed as Andy looked down at his own hands. "Forgive me," Andy suddenly said. "Tell me how you're feeling. Think you broke a few ribs, but besides that, you seem to have gotten off pretty much unhurt."

Leo grumbled. Unhurt! Unhurt. Yes, he was unhurt... The strange dream murmured at the edges of his consciousness. There was so much he had to do. Above all, he had to take care of the institutionalization of Uncle Rubin. Lock him up. No time to lose. Who could he call to have the old man driven to Dr. Hartenstein right away? No time to spare. From the dream he knew that much.

"And by the way," Andy added, "your wife tells me your mother's alone in the hospital now. We should hire help to keep her company."

His mother... yes, more than his uncle, he felt for his mother—urgently.

He didn't want her to die. For the first time he realized that he wanted her to live so badly that he would do anything to keep her dark eyes blinking and smiling and dancing in this world. Why did he forsake her? Why did he abandon her? Why hadn't he given himself as a sacrifice to the one cruel God that can keep her alive?

And a river of tears surged from his eyes. For the rest of his life, Leonard Stern would be a religious man. Here I am, Mother—Hineini! Here I am!

8

Sacramento

We only had one day and one night in Sacramento, so we had to make it count. The city was bonfire hot. We got there at 10:30. Parked the car at our cousin Lucy Wessel's apartment. Brunch at a diner, years of catch-up. I ate two pancakes and an omelet and let Becca do the talking. Mom had called up her cousin, Lucy, a pleasant woman in her late 20s, non-profit consulting. Sunhat, wood-frame sunglasses. She was hosting us for the night, so I was sure to be polite, but I was restless. I wanted to get out to Walerga. Brunch ended at 12:30 and Becca and I nodded at one another.

The sky and street was full of birds, chirping bluebirds, strutting pigeons, squawking crows, and eagles flat like crosses against the sky. Becca wore a tank-top (unshaven armpits loud and proud) and a Giants cap and had her hair in a ponytail, which was a surefire sign she was in a good mood.

"North Highland Road, Walerga," I read from my own notes.

Becca nodded, punching Walerga into the GPS. "Can you remind me which story that is?"

"It's pretty far back. We're talking 1945."

"That's going *way* back."

"Yeah, but it's the most important clue in this part of the country," I said. "Rubin Yakovlev was confident that the bracelet was here. He heard about a man who had escaped the Japanese internment camp thanks to a magic amulet, from a bunch of sources. Grampa Andy highlighted it, too."

"North Highland road, you said?" Becca was reading the GPS directions.

"Yep, that's it."

The GPS told us to make a U-turn. Becca looked up at me.

"This isn't going to be easy," she said. "If we're talking about 1945... well, Matt, that was 70 years ago."

"So what?"

Becca shrugged. "I'm just trying to get you ready for disappointment. We might not find the bracelet here."

"I thought you were the one who had a feeling we were gonna find it."

"Yes, Matt, but not necessarily in Sacramento! We should be prepared to not find it today, or anytime soon."

"Okay, okay," I said. "But this *is* the only way, right? We need to go and try to find someone who might know about it. You can't just *feel* your way through time and space."

"Is there nothing else written?" Becca asked.

I peered at the yellowed pages, hoping that something new might magically appear. "Zilch."

"Well, let's give it a shot. Just remember—no matter what, you can't tell Mom we're looking for the bracelet, or she'll blow it. The fuck knows why."

So there we were in Sacramento, suitcases full of clothes, Altoids and plastic sunglasses on the dashboard, one week after my smashing rejection of Becca's renewed offer to go on the road trip. Surprised? Don't be. Teenagers are fickle. Allow me to explain the workings behind my change of heart.

Step 1: Things get worse. Steps 2: I almost lose my virginity. Step 3: I get the fuck over myself.

First of all, after GGB, things *definitely* got worse. When we got home, Mom was in tears. Wet cheeks, red eyes, the works. She was holding a copy of the *Chestnut Creek Jewish Times* and she wouldn't tell us what happened, just kept crying, which freaked both of us out. Becca started yelling at Mom. Mom kept crying. Dad got home. He tried to calm things down. Mom finally said it was a fight with Uncle Michael, and Dad nodded ponderously, before yelling at Becca for yelling at Mom, so now we were all angry. I was with Becca on this one and called BS. Uncle Michael and Mom don't talk on the phone.

Then—I kid you not, exactly then—we heard a knock at our door. I went to open it and found myself looking at Christine. I hadn't seen her in weeks. I was stunned into silence.

"Who's there?" Dad called.

Christine jerked her thumb towards her brother's car, peeking out behind some pine trees down the road, and winked. I felt so relieved I almost started crying. *I have friends*, I realized, *Baruch Hashem!—gracias a Dios!—thank god to all gods.* I kept my cool and told Dad it was a salesman. Christine ran out to the car and I ran upstairs to get the condoms I had bought six weeks ago and hidden in the soccer ball pillow on my bed.

Christine's brother Joe and his friends were driving past our house on the way to the beach, blasting Mobb Deep and the Foggy Mountain Boys, and agreed to drop us off back at her house. After Christine chastised me for not texting her, we got busy pretty quickly. But when it came to the big moment I found—how do I put this? While my member was in fine working condition in the open air, the moment it surrendered its freedom to the contraceptive's confines, it seemed to have second thoughts about the whole ordeal. We laughed it off, got each other off, and were about to give it a second shot when we heard the rumbling of a car outside. Joe had forgotten his feng wan.

At that point, Christine and I decided to wait until some other time, that day already in smoking ruins. Somehow, though, it made me feel better.

When I woke up the next morning, I felt a surge of self-hatred at how I had treated Becca. What was I, an ill-tempered bonobo? I went to her and apologized. She was in a similar state of self-reflection. We agreed on all accounts: that we should apologize to Mom, find out what was up, and that we *should* do the road trip. While we never did find out what had happened to Mom, we *did* pack and take care of incidentals (got my license like nobody's business) and hit the road just a few days later.

Our days of packing and planning got so busy that by the time we were on 680 North with Becca at the wheel, I was opening up the folder of Rubin Yakovlev and Grampa Andy's notes for the first time in a while. I was also grumpy because I had fallen asleep for the hour and a half to Sacramento, so

I missed my first glimpses of presumably majestic road trip scenery.

Becca jerked us out of parallel parking and into the streets of Sacramento. I hadn't been to Sacramento before and knew nothing about it. I got to see the ordinary side of the city. It had plenty of trees, and a much richer color than the faded stucco and dusty hills of the Bay Area. My theory is that in the mountains of central California the ocean winds don't wear out buildings, so the paint sticks better and keeps its luster—Sacramento is a deep twilight color, as opposed to the pale dawn of San Francisco. We crossed a big bridge with stony watchtowers. I saw the river. The water looked clean. I saw people outside. It was a healthy city. Surely it had its own set of problems, but it looked like a city that could support healthy and even meaningful human life.

Before long, we left city limits. Away from the river, it felt like we were in the desert, surrounded by tangled shrubs and short pines. Becca was quiet at the wheel, tuning through different radio stations. I looked out the window and wondered about Rubin Yakovlev and all the radio stations he might have tuned in to, all across the country. He must've seen so much of America, but because of his obsession with the bracelet, also so little. Still, better to go somewhere with a purpose than to go for the weather or the gambling. For the first time I wondered: who really was that man?

"I think this is it," Becca said.

We had pulled onto a side road, approaching a small pavilion surrounded by a wooden fence. Behind the pavilion I could see a gray building and a cell tower with a rotating antennae. There was a park across from the pavilion, an open field of brownish grass with a few groves of pine and flowering trees. We parked next to the pavilion in a big lot with two other cars and walked in through an opening in the fence. A small sign fronted with blue tulips read "SITE OF CAMP KOHLER: 1942-1947".

Becca and I wandered under the pavilion, but there wasn't much there—some picnic tables and a display explaining how over 4700 Japanese-American men, women, and children were held at the facility for three years until they were released at the end of the war, and that the site was destroyed by a fire in 1947.

A couple ate sandwiches at one of the picnic tables. We noticed a booth under the pavilion that seemed to operate as an information center. It had pamphlets on the history of Japanese internment written by the Japanese American National Museum in Los Angeles. I was sweating in the heat.

"No one's here," Becca said, leafing through one of the pamphlets.

I scoured the booth for information. A small sign said the Saturday hours were 12pm-1pm.

"There should be someone here," I said. "It's only 1:05."

I heard a door close. Someone had just left the booth. I peeked around the corner and saw a tall teenager in a collared shirt locking a side-door.

"Excuse me!" I called. "Can I ask you a question?"

He turned. "We just closed."

"It's really fast."

"What's your question?"

I glanced at Becca, but she was still looking at the pamphlet. "Uh..." I had to buy time while I figured out what the hell I could even ask this kid. "What is this place? Why is there just a little booth here?"

"The Japanese American National Museum runs a booth here," he said disinterestedly. "We don't get much traffic here so we don't stay open long." He turned to leave.

"Wait!" I said. "One more question."

He turned.

"Well, I had a specific question about the history of the site. I was wondering who I could ask..."

"Anything that you'd want to know is there in the pamphlet."

"Oh." I scratched my head. Was that it?"

"Have a nice day," he said, starting to walk away.

My armpits were sweaty and I felt lightheaded. That couldn't be it. Could it? Was it over? What the hell was I even supposed to ask? What did I think we could gain from coming here? Why hadn't I made a plan? Or written a whole notebook full of questions? Apparently, I wasn't smart enough to act and think at the same time, like Grampa Andy, or even Becca, who glanced at me and said, "Is that the best you can do?"

"What?"

"Come on! You wanna find the bracelet or not? Shit, Matt, you're useless." She flung the pamphlet on to the table and went after the kid.

I stood still, stunned silent, mind stuttering. No thoughts. Fucking thoughtless, fucking useless.

I have no idea how long I stood there. I just know that at some point, Becca came running back with her baseball cap in hand and a smile on her face. "His boss was incarcerated here as a kid. Old Japanese dude. Comes to lock up the gates here at 6:00 every day, never late, no phone number. There's no one better we could ask. But there's no point in waiting here. Let's go." She pointed to the car. "You alright?"

I nodded.

She handed me the pamphlet. "It's got a lot of detail. People were forced to live in these tiny shacks, twenty people to a space built for four. Overt *and* institutional racism, no surprise there. You should read it. There are still issues with reparations going on today."

I followed her back to the car.

We drove into downtown Sacramento for ice cream and spent a few hours walking by the riverside. We saw the kitschy historic district, reconstructed old-timey buildings and gold-rush themed restaurants, and Becca educated me about *Mujeres Libres*, a Spanish anarcha-feminist group, eventually concluding that they weren't nearly radical enough. "Very bourgeoisie," I concurred. Meanwhile, I couldn't stop thinking about how I had utterly, completely, miserably, embarrassingly, comically, radically, failed.

We drove back out to Walerga. There was some traffic, but we squealed into the empty parking lot at a healthy 5:25 PM.

We went and sat in the pavilion. Becca read the pamphlet from the Japanese American museum a second time, and I got out some energy by jogging around the park across the street despite the sweaty gym-sock heat. The afternoon sun was bright and far from setting.

When I got back from my jog, I still didn't see any cars besides our own in the lot. Becca was lying on her back on top of one of the picnic tables.

"I'm exhausted from all the driving, so I'm going to take a nap," she said, and did.

I sat cross-legged on the cool pavilion floor and waited, feeling my shit, which I was *supposed* to put together, falling apart. If I couldn't ask the right questions, I couldn't find the right answers. If I couldn't find the right answers, then the trip was pointless. Every person has a reservoir of knowledge and experiences: streams, rivers, oceans and oceans of memories, feelings, facts, and fantasies, that any other person can never access, but you *can* get close, you just have to ask. But how do I know what to ask when all I am is *me*, and the person who is me doesn't know what to ask?

As the clock hit 5:58, a dark car pulled into the lot. Out came a man. Old, definitely old, super old. He limped into the pavilion, bald with slits for eyes, pinstriped suit floppy on a skeletal frame. I watched him unlock the booth, enter, come back out, and lock it again. And then I realized—Becca was still asleep on the picnic table. *Do something, Matt, do something!*

"Excuse me!" I called to him. "Are you closing now?"

He turned, surprised that I had spoken. I walked up to him and smiled.

"Are you closing now?"

"Hm? No, no. Hardly. Well, we're closing, but I won't kick you out."

"Oh, we can move," I said. "My sister's just asleep." What should I do? Should I wake her up? Should I figure out what to ask on my own? Could I? "I just had a question for you," I ad-libbed. "We heard that you know everything there is to know about this facility."

"I was here myself when I was a boy," he said, voice wire-thin and quavering. "Three years, four months, twenty-seven days. It's not easy to forget. Was it the young man this afternoon?"

I nodded.

"He doesn't know nearly enough to run the booth," he grunted. "I apologize on his behalf."

"Oh, no," I said. "It doesn't matter. You see—well, what's your name, sir?" It seemed a good question to start with.

"My name is George Yoshida."

"If you don't mind me asking, I heard you were interned—incarcerated here."

Yoshida nodded several times. "My father had a roadside vegetable stand. When we arrived, there was nothing but dust and it was 100 degrees. Our barrack had a cement floor and tarpaper walls, a tiny room for the four of us, and a mess hall and restroom for every long row of barracks." It was almost a recitation.

"It must've been hard," I said.

"The worst was the food. It made us sick, all of us. Beans and beef... nothing for the babies... terrible for the body. All of us were used to eating rice, and my mother got so sick she couldn't move for weeks. But we improved things. We made blinds for the windows out of the cardboard boxes from the mess hall, and we all had gardens. We made covered patios; it was too hot to be inside in the summer. We even built a schoolhouse. Imagine that! A school in the barracks. It seems unbelievable now, but I know I helped to raise the beams, but refused to go to class. I wanted to apply for outside employment, but I had no one to vouch for me, so I had to stay in the camp." He nodded. "After the war I became an engineer, dealing in semiconductors. Do you know about semiconductors?"

I shook my head enthusiastically, astounded by every word pouring out of George Yoshida's mind. Living must have been hard, but to remember it all—all this detail—now that's an impossible task. I could hardly believe the detail compressed into one man's mind.

"They are materials with conductivity between metals and insulators. These things are useful to know. I only retired five or six years ago and have been managing the museum's Sacramento initiatives ever since."

"That's incredible," I said. "It must have been depressing to live there."

"Oh, I don't think depressing is the right word for it. There were all sorts of peculiar people and curious matters to distract from the worst of things."

I felt a little lightbulb flicker in my head. "Like a magic bracelet?"

"A magic bracelet?"

"I heard a story about this place," I said, "that I wanted to ask you about." Now it wasn't just his words that were exciting me; my own words, too, started blowing bubbles and balloons in my chest and stomach. "I heard that there was a man detained here in 1945, a man who supposedly had a magic amulet. A bracelet, but then he managed to escape the facility. Does that ring a bell? Someone with a magic amulet?"

Yoshida furrowed his brow.

"No?"

"No," Yoshida said, and then laughed a little. "There was a boy. A tall, tall, skinny, skinny boy. He was a lowlife—a good-for-nothing thief. He wore a bracelet that he said he had stolen from a cowboy in the desert, a bracelet with a gold coin on it."

"That's it!" I cried, turning to Becca. "Wake up, Becca! He knows! Sorry, Mr. Yoshida."

Yoshida didn't mind. I liked him. He was a chiller. I could never tell if his eyes were opened or closed, which was nice because there was no uncomfortable eye contact. He continued as if I hadn't interrupted. "I remember him. Oh, I remember. He hid the bracelet from the guards and snuck in and out of the camp almost every day. He was so skinny that he could slip between the bars of the fence, and his arms were long so he could climb the walls. He went out in the fields to steal strawberries to eat and lemons to suck."

"He wore a bracelet with a gold coin?" Could it be? Could it *really* be?

"I don't remember," Yoshida said. "It may have had a gold coin. We talked often. The buffoon had his eye on my sister, and gave her presents: mostly strawberries. She made him bean cakes, saving up food from our garden—we had to pay a caretaker for the seeds. My sister was head over heels for the rascal!" Yoshida wagged a finger. "We tried to stop him from sneaking out by telling him the story of the woman who tried to run away and was shot in the foot. She had to have her foot amputated—an awful scene, and we could hear the screaming, all night long. But he didn't care. He wasn't afraid of losing a foot. In the end he ran away, of course, and was not shot in the foot. He would never keep a promise to my sister."

"What was his name?" I demanded, hands trembling. I was on the bracelet's trail—I was on the verge of a discovery! I felt a surge of kinship with Grampa Andy and Rubin Yakovlev, the thrill of tumbling into the river of history and gripping its white water like rafts hug the Colorado River.

"What's his name? What happened to him?"

Yoshida smiled. "My boy," he said, with a light-footed air of not-quite tenderness, quelling my blasting river to a stream, a creek, a pond, a puddle—"nobody knows. When Yamamato Hiroya ran away, he disappeared completely, like the wind."

9

Pyramid Lake

Holy *shit* was I excited. I was so goddamn excited that I nearly pissed my pants on the way back to Sacramento. We had to pull over and I peed into a ditch. I watched the dry soil moisten. It felt symbolic, like I was the gardener of the Earth. The element pouring out of me animated the universe. It changed the color of the soil.

After the conversation with George Yoshida, I woke Becca up and told her wisely that I would explain everything later. We left the pavilion and he locked the gate behind us. He got into an old Jeep and we got into our old Volkswagen. He waved at us as the jeep sputtered out of the parking lot. Good guy, quality dude.

As we drove back into town to our cousin's apartment, I retold the story to Becca with an irrepressible grin.

"So we need to find Yamamoto Hiroya," she said, an eyebrow raised.

"Well, if we can find him, he can definitely tell us what happened to the bracelet!

"*If* we can find him. *If* he's real."

"What do you mean?"

"Just trying to be realistic, Matt. Old people can be kinda crazy. Sometimes they misremember stuff, or make shit up."

"Well, I just so happen to have a *feeling* that this is gonna work out."

My feeling was misguided. A thorough investigation at the Sacramento public library the next morning returned precisely nothing. No Yamamoto Hiroya, no relatives, barely anything on Camp Kohler, and now that it was the weekend, we'd have to wait till Monday to find George Yoshida so we could learn if there was anyone else we could ask, and we didn't have the time to wait all weekend. I didn't let it bother me. You say the first stop was a failure because an Internet search returned zero results? Because I was a few good questions short? "The trail has run dry," you say, but you're wrong—I had discovered a more essential trail on that hot, spectacular Sacramento day, a trail that leads into the misty caverns of past, and the true search was on.

I wrote notes detailing George's story in a journal I had bought. If we kept following the notebook's clues, with just a little bit of the luck we'd had in Sacramento, sooner or later we'd find it, no problem. We just needed to be patient.

Next was Reno. Well, not Reno, but forty-five minutes North to Pyramid Lake and the Indian Reservation there. It took me the first hour of the drive to go over all the notes, since Rubin Yakovlev went there three times in the 1940s, and Grampa Andy went one more time in the 90s.

It was a weird story. Rubin Yakovlev had been confident that another man was competing with him to find the bracelet throughout the 40s—the same man who had originally purchased the bracelet from my own great-grandmother. This man, referred to by Rubin Yakovlev as "the cowboy," considered the bracelet to be his own, and, with it having somehow or another fallen out of his possession, was frothing at the mouth to get it back. The cowboy was a murderous, evil man, a cold-blooded Indian-killer through and through, whose lifeblood was violence and spectacle. Yakovlev wrote in 1943 that a Paiute man living at Pyramid Lake took the bracelet from the cowboy, surmising that the cowboy might be lurking around Pyramid Lake to snatch it back. He described a few crackpot theories on an elaborate revenge scheme by the Paiute tribe and seems to have asked around Pyramid Lake, Reno, and eventually El Paso, where he suddenly heard news that the cowboy was elsewhere, in Bend, Oregon. There was even a copy of a weird letter written by Grampa Leo to a psychologist about the whole ordeal. It seemed like a dead end.

But the dead ends are where things get interesting. Grampa Andy, perhaps on a whim, went back in the 90s. On his way into town, he caught wind of some intriguing tall tales from a Reno local. There were two stories that stood out.

The first was a rumor—partially confirmed by a copy of a black and white photograph—that a Texas rancher fished up a massive 36" trout that had a bracelet with a gold coin in its belly. The picture, on display in a Reno bar, showed an overweight man in a muscle-T proudly hoisting the enormous trout over head, but Grampa Andy could never locate the rancher's name or address.

The second was a tall tale about a she-wolf devouring children around Pyramid Lake. Some men went and killed the wolf and found that the wolf *also* had a bracelet with a gold coin in its belly. Surely, it's more than a coincidence that the bracelet showed up twice in Pyramid Lake, even if the stories aren't true.

So ten years later, I figured it would be worth a shot. Plus I had heard good things about Pyramid Lake.

When we crossed into Nevada from California, we were in the full-blown mountains, ghostly clouds crawling across pine-covered peaks as far as the eye could see. (Becca played a Patti Smith CD. Moods were not matched.) But as soon as we passed Reno, we were in the full-blown desert, tumbleweed and dusty shrubs rumbling out to distant tan boulders. The desolate expanse was grim as bone, and I kept my eyes on the notebook most of the time. We had forgotten to get lunch after leaving the library in Sacramento, and had to stop at a McDonald's in Sparks, Nevada. All of the houses were either white or terra-cotta colored, the McDonald's the lone exception, a red plastic toy lost in the desert. We followed a dry gulch in the cracked stone for another hour, passing some impressively spiky boulders, before arriving in Dixon, a few dozen trailers and run-down slate houses connected by a maze of power lines, distant gray water towers looming like a cheapo skyline. There was no grocery store, and the elementary, junior-high, and high school were in the same one-story building. We didn't see signs for the Indian reservation, but there was a ranger office where you could buy fishing permits, so we went in to ask.

Becca and I were surprised when a big-bearded man told us that this *was* the Pyramid Lake Paiute Indian Reservation. We got directions to the lake and decided to go to sight-see.

"How is this an Indian Reservation?" I asked, climbing back in the car. "It's just a tiny town."

Becca shrugged. "Native Americans don't live in tents and wigwams. What did you expect?"

I don't know what I had been expecting, but Dixon was such an ordinary town that I almost felt depressed as we drove to the lake. I mean, I knew that the situation for a lot of Native Americans is not so hot, but I hadn't understood that meant people lived in the most ordinary sort of American poverty: gas stations, cigarettes and soda, hunting and fishing and God and gambling and divorce. Becca picked up where my thoughts left off, rambling on about possible causes behind various economic problems—the end of American industry, segregation, corporate malice—but ultimately decided that it was nothing but a direct lineage from the unthinkable violence directed at Native Americans throughout our country's history. Murder, forced relocation, forced assimilation, murder again, relocation again. There were no economic forces at work: only hatred and evil. "It speaks to the strength of tribes that they are doing as well as they are," she concluded in her noblest tone.

Becca's use of the words *forced relocation* struck me. After all, forced relocation to government-designated reservations was just like the Japanese-Americans at Camp Kohler. And that was just like the Jews of Poland and Ukraine, before the final solution. "Forced relocation." Words tinged with genocide? What does it mean to move? When you can't move, when you're forced to move... This, definitely, signified the beginning of the end.

But even the memory of Pyramid Lake—once you get past a crowd of sputtering RVs—makes none of this matter.

It wasn't a desert oasis. No emerald trees studded the shore, and past the RV camp there was no sign of human life, or any life at all. Pyramid Lake was rather a geological ecosystem. It was an etching of an age ten million years gone by, when Nevada rolled with dark blue waves. The dried-out desert sea tossed around us in tan tumbleweed-stung stones, scattered in the shape of spreading eagle wings. There were dark, craggy rocks that snapped like turtles on the shore, and the lake, blue rippling out to the shadows of ocean-bound monuments of rock, dozing bison by their watering hole. It was beautiful.

The air felt cool by the water, so Becca and I sat there for a little while. We put on sunscreen and went for a walk. We saw different pale rock formations sticking out of the lake. I examined them carefully, in case an omen were to manifest. The only thing I saw was a white bird flying low over the water, but I couldn't parse the meaning. We spotted a group of fishermen about ten feet out into the lake, bearded men in their 30s, dressed in tall boots, gear and goggles, water halfway up their legs.

I felt a pulsing thrill. "I'm going to ask these people about Grampa Andy's story," I told Becca, and hollered out a greeting to a guy splashing back towards a tackle box on shore. Becca trailed after. Watch and learn, sister. I can ask questions now.

"Doing just fine, and yourself?" he said, bending to sort through the box.

"Fine," I said. "How's the fishing?"

He looked up, big chin, yellow teeth, red beard. "It's been incredible all season. Never seen anything like it. It gets better every year. My old man tells me ten years ago the lake was dead. Now it's full of king-sized trout."

"That's great."

"Can't bring small ones home," he said. "But between the five of us we can get five big ones, ice 'em, and bring 'em back to Sparks."

"Are you all from Sparks?"

"That's right, towards Carson City, not too far."

I smiled at Becca. "We stopped there for lunch today. We're headed east from the Bay Area."

"Really now?" He stood to return to fishing. "The only tourists that ever come up are on their way to that Burning Man satanic bullcrap, blue-haired hippies with foam coming out of their mouths and dirty Jews. What'd you think of our little town?"

Excuse me? I opened my mouth.

"The McDonalds is good," Becca said, and the fisherman laughed. I glanced at her and decided to shut up. I was impressed by her, given the circumstances. I mean, how was he supposed to know we were Jewish? Shocking as it was, I had to keep going—I couldn't let it get the best of me, not now.

"Ever hear any stories about giant trout with gold inside them?" I asked.

"Where'd you hear a story like that?"

"My grandfather. He said it was a local story."

"I never heard that." He thought about it. "The Indians have their stories."

"You know any?"

The man shook his head. "You can go crash that Indian language class if you want to hear some. I've met the teacher, Martin Hawley, and he always likes telling Indian tales."

"Do you know where?"

"Dixon. And Dixon ain't big. You'll find it."

I grinned at Becca and the fisherman went back to his fishing.

Becca nodded. "You seem to have learned something."

"From you? Hell no. That was all improv, young Padawan. Follow my lead." I was frolicking ahead to the car, the Jew comment in the rearview mirror.

We drove to Dixon. We stopped at 7/11 and bought a gallon of water. I drank half of it right away. I had good feeling about Pyramid Lake. Clear blue skies, cool strong wind—nature was on my side.

We drove in circles around Dixon before we found the old classroom building next to the permit office, back where we started. We got there before the community Northern Paiute Languages & Cultures class at 6:00 but couldn't interrogate the teacher before class began because he didn't arrive till 6:06, and dove right into his lesson. We would have to sit through the class.

Becca and I tried to hide at the back, but there were only six total students: three kids between the ages of five and seven, a preteen girl who sat on the edge of her seat, a fat and surly-looking boy with a ponytail around Becca's age, and a trim and tiny middle-aged woman with spectacles hanging off her nose. The teacher, Martin Hawley, had broad features, dark skin, and bright, flickering eyes. He wore a bowtie and stood completely erect at the front of the small classroom and stained chalkboard. He looked ageless and could've been anywhere between thirty-five and sixty.

"*Yaa uu pesa petuhoo*," he said, and the students mumbled it back.

The class was more of a lecture and didn't involve much Paiute language, and more importantly, it was clearly the most elementary possible level, so Becca and I could follow along. They counted to ten—*sumu'yoo, waha'yoo, pahe'yoo, watsuggwe'yoo*—and practiced pronunciation of basic words, *panunudu* for lake, *ma'oohooka* for desert, *baa'a* for water (which really stuck with me. I think that word whenever I'm thirsty—there's something intuitive about it. It's like saying it dries out your mouth and turns the words into reality. *Baa'a,* I need a fuckin' drink). In between having the students stand up and recite Paiute straight up Hebrew-school style, Mr. Hawley went on either tangents or lessons about the Paiute wars from the 1850s, imploring the classroom to remember history. He talked about the Comstock Lode and the Williams Station Massacre and women trapped in vegetable cellars and I couldn't tell if he was criticizing the Paiute or white people or both, but I confess I wasn't listening closely. The woman was paying attention; the kids played silent games among themselves; the older girl was trying to pay attention but kept up retying her shoelaces; the surly kid's eyes glazed over as he picked at a scab on his wrist. Becca was listening like her life depended on it. I zoned out and watched the surly kid rub his punctured scab in a meditative circle. His forefinger was bloody. He licked it. I wasn't repulsed—in fact, I connected with this motherfucker. He was like an uncensored version of myself. I personally wouldn't pop a scab in class, definitely not with Chelsea around. But I won't say the idea doesn't intrigue me, doing violence to oneself to focus, and turn inward, as Mr. Hawley spoke of the outward. I think Surly was really listening to Mr. Hawley's every word. He probably soaked up the information all the better thanks to his inward turn, his popped and bleeding scab. Then he suddenly jerked around and looked right at me. I nearly leapt out of my seat and slapped my gaze on Mr. Hawley, heart sprinting like a horse after gunfire.

At the lesson's conclusion, Mr. Hawley handed out homework assignments and the students turned in their old ones, but Surly turned in nothing. My curiosity came back, because in this case, he was different from me. I *always* did my Hebrew school homework—they were easy worksheets, just alephs and bets and the Six Days War comes before the Yom Kippur one, and the midrash is about the mishnah and not vice versa. But Surly did not appear to think the dotted i's and crossed t's of the declaration, *I am Paiute!*, was worthy of his time. Was this foolish or wise?

The kids dashed out of classroom and the woman gathered her belongings and followed. I glanced at Surly as Becca approached Mr. Hawley, gesturing at me, while the teacher was packing his old-fashioned black briefcase.

"Mr. Hawley," Becca was saying. "I'm so sorry. Could we speak to you for a moment?"

I hurried up beside her. He looked at us and seemed to inherently disapprove. Up close he was tall and the stern, horizontal lines of his face nearly turned me away. Becca thanked him for the lesson and explained who we were. He nodded.

Becca nudged me, so I gathered my courage and asked him about the story of the trout.

Mr. Hawley nodded. "It's a local fable," he said, "and not a Paiute story, if that's what you're asking. Our own myths have little to do with trout, and nowadays the lake is stocked, but ever since whites started fishing here a hundred years ago, it's become a local legend that the father trout grow gold in their stomachs. If a fisherman finds a father trout and a gold coin when he guts it, it's an omen. In times of peace the gold coin is an omen of war. And in times of war the coin is an omen of peace."

Interesting, but irrelevant. "So there was never a a trout with a gold coin bracelet on it?" I asked. "I had heard that the coin was on a bracelet."

"There is no bracelet," Mr. Hawley said. "From time to time you hear that someone fishes up a father trout. For example, you may have heard that the day before 9/11, a young boy fished up a trout with a gold nugget the size of a fist. Nowadays they're even saying that before the Europeans came to this land that fishermen were finding gold in droves. They're not true—tall tales, just stories."

I bristled internally. "Are you sure there isn't some sort of basis to these stories?

Mr. Hawley chuckled. "Well, if you believe in magic. Do you?" he asked, but before I could answer he continued, and I realized it was a rhetorical question. "Do you have Paiute blood?" he asked.

Becca and I shook our heads.

"I may as well explain," Hawley said. "Stories like that are meaningless. Even Paiute legends and myths only matter to *us,* not to you. Why would they have meaning to you? You can't follow our story. You don't know anything about it. But when it comes to you *and* us, h*istory* is the thing that matters. Thirty years ago, forty years ago, Pyramid Lake was dying. There were mines upriver, polluting the lake and killing the fish. Putting aside any native *pooha* of stones, water, and mountains aside, to you children, we only survived thanks to the fickle whim of history—that the mineral deposits in Nevada were shallow enough that the mines died before our lake did. Now all the gold and silver is gone, and our lake is healthy, even though when the weather is good the whole town stinks with RV exhaust. Don't put stake in tall tales, and consider history instead."

Even though I hadn't yet told him about the story of the wolf, I figured I couldn't ask him about any more tall tales. Mr. Hawley curtly nodded, snapped his briefcase shut, and walked out of the classroom.

Becca scratched her head as we left the crusty old building. "That was interesting," she said. "I'm sure you thought of Hebrew school, right? Like our teacher who made us recite parshah after parshah, droning on and on as if memorization is really learning anything—do you remember her? Old, red wig..."

We noticed Surly standing outside on the street, with a scratched Muhammad Ali skateboard in hand.

"Do you need a ride or something?" Becca asked him.

He shook his head. "I'm waiting for my friend to pick me up." He flung the skateboard down. "Nearest skate park's in Reno."

Another surge of kinship. "That's sick," I said.

And then we kinda just stood there for a moment. Surly nodded at us and looked away. He didn't look particularly Surly anymore, so I figured I should ask his name, but Becca was already walking to the car.

Even though our friendship ended before it started, I think about Surly now and again, wondering if he pops scabs in front of cute girls in class, uncompromising in his approach to understanding history.

Becca and I fell into a long silence as we drove away from Dixon, towards the highway. I was thinking about Surly. Who knows what Becca was thinking about, but eventually, she said:

"Why do you want to find it?"

Obviously, she was talking about the bracelet. What else could "it" be?

"For Grampa Andy," I said. "More or less. He's never failed us before, and I don't think he will, even in death."

Becca nodded slowly, shifting the car along the subtle curve of the road. The car barely turned, but the road bent in a long, long arc. Soon enough, I could no longer see that one especially tall and spiky stone, representing the gateway to the world of Pyramid Lake that now we were leaving behind.

I *do* have manners, so I returned the question:

"What about you? Why?"

10

Salt Lake City

Becca never did answer my question, but it was a long journey to Chicago, so I'd have time to grill her later, or so I thought. I mention Chicago because that's where things changed for good. That's where we met Cowboy Jim. Until Cowboy Jim, bear with me.

We could've made another stop in Nevada. Remember how the racist fisherman had mentioned Burning Man? Well, those words were percolating in my brain on the open road, and all of the sudden I remembered I had heard those words before—in the notebook, in Grampa Andy's handwriting. But by the time I remembered we were approaching Utah, and since Burning Man doesn't happen till late August, there wasn't much we could investigate. So I just had to keep this story in my back-pocket.

1998. Grampa Andy went to the Burning Man festival in the middle-of-nowhere Nevada. Harsh conditions. He described the festival as a post-capitalist fantasy wonderland where everything is art. Grampa Andy had a brief conversation with Lisa Montana before the 1998 art-and-guns festival descended into a nightmare, preceded over by the blazing effigy, cackling flames to the white-dust sky, mohawked biker gangs riding their motorcycles into the flames, women that looked like Joni Mitchell dressed like Princess Aura dancing in the desert sun, while a man in cowboy boots fires a shotgun over and over, the blast booming across the dead plain.

Before all of that happened, though, Grampa Andy heard the story of a singular Lisa Montana, some washed out beat-now-revived-via-Burning-Man woman. This woman supposedly encountered a magic bracelet in a desert trip with Gary Snyder's nephew. This is how, according to Grampa Andy via Lisa Montana (and of course, to you via me), their little adventure went:

Lisa & co. departed from West Wendover, a town of 3,000 citizens and three casinos. Over the course of six days driving across the desert all the way to Joshua Tree, the group consumed increasing doses of LSD until they couldn't contain themselves and made explosive love beneath the stars, only to have their seismic orgy interrupted by an apocalyptic vision of a bracelet with a golden coin attached. They follow the omens to a canyon and saw a leather bracelet with a gold coin lying in the ditch, alone, as if abandoned, thrown aside. A few months later, Lisa Montana was approached by a tall handsome man in a cowboy hat at a bar; the pair slept together, and in the morning, the man and the bracelets were both gone.

It read like nonsense. How the hell did the bracelet get into the middle of the desert? Could someone prior have thrown it away? Could the vultures and the packrats have yanked it across the sands one mile at a time? Into a canyon and the tanned, long fingers of Lisa Montana? It was a story so absurd that it didn't seem worth verifying, and it was too late, anyways. We were in Utah.

Though Becca did most of the driving, I took the wheel now and again. I had never driven more than a half-hour before, and it was a four hour leg to Salt Lake City. I was so nervous that I got carsick *while* driving. Becca was not happy when I woke her up. I tried to pull over on the highway, but Becca freaked out and made me swerve back and a pickup truck honked as it jerked into the left lane and blazed by. We got off at a gas station three miles later and switched. Every time I closed my eyes Becca gave me a hard pinch. "If I don't get to sleep, you don't either," she said.

All that day we saw nothing but desert. Hot and dust-colored. Hour by hour it weighed down on me, like falling snow. Desert snow—now that would be a sight. Becca wanted to step out of the car every once in a while to take a picture of a big sky or striated cliff, but I was happy to stay in the car. I don't like the desert. It's dry, and lonely, and it kills things. Some things live, but in stunted, skeletal forms. There's dark magic in the desolation, keeping winds sharp, keeping rain away.

I did sense a redeeming quality, quietly filling the dry air and whistling hills: the space, promise, and possibility for life. If I could cast a spell and make it rain, even Nevada could be a beautiful place...

So it felt great to get to Salt Lake City, to be back in some sort of civilization, even if we were only gone a few days. We checked into a motel on the city limits on Friday afternoon. We drove through downtown and had Chinese food. Salt Lake City's plenty large and bustling, made extraordinary by the backdrop of stunning mountains, gray giants with broad shoulders and pointy ears. We asked our waitress what to do in Salt Lake City, and she responded that most people come for the nature around it, like Cottonwood Canyon and the Great Salt Lake, but that the zoo and history museum are nice. I suppose that's life in the American west. And I don't mean the west coast—I mean the wild west. Out here, the landscape is everything. And if human civilization happens to exist within it, even a city this big, then that's just a big convenience.

We came to Salt Lake City for the Mormon Church. We checked out the Temple Square Saturday morning. It was impressive, pristine spires reaching for the sky, the heavens, presumably. You wouldn't learn anything about Mormonism by going there, though. I only know one Mormon kid from school, and the only thing I know about her is that her sister got married at the ripe age of 18.3. Fortunately, Grampa Andy had taped some educational encyclopedia cut-outs into the notebook. Turns out—Mormons are positively bananas. *The Book of Mormon* claims the Israelites migrated to America in 600 BC and built a great civilization. Eventually Joseph Smith came along, and with his handy-dandy pair of magic spectacles interpreted ancient Egyptian glyphs left by the last prophet of the Israelites before their civilization was destroyed by the 'red men'. It's a whacko re-centering of Christianity around the good ole US of A. Joseph Smith founded the church in New York, but facing violent persecution (classic heretic problems) they moved around to Missouri, and after Smith was killed, to Utah.

Grampa Andy wrote about this outlandish Mormon dude named Walter Miller. He was an important figure in Mormon life in Salt Lake City and helped manage sites along the historic Mormon Trail (kinda like my buddy George Yoshida!). But over time he became an outcast from the church. He claimed to possess Joseph Smith's golden spectacles, Brigham Young's compass, and some eight or nine other sacred artifacts associated with Mormon history. There's this 1974 newspaper clip about the different objects he claimed he had, and one of them was a bracelet, recovered from ruins of the Israelites. The bracelet had a gold coin.

You bet it did.

Grampa Andy came across the clip because one of his topics of historical research in the late 90s was Mormonism's claims over Native American ruins and artifacts. Now it was up to me and Becca to unravel the mystery. I was excited. Each place we stopped felt like a passage into something greater. Each place was a place in itself, but also a place on the verge of a place that was more—a *more-place*, or maybe a *place-place.* And that *place-place* was the real place: my family story, wrapped in the cloth of American history, ribboned with a Star of David.

Salt Lake City was no different. We needed to find the door, the way in. We did a mini-driving tour of Salt Lake City, scoping out a place to do research. We found a public library and decided to look for a copy of the old newspaper that Grampa Andy had glued into the notebook.

After talking to three different librarians, we found out that the church in question, the Sterling Church of the Latter-Day Saints, had been closed for several years, but in fact had just reopened last year. One librarian, a superbly whiskered man, helped us find copies of the church's old newsletters. In July 1974, a new pamphlet was published every week, and in some cases on consecutive days.

I read the pamphlets, July 5-23, 1974. Written by Rock Jones, Mormon kid, journalist extraordinaire. The events rose into a theater in my mind, and I swear I was really standing there in the crowd. Heavy sunbeams beat me down. Dry air scratches at my throat. Walter Miller gives a speech. He professes his ability to make miracles. Half the congregation erupts in rage, half in profound awe. I hop in the back of a sedan with Rock Jones and we follow fifty congregants into the desert. Before our eyes, Walter Miller draws crystal water from dry sands. He calls two rattlesnakes from the thrush, provokes them, and survives both bites, sending the snakes slithering away. He holds out his arms to display the twin bites, sacred mirrored wounds. And he calls to the crowd:

"I am Isaac and Avraham before the LORD!
Stretch thy hand out not against me,
Do not do anything against me!
For I am in awe of God!"

And with a madman's fury he cries:

"Mounting through the spires of form
The Worm strives to be a Man,
And speaking all languages rises forth,
Breathing out omens and seeing great lengths,
A fluid chain of countless rings
Built by the Worm, the phenomenon perfect!"

And he bends low, as if to quake in fear of his own word:

"Let the one set-of-words baffle us not;
Let us mount the solstice desert of Ourselves—
Let us fill nature with our overflowing currents—
I have ascended to the realm of God and I dare you all to follow—"

And with that, Rock Jones and I absolutely lose it. Rock admits in the article: "In the resulting chaos I have become unable to remember and therefore record any further events."

If that isn't wild, I don't know what is. I could not be more excited to meet Walter Miller.

I raced through the rest of the pamphlets. Turns out Walter Miller advocated a transcendental spirituality, where humans can become gods by joining the spirit of nature. He thought he had bridged the gap between Man and God.

It almost makes sense. Think about atoms for a second. If all atoms in the universe are recycled, and we really *are* stardust, since exploding stars churns out heavier elements like the carbon and iron that make up our bodies, then humans, somewhat straightforwardly, consist of eternity. Our bodies and minds have already got Nirvana, the universal spirit, endless void. That means there *should* be a way to reconnect with our immortal matter, and therefore "god". Just like people, no matter where they come from, can be friends if they can speak a common language—or even if they can't.

"He's a raving lunatic," Becca remarked, throwing a pamphlet down.

"Oh, no doubt," I said. "We need to meet him."

However she felt about it, my enthusiasm bull rushed us out the library door. A few maps, a call with Mom, Becca's theory that Bush would use the London bombings as an excuse to invade various Middle Eastern countries, and one bathroom-stop later, Becca and I were at the doorstep of the Sterling Church of the Latter-Day Saints.

Only when we were approaching the church did I start to get nervous. I think I was more nervous than Becca, likely due to prejudice (Mormons always freaked me out for some reason). We stared up at the tall white church, fronted with a thirty-foot stained-glass window. It was a gorgeous building, walls white and flat and broad. The parking lot was separated from the building by a hedgerow and lawn, and a backyard of irrigated trees gave the church its own landscape. The green and red of the stained glass glared down as us like a burning forest, the Burning Man himself.

We followed a sidewalk around to the back and entered an ordinary looking office door. A noisy AC unit rattled behind a dying bush. We came into a quiet lobby with a tile floor.

"This is kind of like Beth Shalom," Becca said.

"Not everything needs to be like Hebrew School, Becca," I said. Though there was definitely a tile floor in the Beth Shalom Hebrew School lobby. I thought about how I hadn't been to synagogue in a few years. Dad went the weekends he was around, and both of us were Bar/Bat Mitzvah-d, but he stopped making me go when I started high school. I always hated the place, and I didn't like the comparison. There were no mystical secrets at Beth Shalom, only a big tree with a swing out back, kids that smell like pee, and fat Rabbi Isaac Kornfield, a little too willing to hug you tight.

"I don't know about this," I said.

Becca looked at me with her head cocked sideways, a look that said, *we are literally standing in a perfectly innocuous hallway with an old tile floor.*

We went in and knocked on an office door. When I saw an old secretary with dyed blonde hair, more Beth Shalom memories attacked me like a swarm of rabid bats (Julie Appelbaum kisses me on the cheek. I draw on her face with a marker. I am six years old.), I felt even more nervous. I wanted to tap Becca on the shoulder and tell her, never mind, let's forget it. I don't know if it was a dire aversion to 80s hairdos or plain old cowardice, but I couldn't go into the office. All faith that this new-old beautiful-boring Mormon temple would lead us to the bracelet drained away. I waited for Becca and heard the high-pitched, cotton-candy voice of the secretary respond to Becca's questions.

According to what I overheard, the secretary remembered the events well. She called Walter Miller a psychopath. She hated him for ruining their community. She saw faith and family as the twin pillars of life, but Walter Miller had to go off about becoming a God and nearly destroy their community in the process. Everyone in the congregation had to respond to Walter Miller—you were either with him or against him, and if you were against him, you might've been subject to threats or even violence. She and her husband had stood firmly against, lost their son to a hippie commune in Santa Barbara and their cat to a fire, seen the church close and reopen. She had never heard of a bracelet.

My armpits were stained with sweat and I just wanted to leave, but Becca was harassing the secretary for Walter Miller's daughter's address. After gentle protest, the woman gave it to Becca, and told her to have a lovely day.

Becca grinned at me. "I crushed it, didn't I?"

"Yes," I said, picking at my sticky shirt, "so can we please go?"

According to the map, Miller's daughter lived way out in the suburbs. As I sat there miserably listening to the Pretenders fight the system, I thought about how I didn't come on this road trip to interview sad Mormons. I wanted Walter Millers and Lisa Montanas, not church secretaries and tile-floor lobbies.

We arrived at a gray apartment building that existed for no discernible reason. It was just a highway exit and a gas station, and some sprawl connected to nowhere. We got out of the car onto a scorching blacktop. The building was decaying and the lights in the lobby flickered on and off. We waited two minutes for an elevator before taking the stairs. We climbed to the sixth floor. We knocked on the door as I tapped my foot. A moment later, Walter Miller's daughter, over 50, greeted us in a gray bathrobe.

Becca apologized and explained to her what we were looking for. "Yea, yea," the daughter said several times. "Yea, yea." She was busy, told us what happened, and shut the door in our faces.

Walter Miller had given her the bracelet in his will after he died in '74, just a few months after the incident. Yep, one and the same—it had a gold coin, a silver spear, "California" written on it. But she pawned it off. She had been addicted to heroin and needed cash. She sold it to a handsome older man, tall, leather jacket, hat and boots. Strange accent. He gave her $500 for it and she never saw him again. Never did heroin again, either, so that was good, she guessed. We were only 30 years too late, and she had no leads for us.

11

Sacred Spring

I used to love dinosaurs. Dad bought me these big colored cardboard blocks and I made dinosaur cities out of them. After that, the fun began: I placed toy dinosaurs all around the city. The T-rex was always the mayor, with a mini-pterodactyl advisor and a triceratops chief of police. The rest of the dinos lived their regular lives, going to the grocery store, picking up their kids from school, philosophizing in cafes—you know, dino things.

I was most fascinated by the mystery of their extinction. I stayed up late at night wondering how and why they disappeared. How could such mighty creatures, rulers of the Earth, simply vanish? Looking back, I think I know why my dinosaur bubble eventually burst. I remember watching National Geographic one time when a feature about mass extinctions came on. I learned about the mass extinction of megafauna in North American 15,000 years ago, and I realized that dinosaurs weren't the only legendary animals of Earth's storied past, and that dinosaurs weren't the only creatures that could suddenly and mysteriously vanish.

I had forgotten about my dinosaur phase until I read Grampa Andy's notes about an archeologist named Salvador Mancuso, who lived in Laramie, Wyoming, excavating dinosaur bones in the mountains. He was born in Italy and came to America to marry an architect, Louisa Castle, famous in her own right for becoming a pioneering woman in the field. When I read the notes detailing a few of Mancuso's incredible excavations, including the *Allosaurus* (a vicious predator) and the *Diplodocus* (a spiny dude a hundred feet long), I plunged headfirst back into my dinosaur phase.

The story of Salvador Mancuso wasn't a promising lead. Becca and I decided to try and find him because there wasn't much else to do in Wyoming. Grampa Andy seemed to have written about Mancuso mainly because he found him a fascinating character. There was a vague link: in 1954, Mancuso excavated a *hadrosaur* (quadruped with a headgear-crest not unlike a Nefertiti cap), and Mancuso had also inexplicably uncovered prehistoric jewelry at the same site, listed as "two stone necklaces, crude leather bracelet and coin". Finding human artifacts in rocks geologically one hundred million years old is, of course, scientifically impossible, which is likely why Grampa Andy never ended up going to the University of Wyoming. But Laramie was on the way, and we needed to sleep somewhere.

Fortunately, Becca had the foresight to call ahead from our motel in Rawlins. No one except this old geezer who could barely hear us remembered Salvador Mancuso at all. Turns out Mancuso hadn't lived in Laramie since his wife died twenty-five years ago. Instead, he was at a place up north called Sacred Spring.

We didn't have time to research Sacred Spring before going there, so neither of us had expectations. We just drove on up on winding roads through America's spine, the Rocky Mountains. For the first time, I truly understood the beauty of the mountains. The contrast in the might and weight of the entire Earth heaving to the purity of the sky was stunning. Nickel and iron, magma, limestone, sandstone, diamond and coal, redrock, a hundred thousand trees, great slabs of ice, all together mounted against a single emptiness. My jaw was below my Adam's apple most of the way to Sacred Spring. There were tall pine trees to our right, and scrubby grasses fell down sharp hills to our left, displaying the kind of sterling triangular mountains you think only exist in Mario games. The colors of the world—dark mountains, light sky, each of them staining the other—together, they were beauty.

Salvador Mancuso lived in a one-hundred-twenty square foot apartment made of stained pine boards and Plexiglas windows overlooking a greenhouse and a valley. The insects were loud and the ground was hard. I know the specifics because it turned out Sacred Spring was an eco-commune, a small community principled around sustainable design. When we got there, we saw a single chain of buildings, a four-story rustic cabin connected to a dome, and jutting out of the side of the dome was a series of wood-cabin housing units. Glass was hard to transport up there, so they used Plexiglas, and the windows were precisely arranged to provide shade in the summer and maximum light in the winter, and wood was good for heating up quickly in the frigid high-altitude. We went to a visitor's center, the top floor of the cabin, where they sold native wood carvings and hot bread. Sacred Spring was an intentional living community, where people who love the frozen Rockies came to live with zero carbon footprint, since the trees on their land trust absorbed anything they emitted. They had a tree-farm on the mountainside. The main cabin and dome ran on geothermal energy. The main cabin had a visitor's center, a kitchen/cafeteria, and storage room. The dome was a performance space and art installation. Supersized bronze coins hung on wires from the dome ceiling, humming softly and filling the arched dome with sound like the echo of a massive bell. The air was fresh and tasted like pine needles. The greenhouses overflowed with vegetables, and they had planted flowers on the hillside past the twelve-car parking lot. We asked for Mancuso, and we got him, as we watched a crew take down the bronze bell art exhibit to allow for a new one.

Mancuso was ancient and had a throaty voice and incomprehensible Italian accent, but what I did hear from him disturbed me. He had never seen a bracelet with a gold Spanish coin in his life. So on that account the visit was a failure.

Nevertheless. The first thing that disturbed me was the failure of the commune. They, "like our *compagni* at Arcosanti", had hoped to house a thousand-plus people on a fifteen acre lot, a substantial city and model of urban efficiency. Instead, less than fifty people lived there and they had never exceeded one hundred. While the planning for Sacred Spring was airtight, people didn't want to move to the Wyoming mountains to bake bread, chop wood, and host conferences, even if it had all the efficiency of East Asian urban living with a mountain backdrop to boot (as Mancuso told us, American cities were nothing but miserable sprawl). And despite all the innovation, its tenets had yet to be exported and implemented into real cities. Apparently Boston had considered some of Sacred Spring's plans for a greening of downtown, but ultimately rejected them ("Boston has always been a city of *borghesia* and white trash," Mancuso hissed).

The second disturbing thing was Mancuso's misery, despite the spiritual living conditions. At first glance he was your average grumpy European Marxist, but I realized it all came down to his wife. His wife was one of the founders and designers, and Mancuso had loved her with a passion that, to me, seemed surreal. When he spoke of her his voice softened. His voice was full of her laughter and the way she held him. He *a-loved* her. He said the words so many times that they grew twisted. I could taste them in my mouth, overripe fruit, weeping pungent juice. His wife died long ago in an unimaginable accident, a car crash that tore her body apart. I was suddenly grateful that they had never found Grampa Andy's body in the train wreck. I didn't know if I could bare to see his body smashed to pulp and his twinkling, mischievous eyes slashed like raw fish. Mancuso had never gotten over his wife's death. He *a-loved* her. The word stayed in my ears for days after. Not love, but "alove." It was something deeper, more amazing.

The love is important because without the love of his life, this guy had no reason to hold back. His life had been stripped to its rawest components. So the *third* disturbing thing had a lot more impact than it would have if he was still a lover with earthly possessions and desires.

It's one of those things you can't think about too much, because if you did it'd drive you crazy. When the bracelet lead fell flat, I decided to ask him about Sacred Springs: why did he think it was important?

Spittle shot out from between his teeth. "You do not know?" he snarled. "You cannot tell?"

We could not.

"Simply put, if we do not implement massive and far-reaching changes in our lifestyles and political and economic systems, there will be what I refer to as *abrupt climate change and societal collapse.*"

"Global warming?"

Mancuso smiled darkly. "People dismiss me as an alarmist, but built into every calculation and study about the effects of global warming is this: the assumption of human adaptability."

"Well, that's makes sense, doesn't it?"

His smile disappeared. "No. It does not make sense. Humans can adapt, yes, but more often we are reticent, unrelenting, stubborn, stupid. The effects of global warming that we experience today are from 30 years ago—it takes carbon 30 years to infiltrate the atmosphere. That 30-year gap between the warming we cause and the warming we experience will cause our demise."

"How?" Becca asked.

"You do not see? We adapt to information that is 30 years *alate*. Even if we acknowledge this fact, most people only react to present circumstances, not future ones. Scientific studies do not account for the delayed reaction of human adaptability. They assume that we will react on time, but we will react too *alate*."

"And what will happen?"

The smile was back, and it was even meaner. "By melting and exposing more surface area to solar radiation, the Arctic ice shelf will disappear in fifty years, and the Antarctic in one-hundred-fifty. Without ice to reflect the sun's rays, the ocean will absorb heat and warm five degrees, eliminating 99% of ocean life and causing unpredictable shifts in oceanic currents. Air temperature will rise six degrees compared to 1800 levels by 2100, making life in equatorial regions near impossible to live in. One third of the Earth's population lives in these regions. Most of them will become refugees or starve, as agriculture becomes unfeasible. Even if we adapt to climate change at a reasonable rate, 5 degrees of warming will cause 75% of the earth's species to go extinct within 150 years, and war over limited agricultural resources would result in widespread violence."

"And we can stop it by creating cities around the world like Sacred Spring?" I asked, trying to connect the dots.

Mancuso laughed. "You can stop it by selling your soul to the devil," he said, "*Li mortacci tua!*", and didn't speak another word. Becca and I ate hot oat bread with honey at the counter downstairs.

I didn't realize the fourth, final, and most disturbing part of the whole affair until Becca pointed it out to me. We were walking down the crumbling stone steps from the cabin to our car, alone in the visitor's lot, shaded by pines.

"You know, I was trying to figure out why he had switched his work from paleontology to global warming," Becca said. "But it makes perfect sense."

"Why is that?" I asked.

"They're both about the extinction of life on Earth. He spent all that time looking at things that went extinct, before realizing that that's all of us, too."

I looked at my hands. Becca's right, I thought. We're not that different from dinosaurs. And while I'd still say that dinosaurs are pretty rad, it was depressing to think we weren't fundamentally different from supersized lizards that only got that big because everything else was pretty big, too.

12

Ogallala

Becca closed *Cien Años de Soldedad.* "*¿Qué tal?* Is something wrong?" she asked.

Loneliness is a strange thing. It doesn't have much to do with how many people are around you—it's internal and can show up at the strangest times. After crossing the border into Nebraska, when there was nothing but corn and the occasional tree, I had realized that I was a week's travel away from anyone I cared about in the world besides my sister. So when I saw a hitchhiker waving a bandana on the side of the road about fifteen miles past the border, I didn't give it a second thought. I slowed down and pulled over.

"There's a hitchhiker," I replied, as the man jogged up towards us.

"We can't pick up a hitchhiker!"

"Why not?"

"He could be a serial killer!"

"You don't really think that."

"He really could be!"

"In the middle of a cornfield."

"Matt, it's the 21st century. We can't just pick up someone off the street."

"But he might need a ride. What if we got stranded way out here?"

The man smiled a buck-toothed grin at us through the window, waiting.

"Let me just talk to him," I said, rolling down the window.

"How are you doing today, sir?" the man said. He spoke slowly, opening his mouth wide. He had a huge forehead and a hairy nose. He wore dirty overalls and a White Sox baseball cap.

"Good," I said. "And you?"

"I am not doing my best." He paused and wrinkled his nose, snorted as if he had some phlegm in his throat, and swallowed. He rose his arms wide and smiled sheepishly. "I'm lost again."

I looked at Becca. I gave her a grimace that meant, *look, this guy seems pretty harmless, doesn't he?*

"I think I saw a sign that said Ogallala was a few miles ahead," I said. "We could drive you there."

"That's where *I* want to go!" he said proudly. "I'm from Ogallala!"

"Well, get in the back," I said, "and we'll drop you off. Push anything that's in your way."

He opened the door and hopped in. He picked my backpack off the seat and placed it gently on the ground.

"My name is Bucky," he said loudly, as I pulled back onto the road. "They call me that because of my teeth, even though my birth name is Ryan. Sir, may I ask you a question?"

"You sure may," I said. Becca had reopened her book but was staring at Bucky in the rearview mirror.

"I would like to know what your name is. And then I would like to know where you are going."

I almost laughed. They were such simple questions, but he said them as if they meant more than anything else in the universe.

I told him—I was Matt, and this was my sister Becca, and we were from California on a road trip east. We had gotten the car from our uncle, who asked us to find a missing family bracelet, a bracelet with a gold coin. Bucky listened quietly, occasionally bending his head towards us to hear better.

"That's very interesting," he said. "What you say about the family bracelet is the most interesting. I like gold things very much. So does Father. In fact, I think Father has what you're looking for."

"What do you mean?" I asked.

"Father has an old bracelet with a gold coin. What if it's the one you're looking for?"

My heart started pounding and I slowed the car a bit so I would be sure not to swerve off the road and crash into a cow. "No way!" I said. "You're saying he has a bracelet with a gold coin? How'd he get it?"

"I think you'll just have to ask him that question for yourself, sir," Bucky said. I heard him shuffle in his seat. "But boy, wouldn't that be great? If you could find your bracelet right here in Ogallala. I'm sure Father has it."

Could this be it? I turned to Becca, heartbeat off at the races. Becca looked forward, disguising whatever emotion she felt. "Can we go?"

Becca's lips were parted and she swallowed. "It's not possible," she said.

"Ma'am, don't be close-minded," Bucky advised. "You never know what could be possible!"

Of course it was not possible, but that only made it all the more possible. I started thinking about what I would do if this *was* the bracelet. Would I go home right away? Continue to New York to meet Kaori? How would we pass the time between Ogallala and New York? Bucky gave us tentative directions through Ogallala. It was a tiny highway town, a tractor island in a sea of corn. Bucky lived on a dirt road beside a field. He and his father lived in a one-story trailer attached to a mechanic workshop. His dad was a mechanic for trucks, trailers, tractors, and tractor-trailers. Their own trailer had a few pieces of furniture and no decoration. It made me feel a little queasy: the tiny space, the television from the 1970s, the dirty windows. If I had to say one thing about much of America, it'd be that some things are just much simpler than you'd expect. I might've guessed a Nebraska trailer-house would be decked out with rifles and a confederate flag. But it wasn't decked out with anything, and probably never would be. All the sudden I felt awful about something that I couldn't understand.

Bucky's dad wasn't home and didn't seem to be coming, despite Bucky's insistence that his dad would arrive any minute. We ended up going to McDonald's with Bucky and ordered him ten chicken nuggets. He finished them quickly, eating each in two identical bites. Becca and I got hamburgers, but I could hardly make a dent in mine. I wasn't hungry. I couldn't stop thinking about it—what if this was the end? What if the bracelet was right here, on the western edge of Nebraska, in a mechanic's trailer-house? I was afraid for myself, because I had realized that I wasn't ready to find the bracelet yet. Somehow, it wouldn't be right.

After we got back from McDonald's, Bucky told us about his friends. Bobby, the mailman, who had three cats. Luisa, the preacher's wife, who was from Ecuador and blessed everyone in Spanish. Dawson, an old Black man that had lived in Ogallala since the Civil War. He counted them on his fingers. Five, seven, more than ten! "There are so many wonderful people in the world," Bucky said, "and I'm glad that I can add two more friends. Matt and Becca." He asked us about the bracelet and I told him how it had made its way all around the country, meeting all sorts of people, like Bucky himself. This made him all the more excited, and he promised us thirty-three times that he knew all about it, and that Father would know exactly where it was. Then he declared he was tired as a boot and went to bed. I tried to watch some baseball on their TV as it got dark and then darker, but they didn't have cable and the sound came out fuzzy.

Becca read her book, and I glanced impatiently out the window. When I finally heard a car engine growling to a halt and keys jingling outside, my nerves shot out the chimney.

The door opened. Boots stomped. A tall, balding man with thick shoulders and a salt-and-pepper goatee saw us and sighed.

"Did Bucky bring you?" he asked.

We nodded, standing quickly to introduce ourselves and apologize.

"Don't bother. Ya'll from out of town?"

I tried to explain why we had come. He opened a beer from the fridge while I talked.

"Look, can I offer anything to eat or drink? I reckon you must be hungry."

No, we weren't. We just wanted to know about the bracelet. I told him what Bucky had told us. The words came fast, slurred, stuttering. "D-do you havea b-racelet like that? Brown l-leather, gold coin hanginfromit?"

Bucky's father snorted. "Damn, that boy has a way of doing this sorta thing."

"What do you mean?" Becca asked.

He wrung his hands. "I mean, each person's got a crazier story than the last. An ancient bracelet's not the craziest I ever heard, but Bucky certainly couldn't come up with that." He frowned. "Sorry kiddos, I don't have your bracelet."

"Have you ever heard of it?" I asked. "Maybe someone you know—"

He shook his head. "There's nothing. Bucky does this all the time. He finds people who're looking for something, tells them he's got it. Brings them over here and lets me clean it up. Look son, Bucky is retarded. Always was. Even when he was a little kid he couldn't do half the stuff other kids could. Wasn't potty-trained till he was damned eleven years old. He can do enough stuff himself now, but he's almost thirty."

"He's really nice," Becca said.

Bucky's dad nodded. "It ain't so terrible. He goes along the roads and looks for missing cats and dogs and chickens. He's got a knack for finding them. Kid was always good with animals. The neighborhood folk understand what he's like, so they pay him well for finding things." He straightened. "I don't think we've lost a single rat around here. Sure, some animals end up roadkill, but Bucky always finds them."

The nervousness left my stomach. Suddenly I was starving.

"But..." I trailed off. "Why do you think he tells people that he can help them, when he can't?"

"Bucky doesn't have any friends," his dad said. "He goes looking for dogs and cats till dusk, and hitchhikes back into town. Chats with whoever he meets. Brings 'em back here if they're willing, if he can find a way to get them to stay. He'll be upset when you're gone tomorrow. He always cries a little bit when people leave."

We thanked Bucky's father, and Becca refused his offer to cook us dinner. We went back to McDonald's because it was the only place still open.

13

Omaha

The lead that Rubin Yakovlev had about the bracelet in Omaha was pretty old but Becca and I thought it would be worth a try; plus, it was a big city, so maybe we could find some Chinese takeout. Grampa Andy highlighted and annotated the Omaha section in the notebook thoroughly, but I was starting to feel suspicious about Grampa Andy's highlighting—I couldn't tell if he circled things that were actually useful to the search, or simply interesting.

Rubin Yakovlev traveled all around Iowa and the surrounding Midwestern states throughout the early 1940s before he caught on to any major leads. Back then, he wrote mostly in Yiddish but sometimes in English, and always "the cowboy." "Perhaps the cowboy grips it in cold fingers." "The ruach of the cowboy is steeped in darkness," etcetera. Back then, he read Communist newspapers when they slipped past wartime censorship, and in one of those he found an exposé of the Red Summer of 1919 in Omaha, published in 1943. The summer featured record lynchings of Black people across the country and Omaha was no exception. The article was short and argued that such racial disputes should be of the "Pre-Depression Past", and called, a generation later, for "all noble Negroes in the Sons of Ra" to join the Communist Party, which "fights for the working class regardless of a man's color." Becca took great interest.

"That's it," she told me.

"What's 'it'?" I asked, well aware that her "it" and my "it" weren't remotely related.

"Class isn't more important than race. They're just intertwined. To overcome one, you've got to overcome the other. Race is a barrier that prevents the oppressed from seeing what they share."

"You can't have anarchism if you have communism," I reminded her.

"That's the whole point of communism," Becca reminded me. "The government eventually dissolves." Politics with Rebecca Rosen in three easy steps: 1) Jail the imperialists, 2) Abolish jail, 3) Abolish other stuff. I learned so much from her.

As for the Sons of Ra: Omaha was in labor chaos in 1919, tons of strikes and whatnot, and one day a white mob of 10,000 stormed the courthouse after a black packing-house worker named Willie Brown supposedly raped a white woman. The mayor, Smith, and chief of police, Eberstein (Jewish guy?), tried to deescalate the situation, and, thinking they had, sent the police officers home. Fucking Eberstein. Surely a Jew knows that when there's a crowd of 10,000 shouting "DEATH TO [insert despised ethnic/racial group here]," you don't send the law home! (Unless the police are part of the rioters, of course.) So, no thanks to the historically ignorant Eberstein, rioters set the courthouse on fire, waving American flags. Eberstein and Smith were nearly killed in the chaos, plenty of prisoners died in the fire, and the mob razed Omaha for the color black, bodies hanging at half-mast to replace the flags that had come down. They got Willie Brown and tore off his clothes, dragged him through the streets of Iowa. They tied him to a lamp post, soaked it in gasoline, and set him on fire. Rioters looted hardware stores for weapons. Thousands of Black people in Omaha armed themselves and fought for their lives until the army came two days later. The fucking *army*? Jesus Christ, how many civil wars has America had that we don't learn about in class?

After the riots, some of these Black armed citizens of Omaha formed the Sons of Ra, a militant civil rights organization that throughout the 1920s and 30s committed, depending on your politics, either disruptive protests or acts of terrorism, including the assassination of the KKK-linked successor of Mayor Smith. Strange rumors about the Sons of Ra abounded. Rumors about a bracelet.

Public records showed that a Son of Ra, Bobby Mayfield, had been lynched on three occasions. It only took three or four beers in Omaha packing-district bars for Rubin Yakovlev to overhear rumors that Bobby Mayfield owned a magic bracelet that made him an unlynchable superman. Unfortunately, by the time Rubin Yakovlev found Bobby Mayfield, the police had figured out how to kill the guy: just shoot him. So they did. Rubin Yakovlev managed to talk to Bobby Mayfield's family, and in a 1947 interview, Mayfield's mother confirmed that Bobby wore a bracelet with a gold coin, and that she had tried to get it back from the police. But when Rubin went to the police station, they heard nothing of it.

The story was among the earlier more detailed notes. It seemed to be the first clue after the Jetta Kanosh incident that the bracelet was caught up in a dizzying web of good and evil, although, I must say Rubin Yakovlev didn't seem interested in the moral implications of the bracelet. He just wanted to get it for himself, at times with a passion that verged on the savage.

Per Grampa Andy's recommendation, we decided to look for a descendent of Mary Mayfield. Who knows—maybe over the ensuing generations, the Mayfield family found the bracelet when ours never could?

We stopped by the courthouse to check the records about the case. We told an office intern that we were students conducting research and he helped us fish up an old court document. We cross-checked it with Rubin Yakovlev's notes, which were mainly correct, except for one thing. It wasn't the police that killed Bobby Mayfield, but a man named William W. Hardin. 6'2", white, forties, broad features, hat, boots, jeans, carried two handguns. They released him two months later for good behavior. Why did I feel like I had heard this story before?

Next, we went to town hall for birth records, to see if we could find living relatives of Bobby and Mary Mayfield. Despite our luck at the courthouse, the town hall turned out to be such a hassle that both of us were ready to give in after three hours of bureaucratic stalling. Becca had moved from *Cien Años de Soledad* to *La Casa de los Espiritus*, and then took to reading the notebook, every once in a while exclaiming about scenes and stories I already knew by heart.

We gave up on Omaha.

I would later regret this decision. How could I lose any chance to get closer to the bracelet just because some knucklehead with a bristly mustache is slow at turning pages in a phone book? If we really wanted to find the bracelet, we couldn't let these things hold me back. But in Omaha, we did.

We left. Got in the car. Gave up.

That night, Becca and I persuaded Mom into letting us book an extra night at a hotel on her credit card (yes, a downtown Hilton and not a roadside shack!). After we checked in, I immediately fell asleep face-down in all my clothes.

When I woke up, it was morning, and Becca was asleep. She had managed to change into pajamas and probably brush her teeth before crashing in a more orderly manner. My right cheek felt sore and swollen.

I thought about Omaha and felt incredibly alone. Not only had I lost my friends, family, and even Bucky, but I had lost the coherence of the search, the order of the trip. The omens had abandoned me. There was only the newly constructed Omaha police station, very modern, funky. The Chinese takeout in Omaha was better than Salt Lake City's. Lobbies and offices, litter on the curb, streetlamps, shopping carts of the homeless, downtown revivals and millions of dollars of new construction—nothing that meant anything. I felt more lost than ever. There I was in the middle of America, somehow neither farther from nor closer to my destination.

When Becca woke up, we went to a diner. I ordered three over-medium eggs, rye toast and bacon, and Becca got a veggie omelet. We were served by a tall blond college kid with supersized biceps. Becca set down her fork and shook her head.

"Isn't it awful?" she said.

"What?" I asked.

"All of it. The riots. The lynchings. Murdering a man and getting off free."

"Different century," I said. "Nothing we can do about it."

"But we can, Matt. Racism isn't gone. The war on drugs, war on crime." She picked her fork back up. "We *could* do something. We have to be able to do something."

"All your protests," I said. "Aren't you already doing something?"

"Those are anti-Bush, anti-Imperialist, which is related, but it's not the same. I'm thinking, Matt. I'm trying to rethink why and how we're looking for the bracelet in the first place. The Red Summer sounds just like what happened to our great-grandparents in Ukraine. It sounds like a pogrom."

"You can't make that comparison."

"Because it's too obvious? Here we are, happily in America, where pogroms happen to Black people instead. Black people are the Russian Jews of America."

"I'm not sure that makes sense."

"Of course it doesn't make sense," Becca said angrily. "Because it's worse. At least the Russian Jews could escape to a place where white skin allows you to bargain yourself into the middle class. It makes me sick. I can't eat this anymore. I can protest Iraq all I want, that doesn't change *this.* I'm so delusional! Protest this, protest that, but our very way of life is evil! Everything is evil, the world is evil! Existence is so fucking violent it's gonna drive me insane! And I hate myself more because I *know* I'm going to get over it! I shouldn't get over it, I shouldn't ever get over it, but one day I will, when I'm old and stupid and blinded by a debilitating desire to send my kids to fancy private schools. And to that me I say *fuck you.*"

In retrospect, I could've responded with encouragement, asking her to list acts towards social justice she could take in her daily life. But a certain someone interrupted.

"Whoa there," he said.

We turned to see our waiter, soft-smiling.

"Don't be so hard on yourself," he said. "You can't be expected to solve all the world's problems."

Becca laughed bitterly and shook her head. "It's not that I can't solve them. It's just that by living I make all of them worse."

For a second, I felt like a knife was in my throat. Becca's voice had dropped to a low murmur and the bitterness and choked poison in her words set my heart racing.

Becca...

The waiter calmly thought it over. Neat blonde hair, strong chin, bright blue eyes. "You know, that's not true, because I think you might be able to solve one of my problems. I think you're really bright. What's your name?"

The classic Becca response would be to laugh in his face. Instead she hunched up. "My name's Becca." She sounded like an adolescent frog.

"Well, Becca, I think you're bright, and pretty, too."

"Oh, no," Becca said, more seriously than flirtatiously.

I looked at Becca. Hunky waiter. Becca. Hunky waiter. My eyebrows were in the upper ionosphere.

"It's true." He unclasped his hands. "My name is Keith. Do you have a number? I want to give you a call later."

Becca and I were both stunned. I placed my hands on my lap and stared at the dirty plaster ceiling as if we were in the Sistine Chapel. I'd bet the bracelet that Becca turned as red as the American flag.

"That was rude of me," he said. "I shouldn't have."

"No..." Becca said. I could see her glancing at me. *Nope. I ain't telling you what to do. Esto gringo es tu problema.*

"It's just that I'm traveling," she said. "But what did you want to call me about?" Now her voice was mousey. In what universe would either of us have been expecting this hunky Iowan waiter to ask out Becca? Reflecting on her relatively substantial love life, I realized why it was so surprising to both of us: Becca's too Jewish. She's got the nose, the curly hair, the slightly broad shoulders, the high-pitched Jewish gal voice. That's not to say that she isn't good-looking, but you can catch the whiff of Jew on her from a hundred meters away. I doubted that Becca had dated, kissed, or even held hands with a goy.

He took the bait that should never have been offered. "Well, I wanted to ask you out. To dinner and a movie. Tonight, if you're traveling. I could pick you up."

Becca let out a little choked laugh. "Uh, I guess so! Tonight," she said sternly, eyeing me. "It has to be tonight."

"That's great, I'm so relieved. I'll take you for the best food in town, I promise. What's your hotel?"

Suffice to say that afternoon was awkward. Becca and I didn't say a word to each other till we got back to the hotel, and the moment we got there she buried her nose in *Casa.* I alternated between watching TV and watching her. It creeped me out a bit that my own sister would do something so unpredictable and it made me wonder if I really knew Becca at all, and even if this was a dream, or maybe the Matrix, some sort of intrusion on my life from someone *else's* dream. And all of this was just disguising the terrifying tenor of her voice and the words, *by living I make everything worse.*

I walked up to her until she looked up at me. I opened my mouth.

"Stop right there," Becca said. "I know that it may have made you uncomfortable, but I would like to do this fun thing. I promise I will be back on time. We will be leaving for Chicago tomorrow morning. It's been a long few weeks, and I would like to do this one fun thing."

I was taken aback. That wasn't even what I was going to say! Since when was I restricting her fun? I thought we were in this *together!* And why did she have to interrupt me before I even said a word?

"I don't care what you do," I snapped. "I just don't want to be late."

"We won't be late."

One day earlier, I would've told you that the trip felt like it was moving slowly. And even though we'd done nothing all day, one little event was enough to make me feel like things were completely out of control. Why would Becca go on a date with a rando? It's not like she goes to dances at the private schools and gets invited to college parties. Could she be just trying to get some? I didn't want to think about it. She left in a blue dress around 6:30 and I was all alone. (When why where what who did she pack a dress?!) I had nothing to do. I wanted to talk to someone, anyone, to get these things out of my head. But somehow I was unable to call home. I looked at a few pictures I had packed from disposables. Christine on her longboard. Will in his basement. A group of my "friends" at a pool party. Chelsea was in the picture. Her boobs were bigger than I had remembered. Much bigger. As I stared at them they kept growing. And then the nipples appeared too, poking through the swimsuit, and then they started growing. There was only one thing to do. I got in the shower, thought about a big pair of tits, and fucking wanked it.

I felt mercifully relieved. Afterwards, my mind was something of a blank slate. Thoughts strolled into my head. They knocked on my brain's front door and nodded courteously as they entered. I thought about Will for a while. All the times we spent in each other's basement, fighting with toy lightsabers. I wish things hadn't ended so badly between us. He was probably on his way to Florida by now. Florida! A world apart from California, although also a place where Jews can catch some rays after properly assimilating into American society. Then I realized something.

My mom's family first came to America in New York. At one point, they came west. I'm guessing it was Grampa Leo, moving west to start working in the movies. So to get there, maybe he had done the exact road trip that Becca and I were doing now, in the opposite direction. We were reverse commuting! I saw myself and Becca in the Volkswagen, gliding backwards across the country, sliding back across the face of time. The old Volkswagen lifted its wheels and skimmed the waves of the Atlantic back to Europe and over the old Roman roads all the way to Mother Russia. I could see the shtetl, the potato farms from whence we came. I felt a sense of wonder and pride. I wanted to tell Will about it, Christine and Chelsea too—that what me and my sister were doing had meaning. It's not the *something* that Becca's looking for—the something that would "make a difference," that would end hatred or save lives. But surely we can salvage *some thing* if we push hard enough on this eastbound road. If we dig deep enough into the scum of time, we can find the bracelet. The bracelet will be the past made real, and will have moral and historical lessons, like what Sacramento and Pyramid Lake taught me: that forced relocation is the first step towards genocide. And what Salt Lake City taught me: that the desert is a canvas for magic, real or imagined. We will bring the past properly into the future. And history will be restored, our family whole.

I managed to find peace for myself in that Omaha hotel room. All of the wild bracelet stories and latent teenage horniness had destabilized me, and I needed an anchor: the *realness*, the *trueness* of the bracelet. It was an anchor that would come in handy with the incoming demons. Like I said, *Chicago is the place where everything changed.*

That's when I happened to see the first of those incoming changes, sticking out of Becca's backpack. It was a letter.

Normally I don't mess with Becca's shit. She would never touch any of my shit, and I know she takes her own shit very seriously, which is why it was so surprising that the letter was exposed to the open air. But I was in a mood.

I picked up the letter. It was a thick one—over ten pages of neat handwriting. I began to read.

14

Kaori

Have You Had Any Dreams Lately?

14-44 3-Chome Midori Tsurumi-ku Kyoto-shi Kyoto-fu XXX-XXXX
March 28 2005

Dear Becca,

I'm sorry I haven't written in such a long time. Please correct my grammar when you send back.

Kyoto's spring was late this year. Every year the cherry blossoms (sakura) start to bloom the last week in March, but this year they are not blooming yet. My grandmother taught me how this is strange. You might not know that when I was small my parents weren't around. Dad had a weird working schedule and went between Japan and publishing houses in London and before Mom got promoted at the station, she worked seventy hour weeks. So I spent much time in grandmother's garden.

She would sit in a chair in front of the hanging laundry and sew or read newspapers with little round glasses. I sat on her lap, and she read stories to me. Or she pointed at the garden things. "Look Kaori, a butterfly!" or "Kaori, aren't the hydrangeas very purple this morning?" Many days she took me to the shrine. She was the shrine maiden when she was small, so she taught me charms and how to ward off spirits. We always brought a small pouch of sugar to the shrine as offering. When my grandmother filled up the pouch she let me lick sugar in the wooden spoon. Then she made me up in a coat and pink mittens if it was chilly. My mouth was filled with sweetness and we delivered the pouch, which makes it that a new wonderful thing can happen in the springtime.

I talk about the springtime because I have more Dreams in spring. I see a Dream every night this week. The flowers are late to bloom, but the Dreams are too much on time.

So far the Dream has been the same each night. Once I describe it to you, you will understand why I wanted to write you a letter about it. This is it:

I am walking by myself in the late summer in a shrine. It is quiet and dry and there is no wind, but the sun shines brightly. I pass through the gates and I sense a thing. The pebbles beneath my feet are very small, like grains of sand in a desert. I walk up to the red honden. From far away it looked small but now that I am close I see that it's huge: it is like a banquet hall, and there are many thousands of omikuji, petite slips of paper with prayers written, hanging from the ceiling. They are shining like candles even though the inside of the honden is dark. I walk the hall for a long time as the omikuji whisper their secret wishes. It is like being at the bottom of a deep well and processing in a tunnel overfilled with echoes. I am afraid, because if I were to trip I think that I would go into the world of the dead. I think that something evil is waiting. There is an evil spirit waiting me in the center of honden, but I am not afraid because grandmother has taught me spells to cast it away. Once I dispel the spirit I will take a bracelet from the shrine. Then I will come to New York City and give the bracelet to you. But then I realize that it is not just one spirit. It is a thousand. Or a million or more, they are like ghosts but not ghosts. Their bodies are made of frozen light but they move like water. Then I wake up. Always I wake up when I know that I have to give the bracelet to you.

Do you understand? This Dream is important because it reminds of what happened when you were here seven years ago, when we went to the shrine. There was a strong gust of wind that scared us as we went under the gate. There was a big, dark honden that we can't wander into that we wandered into. There was an evil spirit—of course, I can't know if there really was a evil spirit, or if it was just our imagination deceiving us! I remember how scared you were. We heard groan in the dark and your eyes became big and you were trembling. I didn't want you to be scared. I said every spell grandmother taught me, to make you feel better. And then there was the old priest who made us wash our hands, ring the bell, and bow. Then he gave us sweets. He didn't even realize I was a Japanese until I knew how to wash my hands. It made me feel like we were sisters.

I know I have to wait until August to see you, but I often think about how we met before. I know it has been years, but the Dreams come in colors that sparkle, and I can picture your face perfectly. I just have to wait for your voice to come to me. Maybe it can give me a little of your English. I don't have a plane ticket yet, but I know I am going to come. I laugh a little when I think about it by myself. When did we decide to meet in New York? Four years ago? Or more?

What about you? Have you had any Dreams lately?

I know I have other things to say to you, but most of them aren't important things and can wait. But I want to hear from you everything. How is Aaron? Does Matt do his homework? Did he stop smoking cigarettes? I want to hear all little ordinary things about your life. It makes me less bored.

By the time you get this letter, you will know where you get into university.

I'm sure you get in everywhere. Congratulations! I don't feel bad about saying that because I know you will. But my English is imperfect, and I am not American, and I am definitely not you, but I would like to be. I don't know what the American schools think of Japan. I succeeded in the SAT because my mathematics are strong but I don't think I can be accepted into a good university in America. Even if I did, would it be right for me to go?

Maybe a Dream will tell me what to do. But no, that doesn't happen. I think my life will be simpler if Dreams are about whether to go to college in Japan or America.

It's a scary. If I go to Kyoto University, I will have excellent education and career in Japan. I will get to keep my friends, because they are also going to university in Kyoto or Osaka. If I get into UCLA anything could happen. I might never come back to Japan. I might marry an American boy. I don't want to do this because it's what Mama did. It feels bad to do the same thing that your parents did even if they didn't do anything wrong. Maybe for this reason I want to leave Japan: my classmates all want to be the same. They wear the same clothes. They want the same jobs. Sometimes I want to grab them by the shoulders and yell: "Live your own life!" Becca, can't you help me decide? On my own I don't understand and I can't think about it too much or I start crying.

I'm such a crybaby, but I don't cry about boys or dramas or things like that. Sometimes I start to cry and I can't stop. When that happens, I think: where did all this water come from? I feel like I have oceans inside of my body. Rivers and oceans of a thing I have to do. That's why the tears come—the thing forces out of me. But just what the thing is I do not understand. Is it the thing that the world is full of evil? When our grandfather died and you came to me through the well I was happy. I learned that death isn't always bad. But since then I watched my grandmother die. The second time hurts more than the first. And I know that there is evil in the world. It cries out like birds that I only can hear. I think about the history of the Korean and

Manchurian women that the Japanese soldiers raped. Japanese soldiers who were tortured to death in Siberian work camps. I think about the history of the Ainu that we Japanese have tried to destroy but it doesn't feel like history. I think about Darfur. I watch television programs of people dying and I know everything about the tragedies. I think about Uncle David, who Dad told me was killed by AIDS, and I think about the people who feel so much pain that they can't move or talk. Tears connect me with them. Every time there is a evil or kindness in this world, the tears come. I never know exactly what it is because evil and kindness are always in the wind and in the sky and in the moon and in the morning.

Becca, that's why I want to come to New York. I will wait for you to reply. Congratulations on U.C. Berkeley.

Love, Kaori

P.S. Yesterday I forgot mittens, but I still brought a pouch of sugar to the shrine for both of us.

15

Chicago

In anticipation of Cowboy Jim's debut, remember that not everything that happens on this Earth can be easily explained. Each time the bracelet stumbled into ordinary people with ordinary lives, something extraordinary happened. Up until Omaha, I had ignored it all by focusing on day to day necessities. But after reading Kaori's letter, I knew I couldn't hide from something strange and terrifying.

What the hell was happening? I wondered if this was the real reason Kaori was coming to meet us in New York. I wondered how a dream is different from a Dream. And I couldn't get over how—how in this or any other universe could *Kaori have dreamt about the bracelet before Becca or I had ever heard of it?*

But the part that made me the most uncomfortable was the intimacy between Kaori and Becca. Kaori was so earnest, so trusting. Reading the letter made me feel like I had fallen into her bedroom. No one's ever confided in me like that. Christine did come crying to me once, when she found out her fourteen-year old sister was doing lean. But being there for her didn't feel good. I was scared. I wanted her problems to go away and I wanted to go away from her problems. Fortunately for all of us, the situation resolved quickly—familial intervention brought little Annie Li to tears and sobriety. It faded like a bad dream.

Meanwhile, the mysteries of the bracelet—which I had dismissed as tall tales, or as metaphors for something felt in the human heart but never really seen or experienced—Kaori proved they were real. I had no choice but to conclude that the bracelet is magic. It really did save my great-grandparents from pogroms in the Ukraine. It really did help a young man escape a Japanese incarceration camp, it really did grant a Mormon miraculous powers, it really did make a Black man unlynchable. It was all true.

I read Kaori's letter three or four times before carefully returning it to its place. I tried to remember her. I hadn't seen her in seven years since our family went to visit Uncle Larry in Japan. I remember following Becca and Kaori around, hiding behind a large rock in front of Uncle Larry's house to overhear their conversations. I realized that in seven years I hadn't grown at all.

Suddenly, unexpectedly, I heard the clicking of a key.

I turned. Becca entered in the blue dress she had put on for the date.

She nodded at me. "Let's go," she said.

I blinked at her. "What?"

"Let's get out of this shithole city. Let's go to Chicago. I called Uncle Michael and told him we were coming. He doesn't mind."

"It's late," I said.

"That's good," Becca said. "There won't be traffic."

I couldn't take it anymore. Becca was about to drive me off the wall and I'd lose all the dignity I had if I didn't stand up for myself. I stood to gain my one-inch height leverage over her. (I love that inch. I noticed it when I turned 15 and I will never let her live it down. She may be older, wiser, smarter, and generally a better person, but I'm unquestionably taller.) "Becca," I said, stretching out to a mighty five-foot-nine, "what is going *on* with you? You're all over the place and I can't figure out a thing. And I read the letter. I'm sorry, but I read the letter. It was left out. You left it out. It wasn't my fault you left it out! So I read it." I was becoming hysterical. "I'm sorry, Becca, I didn't want to read it, but I had to. It wasn't my choice. It wasn't me, I swear, I wasn't me—"

Becca stepped away from me and trained her eyes on the door. "Look, Matt, please, let's just get on the road. I promise I'll explain myself. I forgot to put it away, didn't I? But please, let's just go to Chicago. I can't stand it out here.

There's nothing but corn, corn everywhere! I don't even like corn."

Choking down a hot heaving in my stomach, I threw dirty clothes into my bag. I couldn't fight her on anything. I think as a kid Becca brainwashed me by doing too many nice things for me. She made me my dessert, played catch with me on the trampoline, made sure kids at school didn't mess with me, etc. As a result, I've become physically unable to defy her. I am a well-trained lemur.

Why did we have to meet Kaori? Why did she have to be real? I tried to wish her out of existence. She wasn't American. She was oceans away. But she was coming. She ruined everything. She cried at everything. I never cried. I couldn't remember the last time I had cried. I couldn't remember the last time I had a dream. We drove in silence. Unknown lights blinded and sparked. I hated them. They were too bright, and revealed the crags and corridors once lost in shadow, things that were hidden for a reason—because they were ugly, rotten, that scab on my forearm. Like I'd been cutting my wrists in my sleep instead of dreaming.

"So we went to a nice Italian restaurant downtown," Becca said. "It was a pretty happening strip, there were all these neon lights and lots of live music."

I'm sorry that I never told you the full story, she said. I just didn't know what to say.

"Yeah, pretty fun, right? So Keith ordered a bottle of wine, no ID check, and while he drank—because I sure as hell didn't want to—he started asking me all sorts of questions. I gave these super girly long winded answers. I told him that I was studying to be a nurse. Can you believe it? If I was even interested in medicine, I'd be nothing short of a surgeon, but this hunky guy had me so dizzy that I tried to act cute and tell him I wanted to be a nurse!"

How could I? When that fascist dickwad Roger Emerson told us about the bracelet, I was terrified into silence. How am I supposed to tell you that I'd been having dreams about the bracelet ever since Kaori starting having hers? Because—yep, me too. I see it in my dreams.

"Yeah, he plays baseball and studies marketing. Iowa State. Division champs last year. So after dinner we went to a bar and got free drinks from the bartender, one of Keith's friends. I still wasn't having any, and it turned out my instincts were right. At some point I started thinking about you by yourself in the hotel room, so I just told Keith I had to go. That's when he turned into a grade A fuckface. He acted all mopey and tried to hold me and kiss me and get me to stay and grab me in places I did *not* want to be grabbed, but I just got the fuck out of there, leaving horny lil' Keith shouting from the doorway. And that's everything that happened, Matt, I promise."

What kind of dreams? I don't know, Matt, I don't know. But they're there. Usually I'm in a deep, dark well. A deep dark well of dandelions. Big, furry yellow flowers with green beady eyes looking back at me. And in my heart I feel the urge. It's an outward pulse, from my chest to the flowers, begging for the bracelet. I've had the dream twenty times. Maybe more. Sometimes the ocean is flowing overhead, full of stars, and sometimes I can only see the moon. But the bracelet is always there, a little deeper down the well, just out of sight. I'm waiting for Kaori to bring it to me, and I know that if I can just go down the well, maybe I can meet her halfway there, but it's a well, there's a bottom full of water, and I can't swim and I'm drowning in the ocean in the rain and that's where I wake up.

"Dude was huge," I mumbled, drifting off

That's why I know that we're going to find it. That's why

Uncle Michael greeted us at 3:00 A.M. in pajamas and showed us to the guest room. We got in bed, but despite passing out so easily on the car ride, I couldn't sleep anymore. My mind was too full of Kaori's letter.

We didn't plan to spend three weeks in Chicago. We spent the first two days exploring the city with Uncle Michael and Aunt Tracey. I like Chicago. The downtown's clean, the skyscrapers friendly, lean giants of glass and steel, and the brand new Millennium Park sleek and green. Gliding kayaks crossed the rippling blue of Lake Michigan. We went to the Field Museum and had lunch by the river. Uncle Michael showed a refreshing, innocent, and friendly interest in our trip—until I just-so-happened to mention the bracelet. But before I tell you what he said, lemme give you an Uncle Michael rundown.

Uncle Michael's a tall, clean-shaven guy with a handsome smile. He had moved to Chicago three years ago, after but unconnected to one of his many fights with Mom. Mom is fine with us staying at his place, but I'm not sure if *she* would ever stay with him. I think their beef goes way back to when Uncle David died, but I'm not sure how things got so bad. I can remember Mom yelling at Uncle Michael for pretty much anything, even for something as simple as him stopping by the house to let me and Becca play with his cat. I always liked Uncle Michael but had been afraid to talk about it with Mom. I learned when I was young not to talk about it, and those habits stick.

I happened to mention, in an off-hand sort of way, that we had been looking for a bracelet connected with the Yakovlev family. Uncle Michael's gaze struck us like a lightning bolt. Fear welled in his eyes, condensed and hard but melting at the edges, *fear.* I was infected by it and beads of sweat trickled down my arms. He let out a half-gasp-half-sigh.

"You... know about it?" I asked him.

"I do," he said, in the tone reserved for people who just got asked out on a date that they would very much like to refuse. "Who told you about it?"

"Grampa Andy," Becca said. "He asked us to look for it."

"Andy? Why would... how could—" He paused. "Well, it's an interesting story, isn't it? It's an interesting story..." He trailed off.

Becca and I shared a quick glance.

"Uncle Michael, do you know anything about it?" I asked.

Uncle Michael stroked his shaved chin. He was staring at the empty space between Becca and myself, out towards the lake.

"Do you know anything about it?" I repeated.

Aunt Tracey changed the subject.

That night we celebrated Shabbat. I was horrified to realize I had forgotten the prayers, and *asher k'dishanu b'mitzvotav* didn't come to my lips until after Uncle Michael and Aunt Tracey said the first few syllables. I had been a bad Jew. Becca kept Kosher, like Dad, so at least she maintained a connection to Judaism while we traveled. I hadn't even thought about it. I didn't have a problem with not believing in God, but being a bad Jew... I didn't think I was comfortable with it anymore. I wondered what had changed.

On our second day, Uncle Michael and Aunt Tracey left us to our own devices. We went to a park where Rubin Yakovlev claimed this kid Dick Rivers played baseball. It was a decrepit field a few miles west of downtown. I read Rubin Yakovlev's notes aloud so we could remember the details. When Dick Rivers wore the bracelet his team won, and when he didn't, they lost. Classic bracelet move. It was honestly getting predictable.

We kicked up dust on the field and played with the Frisbee Uncle Michael had insisted on us bringing. Becca was good, even though neither of us had played in years, not since we played with Dad and Uncle Michael before he moved to Chicago. We exchanged a few words about how we might approach Uncle Michael about the bracelet, decided to not push it, and fell silent. The day wasn't too hot, and Becca was great at throwing far, so I ran after the Frisbee, jumped for it, fell down.

After all the revelations about the bracelet and capital-D Dreams and whatnot, I had the sense that the baseball field was a part of another world. Or maybe that it was a border between worlds. I lay down on the grass, working through the sensations. I swear, I could feel that the bracelet had been on this very field, more than seventy years ago. The bracelet was there, living in the world of the past. I was here, living in the world of the present. My fingers touched the border, a thin veil. I could feel the dirty leather, the smooth gold coin. A tingling in my temple and in my fingers. *Omens*, I realized. There are some omens that you can only feel.

Becca and I took the evening to plan our travel to New York. We chose Marsten OH, Bald Eagle PA, and Scranton PA as three evenly spaced stops on the way to New York that had ties to the bracelet. Kaori was flying into JFK in two weeks.

The next morning, we packed the car. Hugged Uncle Michael and Aunt

Tracey. Got in the car. Uncle Michael gave us his blessing, turned to walk away, and then quickly came to the window.

"Matthew, Rebecca," he said. "About the bracelet."

"Yes?" Becca asked from the driver's seat .

Uncle Michael took a deep breath. "I mean, it's been missing for so long. There's almost no chance of you finding it. Why bother?"

Now he was reminding me of Mom. Becca made a skeptical face. "For one, it's been super interesting so far, to learn so much history and family history," Becca said. "Plus, Grampa Andy asked us. We need to at least try."

Uncle Michael sucked in more breath. I wouldn't have been surprised if he blew up like a balloon, the way he kept inhaling. "Andy was a historian," he said, carefully. "He loved anything that lived longer than he had. It doesn't mean it's worth finding. I remember when my Uncle Rubin was looking for it back in the 70s. He started to think he was a cowboy and wore a hat and boots and everything. It had driven him crazy."

"We have very stable personalities, Uncle Michael," I responded, shivering at the thought of the mysterious cowboy Rubin spent so long chasing after.

"I'm trying to say that there's no point."

"Do you know something that we don't?" Becca asked, turning the ignition, but the car wasn't starting, only sputtering. She jerked harder. "It sounds like you're against it for some reason, and if you are, you have to tell us why—"

The car hacked a brutal cough and fell silent. The bang and a sharp inhale of chemical smoke silenced the rest of us, too.

Just like that—Grampa Andy's old Volkswagen—kaput. We had it towed to the shop and they said it would take two weeks to get the parts to fix it.

Yeah. That fucking sucked.

We called Mom and Dad and arranged to stay with Uncle Michael until things got fixed. Mom had us promise that we would drive home when the car was ready—she wouldn't have it any other way. Her voice went all high-pitched. When Becca and I protested, she threw out all sorts of threats: refusal to pay college tuitions, perpetual groundings, the banishment of Christine Li from our household. I don't blame her for being stressed. Becca and I tried to explain that we were fine, and that we still had time to go to New York and back, but she was having none of it. Becca and I promised her whatever she asked of us and gave each other little winks and nods.

There we were. Two weeks in Chicago, nothing to do. It was August now. I started texting Chelsea and Christine. I sent them flirty messages that I hoped would make them miss me. Chelsea encouraged me to keep looking for the bracelet. I tried to impress her with funny Mormon stories, but they didn't seem to land. Meanwhile, Becca sat down with a pen and paper and starting writing and writing. I asked her if it was a novel and she scowled. I had no doubt it was a letter to Kaori.

Becca and I told Uncle Michael and Aunt Tracey not to worry about us, but they still cooked us dinner every day and made sure we had something for lunch. Becca and I thought a lot about logistics. We calculated all sorts of routes to and from New York to get back in time for school. We considered buses, trains, boats and planes to New York and back so we wouldn't have to wait for the car, but it was so expensive, and Mom sure as hell wasn't paying. Becca started sleeping ten hours a day, so I felt like I needed to schedule appointments with her even though we lived in the same room.

In the end, we came to a surprising decision. Becca would take a gap year.

"So you're not going to school this year?" I asked.

"I'll travel and get some work experience," Becca said. "I could volunteer for progressive campaigns. Or I've always wanted to work on a wildlife reservation in Alaska."

"Alaska?"

"Or at a vineyard. That would be cool. The pacific northwest, or Patagonia... work on my Spanish."

I grabbed her shoulder. "Becca. Are you sure you want to do this? That's a huge thing—to not go to college for a whole year."

"I appreciate your concern," she said. "But it's not that big of a deal. In fact, it's really easy to arrange, and lots of people do it. I haven't heard of anyone who's regretted their gap year." She smiled. "You should be happy! That gives us an extra two weeks, so we don't have to worry about logistics—we just need to wait for the car to get fixed. We shouldn't have trouble getting back home in time for your school. It was Berkeley that was causing all the trouble."

I accepted her decision, but I had never felt more concerned about my sister. The dreams, the disturbing ease with which she made the arrangements with our parents and Berkeley. If there was a fight with Dad, I never heard about it. Was she doing all this for me? For Kaori? Or was she hiding something?

Becca and I wouldn't leave Chicago until almost three weeks later. I spent that time in two ways: 1) Working for Uncle Michael for cash, and 2) Visiting Dick Rivers' decrepit baseball field.

I went to the bank and found my balance depressingly low. There wouldn't be enough for In n Out with Christine at this rate. After mentioning it at dinner, Uncle Michael offered to make an arrangement. He was a paralegal, so he had a lot of files, and files need to be sorted. Now, there's no way I'm more organized than Uncle Michael is (you should see my room). But wave a wad of cash at me and I'll do what it takes. I drove with him to his office in the morning and sorted his files by case, and the cases alphabetically. I stayed until 1:00 and then took the L back to the Near North Side. He paid me a solid $10 an hour. He had so many goddamn files that the job took me almost two weeks to finish, but at least at the end of it I found myself a somewhat wealthier teenager.

I mention it because the monotonous hours did something weird to my brain. It wasn't like being high, but the repetitiveness of the task at hand hypnotized me into a daze where my thoughts let loose. They got going and going and gathered the momentum of an avalanche: soon nothing could stop them.

My stampeding thoughts stumbled into a few things. First, there's something fucked up about my family that I don't get. Uncle Michael is a perfectly good guy. So why does my mom hate him? *Something* must have happened. I thought about Uncle David. Mom never talked about him, no one ever talked about him. He must be the key to it all, but why, and how, and when, where and what—I didn't know.

The other thing I realized was that I'm not a completely worthless person. Shifting around file after file, licking my thumbs and turning the pages, my thoughts followed home to Christine and how much I missed her sarcastic remarks and quizzical smile, which led to that night at the pool, which led to me realizing I needed to sort my shit out, which ultimately reminded me that I *had* exercised a few practical skills on the trip. One thing I learned how to do was talk to people. After the rough start, more than talking to people, I had been talking to them *well.* I had gotten some half-dozen people from backgrounds as different as it gets to tell me their stories. It doesn't lead to a career, but it was good to know: I can talk to people. I wanted to call Christine and thank her, but I decided it would be best shared in person. In this small way, I happily decided, my shit is very much together.

One morning in the office, Uncle Michael came back from a meeting and stood at the doorway for a long time. I had been thoughtlessly sorting, and had sort of drifted off before I realized the chill I had felt was his shadow hanging over me.

"What's up?" I asked him.

For a long time, he just looked at me. Something in the office clicked mechanically, softly. And just when he started to creep me out, he said: "The bracelet holds a terrible secret. That's why you must stop searching for it."

A chill knifed through my spine and left beads of cold sweat stinging on my forehead. My body drowned in goosebumps and twitched. I turned away from him and kept leafing through the paper, limp, dry, neither warm nor cold. He knew what was wrong with the bracelet, with all of this. He had to know. Of course he knew. But how?

"What is it?"

I could see his reflection in the window and saw his head hang down. "I can't tell you," he said. He stood in the doorway for a long time. Then he left.

So those were my mornings, full of files, runaway thoughts, and downright terror. And I spent my afternoons at the baseball field.

We usually went there at around 3:00, after I came home and ate lunch with Becca. Becca and I talked about the news and politics, whatever was worthy of skepticism, outrage, or applause—Israel decided to evict settlers in the Gaza Strip, a chemical plant exploded in Michigan, there was a country-wide coal strike in South Africa. Then Becca and I jogged two miles in the humid

Chicago heat over to the baseball field.

For some reason I could never bring myself to share with her what Uncle Michael had said to me. It felt like either that she already knew, or maybe that it didn't matter. I couldn't distill the urgency, the mystery of the warning into a simple sentence, even though the syllables would've been so easy to say.

The field lay bare to the street, no fence. Cars drove by in danger from a home run to left field. The dirt and dust on the field was nearly weightless—walking on it kicked up a rust-colored mist that shimmered in the afternoon sun. Tired grass grew in clumps out of the dirt. In spite of the field's neglect, the surrounding neighborhood seemed to have gotten an influx of money. There were tall trees, big oaks and pines. The chatter of leaves in the wind and the slowly descending dust gave the whole baseball diamond a ghostly sense of motion.

After we got there, Becca and I did our thing. She sat in the shade and either read a history book or a novel in Spanish, and I sat down somewhere in the outfield. Sometimes I closed my eyes and tried to meditate. Sometimes I did pushups and an ab workout or stretches and hip drills. If it wasn't too hot, I lay down in the shade and fell asleep. A lot of the time I ended up walking around the bases over and over again, following the silent trail of Dick Rivers, Becca watching the two of us round them after a home run. No matter what I did, Uncle Michael's voice rang in my ears. *Terrible secret. Must stop. Can't tell.* I shivered in the sizzling heat.

It was Uncle Michael's somber declaration that kept me coming back, dragging Becca along with me. Ever since he said the words—and since saying them, my uncle never made eye contact with me again—I felt like my senses had been heightened. At first it was just a sensation, an awareness of the bracelet's presence. A tingling on my forehead, a heart beating in my knuckles. It was even stronger on the baseball field. The leaves rustled against each other, like fingers snapping, the skin of lovers brushing, a choir humming from the far side of the mountain. The dust that rose in my wake slowly fell. It separated into sheets like layers of bedrock: transparent mist on top, above a darker streak of soil. Orange mineral rust speckled both layers. The mist and dirt faded. The leaves rustled, now low, now loud. Sunlight slipped into shade. Pebbles trickled over the muddy bases. The leaves chattered, whispered. Dick Rivers passed third base.

I jumped the wooden fence by the first base sideline and climbed onto the metal rafters, just three rows of seats.

From there, I was a spectator. I waited in the stands, watching Dick Rivers raise his hands to the silent applause, smelling traces of car exhaust, listening to the leaves. The neat geometry of the field formed a diamond: pure white on green. Sky darkened. Dust vanished. A shadow crossed the field, racing towards Becca, bent over in the shade of a large tree.

"Becca!"

The metal clanged as I leapt off the stands, hopped the fence and into to the pitcher's mound as the wind silently carried the shadow across the field and across the street. The dust was high again and falling. The sun shone hot on my face and arms and glittered against the levitating copper grains, a shipwreck scattering.

"What happened?" Becca was jogging over to me. "What happened?"

I suddenly understood why Becca hadn't told me about her dreams. I didn't know what to say. How to explain myself. What Uncle Michael had said. The shadow was real, and it called to me. Afterwards, I made sure to watch it for a whole week, Shabbat to Shabbat, before explaining to Becca that I was confident that soon, the shadow would make its move.

That morning we went to synagogue in Wicker Park with Uncle Michael and Aunt Tracey. They went to a reform synagogue in a new building with a glass lobby and minimally decorated chapel with gray stone walls. The prayers were in English, and Becca and I didn't know the melodies. There was a silent Amidah. Becca davened, whispering it in Hebrew: Kedushat Hashem, Teshuvah, Avodah, twisting and nodding, Sim Shalom. Behold our affliction and wage our battles... Fulfill your trust to those who sleep in dust... *Umekayim emunato lishenei a'far...* The only prayer that was sung in Hebrew was the the Kaddish, and we both relaxed at the familiar drone. *Yit'gaddal v'yitkaddash sh'me raba...*

The synagogue was impressively full, and the Kiddush luncheon after had some killer lox. I had an onion bagel with the groovy shit piled on high. One rumor about heading east that I hoped was true: the farther east you go, the better the Ashkenazi cuisine. The climax, of course, is in none other than Brooklyn.

It was the first time I had felt comfortable in synagogue in years. The prayer didn't make me feel safer, but it didn't hurt to send some positive energy out into the universe. The day's weather made me nervous. A hot and bright sun made for especially black, refined shadows, branded darkly on the streets like scorch-marks. The shadow would be strong today.

Becca and I were silent until we arrived at the field. I was drenched in sweat, more than usual. The scene was as expected: a silent field below, as leaves clattered and cheered above. We walked around the bases, kicking up fountains of dust. We could taste it even after we went to sit in the metal stands.

"The shadow," she said.

I nodded. "For now, watch the dust settle," I said.

"Okay." She swung her legs back and forth. "I'm going to miss this spot."

"I don't know if I will," I said.

Becca was quiet. She tilted her head and gasped.

"What is it?"

"I hadn't realized it until I was sitting here. But this is it."

"It's what?"

"A dream I had."

I turned to her. Blood rose and fell in my veins. "What happened in the dream?"

Becca squinted in the brightness of the reflective metal. "I was sitting in a stadium, above a field."

"Okay."

"It was bigger than this," she said. "And I was crying. I can't for the life of me remember why. But I was crying a lot, my whole face was soaked."

My heart pounded in my throat. I was no longer looking at Becca or listening to her response: I had my eyes trained on the field, searching every inch for any trace of a shadow. Dick Rivers was jogging from first to second. The dust had settled completely. Dick Rivers rounded third. The wind picked up and the leaf-song pitched into clamor before sizzling away. Dick Rivers slid into home and disappeared. The field was still.

"There!" Becca cried, pointing at first base.

I stood. The dark line, the shadow of the base's canvas, flexed and shivered before warping, growing. It churned across the field in a writhing black net and I clanged down the stands and over the fence. Becca called after me.

I was running towards the shadow, but this time it was not fleeing. It was coming towards me.

I pumped my legs into wide strides as the shadow massed into a black-hole monster and I heard the cracking of a baseball bat. The demon and I were going to meet head-on and I couldn't stop sprinting.

"Matt!" Becca screamed.

I tripped on the pitcher's mound and dirt smacked my mouth and I rolled over to see a figure staring down at me.

He was tall with sun-beaten skin and a wide-brimmed cowboy hat on thinning hair. He had a sharp jawbone, aged but handsome features, and a denim jacket over a white shirt. He wore tall boots and smiled at me.

"The bracelet belongs to me," he said with a country lilt. "Stay away for your own good. This is my final warning." He tapped the pistols holstered on both hips.

I heard the pounding of feet and choked on the dust. The leaves rustled. Dirt filled my eyes. The cowboy boots on the mound resounded in my ears like ocean waves.

Then I heard Becca's panicked breathing, and I felt her kneel beside me. She grabbed my shoulder.

"I'm okay," I mumbled. "I'm okay."

"What did it say?" she whispered. My eyes were closed but I could picture her looking down at me, hands quickly fixing out-of-place curls of her hair.

I shook my head. My eyes were closed but I could see the cowboy grinning at me with sharp white teeth. Tipping his hat and stalking away. Clacking boots on marble. Rustling leaves. Swallowing dust.

Becca leaned over and kissed me on the forehead.

That's why I know that we're going to find it. That's why you can never give up

16

Marsten

The dark secret of the bracelet supposedly revealed (well, more like the fact that there *was* a dark secret and an evil cowboy behind the bracelet in the first place), we booked it for Ohio with grim determination. One night in a roadside motel near Columbus. The town of Marsten. I started seeing the cowboy everywhere. I saw his figure in the shape of Indiana grass and tall green trees, and the symmetry of his twin pistols in the gently curved roads that interrupted square plots of land.

We had made it out of the Great American Desert, but it still wasn't raining. The land had started changing past Ogallala and Chicago dealt the final blow. If it weren't for all the farmland and grassy suburbs, the trees would grow tremendous and everywhere. We passed small ponds as blue as the sky, flocks of geese, the occasional beady-eyed groundhog.

Becca and I had a silent consensus to not talk about what happened on the baseball field. Neither of us seemed sure that it actually did happen, so we didn't want to jump to irrational conclusions based on hallucinations, as vivid as they may have been. Besides the possibility of Cowboy Jim (what I had decided to call him) emerging from a darkness and threatening me with handguns, maybe Becca and I had gotten so worked that we made monsters out of a few summer shadows. For the time being, both of us were happy to pretend it hadn't happened. We drove in comparative silence, listening endlessly to NPR. The Kyoto Protocol was coming into effect, just in time for one heat wave after another. Meanwhile in Gaza, everyone was killing each other. No more music, and certainly no more teasing Becca about Aaron the Big Friendly Jew, or complaining about Dad's politics, or gossiping about Berkeley, or retelling James Bond plots with Grampa Andy as the lead. We were less than human, robots programmed to go east and east alone.

"It just about drove him crazy." I remembered Uncle Michael's warning. Had I lost my sanity? For the first time I felt a painful urge for home—you know, normal shit. Watching Adult Swim with Will. Crashing Christine's brother's parties. Taking the bus to Chinatown, eating xiao long bao. Stressing about the SAT. But I couldn't have any of that, not anymore.

Chicago was the point of no return. When we picked up the Volkswagen all fixed up and headed east instead of west, the decision became irrevocable: we would chase the bracelet to the ends of the earth if we had to, braving threats of demons more fearsome than a country cowboy.

Grampa Andy wrote about Marsten, a town in southern Ohio. Rubin Yakovlev went there for the first time in 1956 to inquire after Janet Perkins, the daughter-in-law of an antique collector who had supposedly bought the bracelet from a dealer in Salt Lake City. She told Rubin Yakovlev that she knew her father-in-law had owned the bracelet at some point. Rubin Yakovlev gave her an address to send him a letter when she found out more.

More than ten years later, a letter came. Janet Perkins had not only heard word of the bracelet—she had seen the thing itself. There was a faded copy of the letter in the notebook, written in Janet Perkins's cursive. Her father-in-law had lost the bracelet a long time ago, but out of the blue, the bracelet showed up at an antique auction in Santa Fe. Her husband ended up paying an arm and a leg for it. ("Nevertheless," Janet Perkins wrote, "it gives my husband and his family relief that the bracelet is back in the possession of our family, its rightful owners.")

But, since he was constantly traveling, a letter had to find its way to Rubin Yakovlev. The letter eventually ended up in Baltimore, where he was busy chasing some other lead. He got the letter on April 4th, 1968, the day of Martin Luther King Jr.'s death. Rubin Yakovlev quit his business and tried to catch a flight, any flight to Columbus, Cleveland, even Chicago, but violent civil unrest had paralyzed the entire city. Riot police beat civilians smashing windows. Rubin Yakovlev couldn't leave Baltimore until the 8th.

By the time he got to Philadelphia to catch a plane to Cleveland, it was too late. He arrived in Marsten to find tragedy. Janet Perkins and her husband had been violently assaulted, and their house ransacked. The husband was dead and Janet Perkins in a coma. Rubin Yakovlev himself was the one who called the police. He was the first to see the fallen bodies and the naked wrists. He inquired after Perkins' relatives. No bracelet.

A generation passed. Babies born on the tear-gas-stung streets of Baltimore had babies of their own; the year was 1995, and a letter meant for Rubin Yakovlev found its way to Grampa Andy. From Janet Perkins.

When she woke up from her coma in 1980, she had amnesia. It took her years to even remember her daughter's name, let alone her father-in-law's, let alone the events of the night of the crime. The letter she sent Rubin was a note, reminding him who she was. There were no specifics. Only an invitation to come to Marsten. A decade later, there we were.

The town was radically changed. I can't speak to what Marsten was like in the 60s, but Rubin Yakovlev hadn't noted anything particular in his journals, so I assumed it was an ordinary American town, three hours from Columbus, with post-offices and banks and contractors and churches, surrounded by farm country. But when we got there the place was a poisonous hell.

Becca noticed a warning sign. Someone had clogged the sink in the gas station bathroom with duct tape, and left a tub of Purell instead. But otherwise, there wasn't an easy way to know. We saw big corporate farms, one or two tractors rambling across them. We saw the town strip with a few vacant buildings and all the major fast-food chains, quaint brick buildings. It was a town that had seen better days, but we didn't know *why* until we spoke with Janet Perkins.

Yes, she was ancient, but yes, she was definitely alive. Jesus Christ could that lady talk. She more or less shouted out of her bed. We lied to the people at the nursing home and said we were her grandchildren, so first we got a nice tirade on the loose morals of her progeny (kid #2 had been divorced three times; grandkid #3 was a professional poker player). When we finally got down to business—the bracelet—she got stiff and a little too much down to earth.

She declared: “I have been poisoned by the devil.”

Okay, Janet Perkins, care to explain? It wasn’t easy, but over the course of an exhausting hour we got the full story.

In order to explain best, I better walk you through a brief history of Marsten.

It all started with school integration in 1970. None of the white parents wanted their kids to go to school with Black kids, so first thing you know, broken glass, vandalized homes, terrorized children, and a few murders written off as accidents; next thing you know, white flight. By 1980, the town was mostly Black. So you went from a mixed community to a Black one, but since most of the white-owned businesses got taken over by new owners, the town wasn’t any poorer. Yeah, that didn’t last long. In the 80s, most of the smaller farms in the area got consolidated into giant Monsanto-style industrial farms owned by a single company.

Meanwhile, Janet Perkins was out of her coma by the late 80s. At first, she couldn’t remember what had happened to her that night she was assaulted. The state gave up on her case and let her live on welfare as an amnesiac. She claimed that bits and pieces of memory would sometimes approach, but that a dark force would sweep them away in the night, a devouring wind. Over the course of many years, she realized that it was the wind and the air: that the air was full of poison. She said that the night she went into a coma, the devil poisoned the night air and blew his icy breath to ensure she would never remember who had murdered her husband and destroyed her home. But Janet Perkins fought the devil’s air. By writing every detail of her memory and daily life in a rigorous journal, day after day, month after month, year after year, she began to gather up the scattered pieces of her life.

She couldn’t identify precisely what had happened to the air, but Becca and I figured it out soon enough. She talked about journalists that were causing trouble, and state inspectors that got run out of town by corporate lawyers. We later learned that ten years back, locals organized protests. The big agro company next door was filling the air with pigshit fertilizer, poisoning Janet Perkins and the town of Marsten alike.

I kid you not. The same company that owned all the local farms slaughtered pigs for pork down in Kentucky, so they vaporized the dung, mixed in some chemicals for good measure, and sprayed it out of airplanes over the thousand acre farms that surrounded Marsten. Naturally, in the wind, shit travels. This went on for fifteen years before the tap water became undrinkable and children started having birth defects. No one could grow fruits or vegetables in their yards. The air became dangerous to breathe. Since all the money went out the window in the 80s, the residents couldn't raise hell, as they were all struggling to get by. Community organizers began to agitate, leading the company to settle and pay all residents of Marsten some trifling sum in 2002 (around $20,000 per family). The company agreed to refrain from spraying the town with pig feces. However, when we went to talk to the gas station cashier on our way out, he insisted that it had started happening again this spring. The people in this town were victims of domestic terrorism. They were being bombed with pigshit.

Now, whether you choose to believe that it was the devil's wind that fucked up Janet Perkins, or it was that she spent some twenty years ingesting the matter that emerges from swine anus, is up to you.

But in 1995, her memory came back.

Janet Perkins remembered who had assaulted her and taken the bracelet.

Guess. *Just guess.*

A man in a cowboy's garb, with two pistols and a devil's grin beat her husband to his death and slipped the bracelet off his wrist. He put the bracelet in between his teeth and slung a pistol at Janet Perkins' skull. All went black for ten years.

The devil cowboy had been poisoning the air to keep her memory at bay. She only wished Rubin Yakovlev ("the Soviet gentlemen") was still around to fight the devil and get the bracelet back.

Becca and I promised we would do it in his stead.

17

Bald Eagle

Becca had her foot nailed to the gas. We rushed through Ohio and blazed through Pennsylvania. I finally found myself looking out on the landscape like it mattered. The trees were tall and richly colored. The smell of wet soil hung over the carving hills. Light pushed through a million leaves. Have you ever stopped to think about how sunlight can do that? The sun has a will to shine, and the leaf a pleasant complacency. Light and leaf cooperate, and a gentle green rains down.

Civilization, too, was suddenly fascinating. Billboard advertisements for shampoo with handsome dogs, bearded motorcyclists, people deciding whether or not to throw their cigarettes out the window. Bumper stickers: Penn State, LIBERAL MOMS, I Bet Jesus Would've Used *His* Turn Signals! The world had become beautiful, and it was because, for the first time, the bracelet appeared to be in reach. According to Grampa Andy, it was in Bald Eagle PA in 2000, just five years ago. So, as skeptical as our journey had trained us to be, we still had hope.

The story goes: a gun dealer in Harrisonburg, Virginia who sold antique rifles rigged up with beautiful old amulets responded to Rubin Yakovlev's inquiry twenty-five years late; Grampa Andy got the mail and went over. The storeowner said he had sold a hunting rifle strung with a bracelet and a gold coin to a woman named Maura Green in 1999. A bit of due diligence by Grampa Andy located Maura Green in Bald Eagle, Pennsylvania.

Like so many other American towns, Bald Eagle was a gas station crossroads strung with power wires. You could play the Pennsylvania lottery and buy some Lays. Or, you could go to Bald Eagle State Forest, Bald Eagle State Park, White Mountain Wild Area, State Game Lands Number 295, State Game Lands Number 255, and State Game Lands Number 92. Apparently Pennsylvanians like their hunting.

Maura Green was no exception. We found her house, a spacious country cabin, past a few oat farms next to state game land, woods hugging Appalachian hills. When we walked towards the front door, a demonic chorus of dogs greeted us. A frail white woman named Fanny, who turned out to be Maura Green's partner, opened the door with a hostile politeness. She did the pleasantries perfectly, but the look in her eyes said *what the hell are you doing here?* The house was full of Black regalia, African pottery and masks and Blaxploitation posters. Maura Green came downstairs about ten minutes later with a beer in hand, a friendly Pittsburgh native who had retired to Bald Eagle after two dozen successful years in real estate. Past fifty, she was a big, fit Black woman. She offered us Yuenglings, which Becca declined for both of us.

"Never did believe in the drinking age," she said. "But suit yourselves. What can I do for you?"

As I had done so many times before, but now with a certain hurriedness, I explained what we wanted to know.

"Well sure," she said. "That was a special trinket. Leather bracelet, gold coin? Real old-looking."

"That's it," I said. You would've thought that news about the bracelet wouldn't get a rise out of me any more, but it still did. The moment Maura Green said the word 'bracelet' my heart started pounding out the roof. Just how many years did that bracelet take off my life?

"What about it? I had a jeweler appraise the coin and he told me it was from the 1600s. He offered to buy it from me, so I went and sold it pretty quickly. The thing was bad luck."

Becca and I glanced at each other.

"That thing mean something to you?" Maura frowned. "It was bad luck for me, anyhow. I took that musket hunting twice. Both times a disaster."

We asked her what happened.

"The two of you are from some big city somewhere, so I have to ask," Maura said. "I like hunting. What do you think about that?"

"I don't have an opinion," I said quickly, before Becca could say that she found it cruel and barbaric.

Maura was shaking a finger. Becca had stayed quiet, but Maura had seen her answer in her eyes. "Don't go judging me, now. Are you a vegan, young lady?"

Becca smiled with her mouth. "Vegetarian."

"Not good enough to keep you from being a hypocrite." Maura smiled. "Animals that make products are treated even worse than the ones they kill. I kill my animals the *right* way. Out in the wild, woman and dogs and damned delicious venison. I don't eat any animals that I don't hunt with my own two hands. I'm proud of that."

"That's good of you," I said.

"You'd do well to not judge people like that, young lady," Maura said. "I hunt animals. I don't know what your hobbies are, but they sure as hell don't cause less harm to the world."

"That's good of you," I repeated.

Maura shook her head. "You don't understand, do you? You're not the fastest learners, I suppose. I'll tell you what happened. The first time I was attacked by wolves. True story—attacked by wolves. I thought they had been gone in Pennsylvania, but with stricter hunting laws and all that, I suppose they've been able to make a comeback. I was by myself with my dogs deep in the woods, and on the other side of the stream I saw them—the pack of wolves. We stayed still and quiet and started to back away, but they noticed us, started yapping and growling and getting closer. I fired the musket to scare them off, and most of them scattered, except for one that leapt across the stream and mauled one of my dogs before I shot the damned beast.

"At first I thought it was just bad luck, and everything was normal until the the spring. Same deal, hunting deer with my dogs. But that time I got caught in a snowstorm.

"It was too late in the year for snowstorm—early April, but the snow was falling all around us and sticking hard to the ground, so soon enough we were trudging through the snow, and what do you know—I saw another wolf. This time I didn't hesitate, though. I shot the bastard right away. I wasn't making the same mistake. I checked to make sure it was dead, and put another bullet in its head for good measure. We headed back straight away.

"Me and the dogs didn't make it more than a quarter mile down the road before we saw *more* wolves. As you can imagine, me and the dogs were scared shitless. But it got worse. Out of nowhere, this tall white man wrapped in a cloak and wearing a big goofy hat appeared, standing there among the wolves like he was a member of the pack!"

"What did he look like?" I asked.

"Can't really say. It was dark in the storm. I can only say he was tall and white and wore a cowboy hat. He called out, asked me to hand my musket over. He said that he would ask me one more time. So I didn't hesitate. I shot him."

"You shot him?" Becca gasped.

Maura turned to her. "I shot him," she said, straightening up. She drained the rest of her beer. "That wasn't a man. It was a ghost. A demon. I don't fuck around when I'm in the woods. Well, once I shot him, the wolves scattered, and me and the dogs booked it out of there. And don't even think of reporting me to the police, because there's sure as hell no proof. Don't betray my hospitality." She finished her beer and clapped it on the table. "I had the gold on the bracelet appraised and sold it separate from the musket within a week. I'm telling you, the thing's cursed."

I nodded slowly. "You're not wrong. He's evil. The cowboy."

Maura leaned towards me, intrigued. "You know him?"

"Cowboy Jim," I said. Becca glanced at me and smiled. I think she agreed with my choice of name.

"*Jim?*" Maura snorted. "Figured he was more of a Colton."

Cowboy Colton. Not bad, Maura.

I shrugged. "It's as good a name of any, isn't it?"

We fell into a long silence. Maura eventually asked Fanny to bring us some lemonade. Becca and I drank it out of tall glasses with straws while Maura scratched her head.

I was so deep in thought that I had forgotten the most important question. Becca asked it for me:

"Who did you sell it to? The bracelet?"

"Jeweler in Newark. Ricardo Dias or something, Mexican fellow. Owns a jewelry shop in Newark. We're talking 2001."

Becca and I looked at each other. I felt nauseous, like we were on a rollercoaster, about to go over the edge. We emerged. We were out of the notebook. We found the bracelet's trail, just four years back.

And the ride was just getting started.

18

Scranton

It's kinda ironic that we ended up drowning in the Delaware River, since we almost went directly to Newark, to go after Ricardo Diaz the jeweler. In that case, we would've made it safely to Newark before Katrina hit the Northeast. But the drive from Bald Eagle was long, and we wanted to stop somewhere. The interesting thing about Scranton is that after Rubin Yakovlev's visit there in December 1979, more than fifteen years passed before Grampa Andy picked up the project. Scranton was Rubin Yakovlev's final lead—he died just two years later. Rubin Yakovlev had finally lost it. In the dense entries leading up to Scranton, he's all over the place. He writes about demons, dybbuks, the cowboy raping and murdering, western-style shoot-outs with the devil in Tuscaloosa and a car chase presided over by the Angel of Death in Montgomery. Grampa Leo even tried to have him institutionalized in '77. You could tell that Uncle Rubin had truly gone insane—there's no details, no substance, and hardly anything comprehensible. A lot of Yiddish. Dreams and fantasies, Hebrew poetry.

The bracelet was much darker than we could've imagined, and me and my sister would pay for our meddling. There's one more story to tell before the Delaware River took us to a new universe entirely.

Grampa Andy wrote a lot on Scranton, even though he never went. The bracelet's history in Scranton wasn't extensive, but remember, Andy Wessel was a historian by trade, so commentary on the prison system popped up.

Grampa Andy wrote a near-treatise on it. The prison-industrial complex, private prisons, prison labor, prison abolition. Becca was all for it. "Prisons are a little medieval if you think about it for more than a few seconds. The idea of putting all the *bad* people in a box until they turn good. What century are we living in, again?" The American prison system: that was Grampa Andy's interpretation of the events of what happened in Scranton. But there is another.

Long story short, a priest in Scranton owned the bracelet until a delinquent kid stole it from him in 1978. Rubin, hot on the bracelet's trail, caught up with the pastor in 1979. He even went to the juvenile detention camp up north where the kid who stole it was being held. But that's all that was written. It cut off so abruptly. Yakovlev noted the location of the detention center... and that's it. No more notes from Rubin Yakovlev.

There were just some Hebrew letters at the bottom of the page. I hadn't bothered with most of the Hebrew and Yiddish that filled the notebook, but since these were the final letters in the entire original notebook, I figured I had to know what they meant. I spent four hours in the library in Chicago using online Yiddish dictionaries and had eventually decided on a rough translation: *I am at the bottom of the well. I am the gear in the clock. The sword of god. All dreams come true.*

I tore the page out, folded it into a tiny square, and stuffed it deep in my pocket.

When Grampa Andy had circled back over the notes, he found out that that same kid was still in jail, in Lackawana County Prison. Becca suggested we visit the prison. I was nervous about it but couldn't reject a solid lead.

This is the story of two men named Mark Jones. From this point onward, viewer discretion is advised.

Mark Jones #1 was a respected Lutheran priest in Aberdeen, east of Scranton, who led a double-life. In the day he led his congregation in prayer. He visited their homes and hospitals to offer prayers for the sick, preached on Sundays, and ran daily services. And at night, he fucked.

Now, I don't know exactly what the Lutheran Church thinks of sex for purposes other than reproduction, but I can say with near certainty that what

Mark Jones did was a no-no. He was a sort of male prostitute. Clients would come to an apartment in a nearly abandoned neighborhood to the northeast of the city. They had received a code for a padlocked door. Mark Jones would be lying on the bed and rise to greet them. In that room, they would have one hour together. He would undress them, kiss them, caress and ease them into bed. He would remove his clothes except for a leather bracelet with a gold coin that he wore on his left wrist.

It was difficult to get connected and he wasn't cheap. Still, people from all over the region came to have sex with him. Because testimony reveals that sex with Mark Jones was a sublime experience.

The clients were all different. Most were women, some were men. Some were young and some were old. Some were sexually active, and others had trouble with their spouses, or were lonely. But Mark Jones wasn't just a hot dude with a nice cock. He *did* things to his clients. The women and men that came were well-off, with troubles, depression, or the general feeling of gaping holes inside their minds and hearts. They had migraines that rattled their skulls all hours of the day, or cramps so agonizing that they would be physically unable to move for weeks. Some were mute, having forgotten how to speak. Some were perfectly normal aside from an empty, persistent longing. And that's where he came in.

He worked precisely, like a skilled mechanic or a surgeon. He made his clients comfortable, laid them down, and got to work. Sometimes he never entered them, only touched or kissed or held them. He did whatever worked. And while Mark Jones was a professional, his clients' reactions were of a different sort. The apartment's walls were heavily soundproofed because of all the screaming. They twisted and squirmed and shut their thighs around him as if he were a magnet, and squirted more than ever and even if they never had, and they all moaned and shrieked and screamed.

At the end of it all, they were happy. Their symptoms disappeared. They tipped him generously. He managed to fill the voids, cure the poison in their lives. His sex somehow restored them.

Was it the bracelet at work? Rubin Yakovlev suspected so after speaking with Mark Jones, who he described as bald and soft-spoken. Jones told Rubin his "operation" (which netted him between one and four million dollars) ended in 1976 after he was walking home one night, and a 'rogue delinquent' punched him in the face and stole the bracelet.

That guy's name was Markus Jones, currently (somehow still) in jail. And we were on our way to see him.

As you might imagine, the meticulously detailed story about the nightmarishly orgasmic intercourse of Mark Jones was messing with me. I was sixteen. I hadn't done it. So, you can only imagine the impotence that I felt while reading about these godlike sexual feats. How could I ever make a woman feel this way? Would I even *want* to make a woman feel this way? There was a fucking creepy world of fucking out there, and it terrified me. I woke up the morning before our visit with a furious erection. I crawled out of bed away from my snoring sister, raced to the bathroom, thought about Chelsea's or someone else's boobs, and masturbated violently until I came into the toilet.

I couldn't stop thinking about it. I know Christine had come plenty of times when we were together, but I wanted to have sex with her. Just normal, missionary, however Puritans do it. That would be great. Or eight times, like an octopus, with all those suckers. Or whips and hot wax while nailed to a cross. *Anything.* But I had missed my chance, either because fate had willed it, or because of my own incompetence. Maybe she had found someone new. Looking back, I was astounded that I didn't feel worse about it as it happened—as I failed to *perform.* Isn't erectile dysfunction something for old men? Was I not fit for sex? Maybe I was meant to be *fucked* instead. I started doing fifty sit-ups a day to strengthen my core and did those Kegel things while standing at urinals but I wasn't sure if I was doing them right.

But sex is only half the tale.

Becca led us with conviction. She had told me many times before about the Prison-Industrial Complex, which I knew was one of her least favorite socioeconomic phenomena. The Lackawana County "Department of Corrections" looked like a library or a museum on the outside, an L-shaped building made of dark brown stone, but it was not quite so intellectual on the inside. Everything was metal: the lockers, the railing, the chairs, even the beds and tables. The place must get cold as ice in winter.

Markus Jones was a middle-aged man, dark as coal. For someone who was supposedly in jail most of his life, his face was handsome and he had good teeth, but his body looked frail and falling apart. Tight skin on the fingers, drooping posture. He was convicted in 1980 of second-degree murder. He pleaded not guilty; jury found him guilty. Arranging a visit was simple. He sat with us in an empty room, wearing a dirty prison jumpsuit, a guard posted at the door, and we listened as he talked. The story started out simple and unraveled from there.

"Revenge," he began. "I stole the bracelet for goddamn revenge. *That* was a worse crime than the murder I never committed. As for the so-called murder—that was involuntary manslaughter, I knew *that* better than my lawyer did. But they wanted to get me in the clink. I had a history. Drug-dealing, drunk-driving, so they got me for something worse than I did, locked me up for life. But at the time, I wasn't about to confess to *nothing*. That's because I had just spent twelve weeks in juvenile solitary confinement. Jesus, you can't imagine what that was like. Solitary confinement for a sixteen-year-old boy. Twelve weeks without seeing a soul. Without escaping the darkness. It destroyed me. I should've become more than a murderer. I should've become a monster. I should've become a devil in that dark. Not just that dark but that bright. Because those bright fluorescent lights were either all on or all off but at random hours of the day, always changing. But no. At the end of it all, because of that bracelet, I came out as quiet as a lamb.

"I wanted to die. There was too much light and darkness, too much pain. I tried to kill myself every day for two weeks straight. That was weeks seven and eight out of twelve. Before that, I was trying to survive. But I was so alone, you can't imagine. I couldn't stand the sound of my own voice. I could smell worms—I think my flesh had started to rot. My eyes never got used to the dark, and they stopped working. I was blind as a mole, a goddamn naked mole rat. Even though I counted the days and knew I was more than halfway done, the half that came before had felt like a century. I couldn't bear the thought of going back to my family like that: a blind, hairless ball of rotten flesh. It was bad enough being a juvenile delinquent. If I had to be a monster, then I may as well be dead.

"So I stopped eating the food and drinking the water. For hours every day I would bang my head against the wall until I passed out. My whole world was pain. Dark, silent, grinding, pounding pain.

"But I lived. I hadn't had food or water in two weeks, and I was still alive. How? *How!* I repeated it over and over in my mind. I kept inhaling: *how how how*. A fucking monkey, *hoo hoo hoo. How* was I alive? How could I survive it if I couldn't die? And that was when I lost my body completely. For a week I lived outside myself. I saw the shape of me lying there, covered in bruises and all swollen and shit. But if that was *me*, then where was *I*? I didn't know, but I had escaped myself and finally had relief from the pain.

"And *that* is when I gave the bracelet away."

"So you had the bracelet?" I asked. "That whole time?"

"Course I did," Mark Jones said. "They didn't know it wasn't mine. Didn't even bother to take it off my body, even when I was stark naked."

"But you gave it away?"

He chuckled. "Damn right I did. I could tell it was morning because of a tiny slit of light. You know the gap between the door and the floor? They came in the mornings and turned on the lights and this tiny slit of fluorescent light sprung through the gap. And that's when I realized I was back in my body, lying on the floor. And that's when someone spoke—the only voice I heard the entire twelve weeks.

"A man's voice. Deep voice. Funny accent. Asked for his bracelet back. Asked me to push it under the door. Oh man, after what that bracelet put me through, I was more than willing."

"Who? Who was this man? What kind of accent?"

"Don't remember much. Definitely not American. Some foreign ass accent. After that I was just trying to get out. The next two years, out of the hole, those was the best years of my life. But here I am." He shook his head. "Maybe I'll get parole someday. And you white children, you should know. This ain't much better than confinement. I'm out there all day making little doodads, toy cars and shit, I don't know what company sells them. Sometimes I wish I was back in that dark chamber rather than making someone else's shit. At least when I was locked up in there they couldn't tell me what to do." He suddenly stared at me. "You ever own any toy cars?"

My face had turned pale as milk. We're Jewish, I wanted to say. I nodded like a bobblehead.

"Well don't buy no more."

I nodded.

"Don't look so scared. I learned a thing or two about economics. The laws of supply and demand. Now if you ain't out there buying any more toy cars, they won't have us make them anymore." He chuckled. "But I suppose then we'll just have to make something else. You know, in my head, there's this possibility. There's this chance that if *everyone* stopped wanting *everything*, then we wouldn't need the clink anymore. But I don't think we could ever get there. Eventually they'd have us make toothbrushes or condoms, shit that people need no matter what."

"Revenge," Becca chimed in. "You said you stole the bracelet for revenge? What revenge was that?"

Mark Jones looked up. "Revenge? This priest motherfucker fucked my girl! He wasn't just some high-flier, no, he went around rapin' motherfuckers, children, too. So I beat the shit out of the priest, and took his wallet and watch and all that. I was just a kid though, and my own homies took everything from me, except that fucking bracelet. That bracelet *did* save me from killing myself in the hole, but sometimes I wonder if I'd be better off that way. That's what I keep thinking about, thinking and thinking, if only that priest had never fucked my girl, and I hadn't beaten him up and stolen his shit, then I'd never have ended up with the bracelet, slamming my head against concrete for seven hours straight—because it was the bracelet that saved my life, I'm know it. It's black magic. I keep thinking through the whole chain of events, and my mind goes spinning down the chain. But then again, I have a lot of time to think, so my thoughts go a little bit further than most people."

Walking to the car, I said to Becca:

"Did you ever consider this is all our fault?"

"What do you mean?" she asked.

"Well, our family brought this bracelet to America. If we had just left it behind, maybe none of these terrible things would have ever happened."

"I don't know if we had a choice. If we're saying the bracelet is behind all of this, didn't it save our great-grandmother from a pogrom in the first place? We had to bring it here."

She was right, but still... I couldn't help but to feel at fault, like history would hold us accountable for the destruction that the bracelet left behind.

Another day, another city. Another lead that led to nothing. Because according to Jones, our uncle *had* the bracelet. But we knew that wasn't true. As we drove back into Scranton, I felt like I couldn't look at things reasonably anymore. I got mad. *How* could the bracelet keep disappearing? *How* could a shadow-cowboy have stood over me with a gun raised? It rattled me, jolted me, this dull, twisted sense of failure, and I knew I must have done something wrong, something horribly wrong. The bracelet, it can't, it must not be real. It must be fictional, fake, invented. *How* could I have been so idiotic to believe in it? *How? How? How?* Mark Jones and I weren't so different, banging our heads against a concrete wall for hours and hours.

The next morning, we drove an hour east to the New Jersey border in a storm that wouldn't stop growing. It hadn't rained once the entire trip, but now the rain fell harder, faster; larger drops. The wind blew stronger, heaving and blasting. The clouds grew darker and the thunder louder. And beneath our car, a trickling stream grew deeper till it flooded the street and sent our car sliding into the river.

What does it mean to die? I remember one time Christine and I were talking about fears. I asked if she was scared of death, and she said no.

"*No?*" I couldn't believe it.

"Nope," she said. "I want to live life until it ends. And when it does end, there's nothing else you can do, right? There's no point in being scared. If you spend your whole life scared of dying, you'll go crazy before it actually happens." She nodded.

At the end of it all, I could see that as usual, Christine was right. Because dying itself is a son of a bitch.

On the one hand, I wasn't as upset as I might've expected myself to be. I was proud of making it so far. I was proud to have done my best to honor Grampa Andy's request. I felt like I had become more like him: picking up hitchhikers, visiting a prison. Things that he would do. I'd lived more in the past month than I had the sixteen years before that. We even knew where the bracelet was—Newark—and not that long ago! If we could live, maybe we could find it. Surely if Grampa Andy had known it was this dangerous, he wouldn't have asked us. There was no room for bitterness.

But on the other hand, I was filled with such an intense rage that I can barely begin to describe it. *How* could the universe be so cruel? I couldn't accept God, not even an Andy Wessel-style humanistic spirituality: I felt no flowing energy, saw no inherent goodness in it all. There were no interweaving threads. There were no invisible links. The bracelet, which seemed like it was tying everything together—history, the country, my family—was no more than the shadow of an immigrant's memory. There were no omens, no signs, no spirits, no gods, no magic, no love, no dreams. There was only chaos. People leaping from the Golden Gate Bridge, comatose women who can't remember anything because their towns are being bombed with pigshit, and people screwing other people, throwing them in jail, fucking with them, fucking them, slamming fucking heads against fucking concrete.

Language always falls short of death. Words are adequate for life, but now that it was death they *aren't*, and even though I was still clinging to something like life they just *couldn't.* I wondered if this was how Becca felt, whenever I looked at her and saw an inscrutable expression bubbling with feelings that may as well be in Spanish or Hebrew or Japanese. I finally realized that even she may not fully understand. Sometimes you just *feel.* It's something churning in the gut or chest, something squeezing with maddening violence. Something that screams. Fuck it, *I* want to scream. I'm sorry I want to FUCKING SCREAM. FUCK EVERYTHING. FUCK EVERYTHING. FUCK EVERYTHING. FUCK EVERYTHING. FUCK EVERYTHING. FUCK EVERYTHING. FUCK EVERYTHING! FUCK EVERYTHING. FUCK EVERYTHING FUCK EVERYTHING FUCK EVERYTHING FUCK EVERYTHING FUCK EVERY THING FUCK EVERY FUCKING THING FUUUUUUUUUUUCKKKKKAKHHHHHHHHHHAHHHAHAH

I screamed into the Delaware River. My mouth filled with water and all I wanted to do was live.

Yit'gaddal v'yitkaddash sh'me raba…

19

Lawrence

The Pros and Cons of Being a White American Living in Akkeshi

1982, Hokkaido, Japan

Lawrence's brother died in his absence. They had spent so much time together in Morningside Heights, in and around Columbia. There were the weekly concerts at Barton's, with Sam Woods and his jazz prodigy cousin, Charly. Lawrence wondered if it was his fault for being abroad, or if it would have happened even if he'd been gone for just a day. Though Lawrence had experienced a lot of change over the past few years, nothing jackhammered the passage of time into his heart as much as David's sickness, diagnosis, brief struggle, and death. Four years ago, Lawrence and David were together in New York. Three years ago, David and Sam Woods moved together to San Francisco. One year ago, Lawrence didn't know David was sick. A week ago, the news came in. It was late at night, and he had driven forty minutes to a ski resort hotel to return an international call from his father.

"Hello—"

"Moshi-moshi—I mean, hey Dad. This is unusual for you, is something wrong?"

"Larry. He's gone."

...

...

"Already?"

"That disease is a monstrous son of a bitch."

...

"You there?"

"Yeah."

"You'll come home this time, won't you? Your siblings need you around."

"I'll buy a ticket."

It was December 26th. He would have to drive four hours across marsh, mountains, and plains to get to the nearest airport.

Rather than procrastinate inside by the fire, reading the same manuscript again, Lawrence decided to go for a walk. He left the temple, wrapped in a blue wool scarf. One monk, as always, was outside the red pagoda, raking the Shirakawa pebbles into waves. Wood-fire smoke puffed from the chimneys of the monk's cottages.

He lived a healthy life here. He ate vegetables and fish, buckwheat noodles, and curry rice. The water was clean and the air cleaner; the sun, weak as it was in winter, became a source of wisdom in the sky no matter the season. Lawrence was always in a place for reflection, and he wrote out truths in tree lines and cloud formations. One thing Lawrence admired about Japanese culture was the building. The garden of Shogyo-ji mapped the cosmos onto a gravel field, marked with lush green fir and gray stones. Different realms of good and evil, joy and sorrow, guilt and responsibility, ignorance and truth lived in the pond crossed by a wooden bridge, and in the three rocks surrounding the old cypress. The temple buildings, measured in their extravagance, held ideas and emotions in balance. Here, he could forget.

He had the time to both remember and forget at his job as technical director at the local TV station. The job was simpler than making movies in Paris and Tokyo. He dealt in the wires themselves—wires and electricity, life's animating force. His days moved one step at a time: *hinode, asagohan, hirugohan, bangohan, nichibotsu.* At lunch, Shizuo-kun talked to him about

American politics. Lawrence tried to argue that Reagan has to go, but Shizuo-kun was won over by the president's charisma.

He passed a graveyard on a muddy hillside and a deserted mill on his way to the familiar forest path. Wind burned in his nostrils. That was one thing he couldn't stand—it was *so* cold here. He thought New York was bad, but when the Pacific's icy breath swirled through the wetlands and into town, leaving the temple became an existential ordeal. The haunting dusk that reigned in day, the ivory fog that swept in from sea, the ice storms—they seized and dragged him to terrifying depths. Sunrise pierced the bay, wetlands, and town like a red sword and plunged into his heart. Lawrence would have happily left his own body for that of a Japanese. Perhaps the climate would become less terrifying. Perhaps the large-billed birds that cawed like devils in the morning would turn to woodpeckers in California groves. Perhaps everything would translate perfectly.

Among the tall trees and following the distant trickle of an ice-clogged stream, Lawrence could relax. The dark-eyed trees were safe and friendly; they bore no relation to him. He was a rat passing through their shadows.

When he wondered who he was—a question that mattered more since leaving the U.S.—Lawrence could only think of his skin and land, having disregarded religion long ago. But the land was stolen from natives and made profitable through slavery. The skin weaponized to create hierarchy and inequality. The merciless, savage violence his own family had participated in and even accelerated—capital, gentrification, drugs. Perhaps he came here to surrender himself to the mercy of others and was relieved to have been treated with kindness. The ghosts of this landscape were not his own. They were not ghosts and gods, but *yurei*, *kami*. The forests, trees, foxes, leaves and bees were spectacles and scenery. He had no ancestry here. Nor anywhere. America and Israel were settler-colonial states where merely living consisted of violent assault on the Other; Europe was ravaged by Fascists and Anti-Semites. Compared to California, this icy wetland haven existed neither more, nor less. It was simply on a different plane.

Or perhaps he came here to flee his family.

Lawrence arrived at the river. It had partially frozen. Weak sunrays hit the water and chipped at the ice. Really, it was a beautiful place, really, he was lucky. The people of Akkeshi were good to him. Though he drew stares, neither townsfolk nor the monks of Shogyo-ji questioned him for being there. At the izakaya, the bartender was happy to get him drunk on sake, and in the market the fishermen advised him on what to buy: *Kore da. Chigau yo. Kore yo. Kore da yo.* He lived at the temple and remembered his chores; two monks took him in and explained the details of religious ritual. He was happy to listen, though he understood just half of what they said. Lawrence pushed aside ferns dusted with snow to approach the water's edge.

Lawrence looked through the clear stream, flecked with blue ice. He saw shadows cross the underwater stones. He realized it was Itsumi Terakado. A year ago, the dentist named Terakado had approached Lawrence, and asked Lawrence to marry his daughter.

She was intelligent, though quiet for his taste, and he wondered if it was only because he was a foreigner that one of the wealthiest men in town gave him any notice. But to marry into a family with a large and comfortable home, let alone a family that visits the coral reefs of Miyakojima every May—such good fortune should not come to a stumbling wanderer. The daughter had just graduated Hokkaido University and loved to ski; the father enjoyed whiskey and Chinese poetry; the mother's squid and eel was marvelous; the son was a lawyer with a passion for boating. Lawrence would be the first to confess that he had never had more fun than when he and Itsumi and her brother went out on the water last June. He wondered if there was a darkness beneath the surface. Both brother and sister were too quiet, too brilliant. He told the brother, "*kawatta shitsumon watashi ni kiku-nda,*" she asks me strange questions, and Taro-kun responded sardonically but with a tinge of darkness, "*Ore sonna koto imouto ni tsuite yurusan zo,*" don't you dare say things like that about my sister.

Meanwhile, Terakado-san was disappointed that Lawrence had yet to move into an apartment, but he couldn't bear to leave the tranquility of the temple. Lawrence lost the dentist's respect as autumn wound on. It was painful to see happiness within reach and be too afraid to grab it. No wonder he was seeing her shadow in the stream.

Lawrence shivered as a second shadow overtook the first. The shadow of David. The sight burned Lawrence's eyes like salt. He wanted to light the forest on fire and, as if in response, a howling waste of wind silenced Lawrence, turning flame to bone-cold ashes: How could you burn the only place in the world that has treated you like a human being?

Lawrence stared at the stones, in endless fractured shapes and turned in myriad directions. No—he was wrong. It *wasn't* David's shadow. It was darker, sharper, the shadow of a taller man. Lawrence's breath fogged out in clouds; his own life-force billowed around him; it was as if his body was breaking into mist. David, dead, David, who wore the leather bracelet on his wrist... Lawrence thought and thought, furrowing his brow at the cracked and trickling ice. Streams in the seeping ice gathered form, one, two. He saw Japanese characters emerge in the water: one, two, water, sound, origin, gate, light, dark. Are the colors of the world dark, or are they light? This, Lawrence thought, is the ultimate question.

The body floated, pale among the ice plates, gold glinting from the wrist.

Gold in the water. Leather on the wrist. Lawrence shivered. He would never be able to forget when his father had asked him and David to take his Uncle Rubin to the hospital, just two years ago. His father had been in a car accident the previous day. Lawrence was in LA, having graduated just a year prior, and David was on summer break. According to his father, his great-uncle, around eighty years old, was dangerously unstable and needed to be brought to the hospital at once. But it sounded like his father only had a vague idea why, and until they checked Uncle Rubin into what turned out to not be a hospital but an old-school asylum, and he revealed to them the full account of his relationship with that bracelet, did they fully understand why. In spite of the horrific tale, David still received the bracelet from Rubin Yakovlev after the old man passed. Still wore it on his wrist until the end.

In that moment, Lawrence had determined to leave. He was already unhappy and yearned deeply for the light and air of a faraway land. But hearing what his uncle had done and watching his younger brother take the bracelet—it gave him conviction to run from it all. The overbearing worldliness of Los Angeles and old worldliness of New York. No reality, only constructions. Dreams, jazz, guns. Allison and Michael's bickering, his father's endless demands. Atheism as betrayal, David is now straight, now gay. Sam Woods is now alive, now dead, anarchists that want Lawrence to drive them to the beach and listen to their awful poetry, 1000 crosseyed pages of film theory as the pathetic prize of his father joining the upper-middle class, the dreams and the nightmares. The sickening thought that his happiness and fate depended on an old leather-and-gold artifact drifting on pale green waves through space and time.

And there were not just dreams but letters, too. The letters from his mother. Lawrence returned from his walk and read one. She never failed to send him an exhausting Christmas letter sometime in November, just in case of delays. Since a lot of Japanese people celebrated Christmas, it never felt out of place, but his mother always assumed that it was inappropriate. He corrected her in his response, but in the next letter, she got defensive. "I feel like you don't want me to send you letters," she wrote, "so I *have* to apologize." He hadn't finished his response yet. He wanted to take a step back from the arguments, and was on the verge of telling her that he *could* get married, and that it might be his last chance before Terakado-san moved on to a more suitable bachelor. He supposed now he might not need to bother with the letter if he could see her in person.

Still, he reread her latest one. He had read it too quickly before; now he could see David's ghost shivering between the lines. David had always written long letters, full of San Francisco weather, medical school examinations, Sam's Oakland cousins' barbecues and house parties, Uncle Rubin passed away, that he would get the bracelet and Michael the old Buick. Lawrence kept David's letters in a manila folder under his futon shelf. When the news came in, he had been overcome with such an unbearable pain that he began to burn the stack in the fire in the main hall. The pure energy of memory vaporizing in the odor of ash. He couldn't get through ten pages before breaking down entirely, while the *Butsuzo* looked on and handed out their judgment.

By the time he reached the final line of his mother's letter, he was so exhausted that he didn't know if he had it in him to go to home, to go to the funeral, to go to any funeral. The return of the bracelet had been full of hope, but since then his family had known nothing but death. Surely, at least he could comfort his younger siblings? The bracelet, it symbolized the murderous and the broken. At least he could ensure that it was buried deep in a landfill somewhere far away.

And if he did make it all the way home... well, maybe he could stay. What if he did go back to California?

No one here would miss him. No, that's not true—the priests would regret his departure, and Shizuo-kun, and the Terakado family, and some sprinkling of others. He thought about it for a while.

And outside his window, descending in tapestries, the Akkeshi snow piled on, and on, and on.

20

Michael

The Golden State

1983, California

For a time Michael lived in a golden state, but he eventually descended into a state of fear. Consciousness was a terror, curling like a snake, pounding like a hammer that misses the nail every time. For weeks he lived from high to high, vaguely sensing hurried meals and mindless sex like gnats buzzing in his mouth and balls. And then his brother died.

By the time Lawrence came back from Japan, Michael had arrived in a state of white noise. At the funeral he felt flecked, ravaged, devoid of thought. Or perhaps the thought was altogether too much and blasted in his eyes like dark kaleidoscopes and in his ears like the roar of a highway of regrets, generators, factories of fear.

After death, there is memory. Michael's memories told him David was the conciliator, arbiter, judge, dividing the lot between him and Allison while Lawrence hid away. David fixed their fights, scolded Michael when he stole his sister's diary, protected him from her sharp tongue, and played football out back, endlessly running the ball between those two palm trees in the yard, taking turns on offense with David as quarterback.

But there is no room for memory in the desert. The sun's too hot, the air too dry. Memories evaporate. Dreams dry up.

So as the desert road flung onwards, Michael didn't remember anything—he just had a headache. Rubble mountains circled the endless valley of shrub. A bighorn sheep climbed the eastern rim. The gray Buick sputtered and choked on the dirt road, passing bone-shaped boulders and clumps of cacti. A few stars glittered over the eastern indigo.

Michael didn't want to go camping at Joshua Tree, with Lawrence of all people, sober of all states. But his parents begged him, and at the moment, he was not in a position to refuse his parents anything.

He had at least prevented the worst, which would have been Allison coming too. Lawrence had wanted her to join, at first. Michael's response was simple: if Allison comes, the trip doesn't happen. So she didn't, and the trip did.

"*Saa,* we should've left earlier," Lawrence said.

"The traffic has gotten worse since you left," Michael said. He lounged with his feet up on the windshield as Lawrence drove with one hand, the other shielding his eye from the red sun stabbing at him through the rearview mirror. "It's always getting worse. Every year. They build new roads, they always do, but the traffic gets worse anyways." Michael scratched his neck. "Say, do they really not do any drugs in Japan? Not even weed?"

Lawrence grimaced.

"Nothing?"

Michael watched his brother stare ahead.

"I thought this was supposed to be a bonding trip for us. We can't bond if you don't open your mouth."

Lawrence opened it, but no sound came out. He closed his mouth and opened it again. "This is a *sober* camping trip, Michael. Whether or not we bond is largely irrelevant."

Michael couldn't kick his feet up any further, so he hunched his shoulders and let his head sag down the seat. He needed a hit.

The tips of yellow coral-shaped plants flurried past. They saw Joshua trees, spiked arms pointed in expressive poses like frozen dancers. They were the guardians that watched over the sacred desert. They kept track of the dawns and dusks, desert squirrels and wood rats, blue-tailed birds and black tarantulas.

"This place is enormous," Michael said. He could see the whole valley in a bowl, and the mountains on the other side.

"It's only the beginning," Lawrence said. "But we need to set up camp before it gets dark."

Michael shrugged and tapped his feet on the windshield. In the dark, out of the dark, whatever. It didn't matter. Michael was used to doing things in the dark. He planned to let Lawrence set up the tent and all that. It might be funny to watch him struggle. He picked at the bracelet on his wrist.

"I wish you wouldn't wear that," Lawrence said.

"Wear what?"

"You know," he said. "It's an ancient, worthless thing—"

Michael rose his wrist. "It was David's. You want me to throw it away?"

"You know what it's been through," Lawrence said. "And it's been around too many of our relatives when they die. It makes me feel weird when I see it on you—"

"Oh, shut up." Michael sat up straight. Yes, he knew the awful truth behind it. David had told him and Allison. Michael felt queasy just thinking about it, but knew that he couldn't bare to cast it away, to fling it into the desert. "I—I've had dreams about it, you know. For a long time. Before we knew anything. It's like a dream come true, to wear it. Dave wore it." He tapped the gold coin, a winking mirror for the sun's last spark. "Think about it. It's been in our family for generations. Uncle Rubin said our great-grandfather wore it against the Rebbe's orders when they studied Kabbalah. He matched up Hebrew letters with the Latin ones to prove that it added up to 613. You know, the 613 mitzvot. It was meant to come all the way through time to me, for me."

"I just wish you wouldn't wear it around me," Lawrence said. "It was on David's *dead body*. Touched his—dead skin. Doesn't that bother you?"

"You're a ghost in America. Doesn't that bother you?"

"Well you could show some courtesy. I'm asking a favor."

"I don't need to show a coward any courtesy."

"Jesus Christ, Michael, a coward? For what?"

"You're afraid of a piece of jewelry."

"You know what I'm afraid of!"

"Cowards run, and you're always fucking running. New York, France, Japan—anywhere that we are not is worth a shot for you." Michael glanced over at Lawrence and took great pleasure in seeing his face as red as raw steak. "You can't bear the sight of the bracelet because you can't bear the sight of *me*—"

BANG!

A huge bump jarred Michael, throwing his head violently into the dash. A steel blast of pain struck black across his vision. Michael returned to the darkness.

The edges of his consciousness trembled: had the car veered off the road, grinding in a ear-rending shriek against the guardrails? But no—there weren't guardrails in the desert. Pain—clogged thoughts, smoke tunnels. He lost track of his body. He might have been floating above the car, or turning in its wheels. The earth writhed as if to shake away its satellites. Then came a blinding flash of white.

Michael was in the endless desert.

It was freezing. When he opened his eyes, the world seemed to have fallen fully into night. He saw the same skeletal bushes, red cacti, and scattered Joshua trees in a dusk of winter gray, hazy violet glow on the horizon. Staring up at a cloudy sky, he could see his own breath rising off his body in thick white plumes.

He felt wetness on his nose and saw that snowflakes filled the air. The flakes were as big as dandelions and fell erratically, like dead leaves dancing in the wind.

He stood quickly. He no longer felt pain in his head from the crash, and for that matter, he didn't feel the constant joint pain that had plagued him ever since being cut off, either. He was standing alone in a dirt road. It was completely silent.

Ahead, he noticed peculiar shadows. He walked towards them, straight down the road. The shadows condensed, blackened, brightened. They assumed the shapes of buildings. Could they be buildings? No—massive Torah scrolls like mountains—no—buildings—tattered townhouses, crowded together, in the middle of the desert. It was a ghost town.

Just as Michael came upon the strip he saw a single street lamp casting a floating yellow haze. A tall figure cloaked in darkness stepped out from the roadside and into the lamplight.

Uncle Rubin?

Michael paused, instinctively grasping his wrist. The leather tightened and squeezed. It wasn't his uncle. The lamp illuminated the figure's body and features in golden glow: a handsome man, wide-jawed with a cleft chin, sharp cheekbones, leathery face and skin that had seen its fair share of desert sun, blond hair faded to a peppery gray, black boots, brown pants, blue shirt, tan vest, and a wide-brimmed cowboy hat, all tinged with the golden aura cast by the streetlamp. He raised his hands slowly, as if surrendering. Stalactite shadows crept down from his hat over his mouth and chin, and from his broad chest down his stomach and legs.

The man lowered his hands. "Howdy," he called, sturdy voice made gentle by a country lilt. "Didn't mean to scare ya. Going for a midnight stroll?"

"I'm not going anywhere."

The man smiled. "Now, that's a good thing." He started walking towards Michael. "Too often I find myself running around when really I ought to *meander* for a change." He scratched his hat. "I would introduce myself, but y'see, I'd prefer not to. As a consequence, I won't do you any discourtesy and ask for your name without giving you mine. I just figured that you're looking for some shelter. Ain't that the truth?"

"That's true," Michael said, enunciating with caution, hands behind his back quietly slipping the bracelet into his pocket. "Is a campground nearby?" He felt the distant tug of Lawrence. I'll find out where the campground is, he thought, and then come back to you. Just give me a moment.

The man laughed a jolly, dancing laugh. "Hell of a lot better than a campground. Lemme show ya. Won't take more than a jiffy. Soft, feather beds, good beer and whiskey, jazz blown in fresh outta San Francisco. Variety of interesting fellers to talk to." He tipped his hat and smiled. "I'm heading there to find something I've lost, and I'm sure as I've ever been that I'll find it there. And hell—if ya prefer to camp out beneath the stars, ya can do that too, just up the hill where I'm headed. So why dontcha come with, see how it suits your fancy? I never saw anybody offer more than perfunctory dissatisfaction. How about it?"

"Is it far?"

"Not far at all. Just follow me, young feller."

Michael followed the man down the street, leaving behind the lamplight streaming gold on the cracked road. When they turned the corner, the heart of the town looked straight out of the wild, wild west. There was a collapsed church, Jesus's left half mounted on a cross visible through the fallen rafters. They passed the bank, the gun store, tobacco shop, town hall. Meanwhile the snow kept falling, from clouds so thin that moonlight passed through them like glass. As they continued, Michael gradually began to hear human voices, laughter, and even music. One warm, male voice in the din sounded just like David's.

"Voila," hummed the man.

The old building was made of wood. It had a small veranda and a mounted sign with the red letters "SALOON". The windows were full of lamplight and rattled with the tinkle of an old piano and dozens of merry voices. David's voice whispered in the din and Michael despite the snow was drenched in sweat.

"Do you hear..." Michael trailed off.

"It's damn cold out here," the man said. "Let's get inside and a get a couple swigs of whiskey in the belly."

Michael hurried in behind the man through the swinging doors. Inside, a few buffalo skulls were mounted on the wall above a fully stocked bar. Amber oil lamps gave life to leaping shadows, shadows that stretched from wall to wall and danced madly and made love. A bartender in a bowler hat served drinks to a crowded bar, his shadow entangled in a passionate thrusting tryst with the shadow of the ancient Black man, who was crooning on an upright piano in the corner. The air was thick with cigar smoke and the smell of whiskey and perfume. The far staircase led to a landing, and through the banisters Michael could see a single, unadorned wooden door. Round tables draped in white tablecloths scattered throughout the room. The crowd was unlike anything Michael had ever seen: women in frilly dresses and feathered hats sat side-by-side leather-jacket-wearing tattooed motorcyclists, and a small crowd of old jowly men in bowler hats and canes played cards with two teenage boys in hoodies. A few servers, mostly young people dressed in trim, old-fashioned suits, carried trays of drinks, chatting with the customers. The saloon jostled with laughter. Michael couldn't hear David's voice anymore, though he scoured every inch of the room for him.

The man in the cowboy hat was waving at Michael from a table by the piano. Michael wound his way through the motley crowd and jostling jazz into a rickety chair.

"Drink up, friend," the man said. "It's gonna be a long night."

Michael picked up one of two shot glasses full of brandy.

"Cheers."

They drank the brandy. Michael was fine, but the cowboy nearly choked on the stuff. Hacking and coughing, Michael watched as the cowboy repeatedly gestured that he was fine. He remembered Uncle Rubin, who could never handle American liquor.

"So," Michael said, after the coughing fit had ended, "what is this place?"

"Good question. It's at the same time an ordinary and a very extra-ordinary place. Newcomers come every morning, shrouded in light as soft as feathers. All these newcomers come like a parade—toddling children race past the old folks, all sorts of peculiar expressions grinning and crying on every face. If they come in the morning, they'll pass Martha, mopping up last night's mess on the floor. At first, of course, everyone's real happy about getting here, knowing that they've still got time, you know. As the day goes on it gets busy, and people start drinking and laughing and playing and having a darned tootin' good time. Sometimes folks run into old friends. Folks share stories. Tell each other about their lives. Listen to some good music, have some good bourbon. And at the end of the night, folks head up those stairs over there," he pointed at the staircase, "and go through that door. You see it?"

"I see it," Michael said.

The man nodded and took off his hat. He placed it on the table next to his empty brandy. "Just about everyone heads through that door."

"Where does it go?" Michael asked.

The man laughed big. "Now, you hang on just a minute—I want you to meet a good friend of mine. I'm sure he'll buy us some more drinks. You like the brandy?"

Michael felt its warmth rising in his cheeks and nodded.

The man smiled. "Good. I'll be back—don't even think about moving!" He stood and set off towards the bar.

Michael sat and rapped the table, listening to the music. A few horn players had joined the pianist, humming warmth and Latin flair. The music got faster and more upbeat, swaying, skipping, luscious and hot.

"Can I get you anything?"

Michael looked up. A female waitress about his own age looked at him, a green bow in her dark hair.

He shook his head.

"Just let me know if I can."

She was about to walk away but Michael spoke up, leaning over the table towards her. "Wait a second—tell me something. What is this place?"

She gave him a puzzled expression. "You don't know?"

Michael shook his head. "I just stumbled into here. My brother and I were driving in the desert and I found my way over."

She closed her eyes and opened them. Her words came out hurried, scared. "I'm sorry, but you should leave as soon as you can. I've been here for a while, working. When I came here, I was like you. I was searching. I thought I could find an answer to my life, just like everyone else. But I couldn't find answers. I couldn't find anything. I've talked to so many people about their lives and I still can't sort out my own." She shook her head and sighed. "You should leave this place. If you can." She wandered off.

Left unsettled and dazed, Michael tried to understand her words, but the tumbling rhythm of the music was more captivating. The music was like a tremendous tree with roots penetrating to the heart of the earth, while words were nothing but the water running through its leaves. Michael looked over at the band and his jaw dropped.

Sam?

Holding his tenor saxophone like a lover was none other than Sam Woods, puffed up and playing along with the rollicking swing number. David must be here, Michael decided, and examined every inch of the saloon again, to no avail. For a while, Michael watched the band. Dancers skipped and clattered across the squeaky floor. The impassioned lovemaking of their shadows nearly drowned the entire bar in darkness.

The moment the band took a break at the bar, Michael dashed across the room and grabbed Sam Woods by the shoulder.

Sam was holding a full mug of beer and turned with a broad smile that shattered when he saw Michael.

"Mike?" he gasped.

"Sam!" Michael cried, hugging him, spilling beer foam on his shirt.

"What—what are you doing here? You're not..." Sam's brown eyes welled with tears.

"It's so good to see you," Michael said. "Lawrence and I were just passing through. We're camping, and I happened to stop by. I don't understand this place at all, but it's fun, and I don't feel like I've got needles in my scalp, and that's enough for me. What about you?"

"Well, Mike..." Sam set the mug down.

"And where's David?" Michael asked. "I thought I heard his voice earlier. He must be here. Is he doing okay?"

"He's doing fine, Mike," Sam said. "He's doing fine. He went through The Door just last night." He jerked his head towards the stairwell. "I was thinking about going through it tonight myself. But Mike..."

"He's just upstairs?" Michael's heart sputtered and his head whirred. "Well, let's get him!"

Sam put a hand on Michael's shoulder. "It don't work like that, Mike."

"What do you mean? I can't go upstairs?"

"You could," Sam said, "but I don't know if you want to. Mike... I'm not sure if you realized. Everyone here is dead."

Michael looked around. The people certainly didn't look dead. They were drinking, laughing, singing folk songs, playing cards, holding hands, kissing. And yet... Sam Woods had died of AIDS on December 4, 1981, just a few weeks before David; Michael had attended his funeral. He had stood in the back of the church with Lawrence, awkward to approach in the entirely Black crowd. Sam's mother had walked down the aisle, grasped Michael by both hands, and cried.

"This place is a crossroads, Mike," Sam explained. "Nobody stays for long, except the workers. People come to stay here while they sort out what happened in their lives. Some people stay longer than others, but eventually, everyone goes through The Door. We enjoy last moments of life here in the golden desert of California, where anything is possible, and we fill the world with light. Then, you get to the other side of The Door, and who knows what's after that. I just know that David is over there now. He's waiting for me. I'm going through The Door tonight, Mike, and I don't think you should follow me."

Michael closed his eyes for a long time.

He pressed them shut. He needed to make the world darker than dark. He needed to destroy sense, crush thought, obliterate his body and lay his soul on the saloon floor.

Sam waited and then spoke gently. "You're not dead, Mike, are you?"

Michael shook his head. "I should be."

"What happened?"

"Overdose." Unconsciously he slipped the leather bracelet from his pocket onto his wrist. He couldn't remember it. Any of it. Not a single goddamn thing. But he could remember the aftermath. He could *only* remember the aftermath. The aftermath was his entire life. Nothing before waking up in the hospital with punctures like black staples in his vision seemed to matter. Every member of his family, every one of his friends—they forgot his entire life up until that near-fatal hit of heroin. Nothing else mattered. No conversation could exist outside of it, no relationship could take root without its brand. He would remain an addict-on-the-brink for such a long time that it may as well be the rest of his life.

Sam shook his head and put his hand on Michael's shoulder. "I'm sorry, Mike. That's nasty. But don't worry—people don't care about that sort of thing here." He looked over his shoulder towards the swinging doors. "Still, that doesn't mean that you should stay."

Michael looked at his feet. "It's warm here."

"It's always warm inside. And it's always snowing outside. The place don't make much sense, cousin."

Sam used to call him that.

"I know you want to see David," Sam said. "I'm going to see him soon, and that makes me the happiest man alive." He rose the mug of beer to his lips.

"You think I'll see him again some day?"

Sam grinned. "No doubt. No need to rush things, Mike. Say, how'd I sound with the band? Pretty damn good, right?"

"Fucking incredible," Michael said. "Better than any living band I've ever seen."

"I'll drink to that," Sam said, and laughed loudly. It was a thin laugh, a bit wheezy, but it had energy and vitality and didn't fade. It kept going until Michael was convinced that the laugh had wound itself into the saloon's air, along with cigarettes and the chatter of the dead and the shadows. His laugh that brought a hurricane of memories. The visits to Columbia: how many Harlem jazz clubs had Michael gone to with Sam and David? David made jokes about the white people there, and Sam laughed his loud, wheezing laugh. How many times had they taken Michael to this or that bar, or set him up with this or that girl and the occasional guy, David, giggling, and Sam, laughing his loud, wheezing laugh? Even the number of times that Sam Woods had been to their house in California was too many to count. Sam had a smooth tongue and easy smile that won over the heart of Michael's mother in five minutes flat. Michael didn't want to leave, although he knew he needed to.

He nodded. Forever gone, forever lost... weekends of splashing in Pacific waves are dust, years of waking to his brother's sleepy eyes are dew.

"I'll see you later, Sam," he said, on the verge of tears, and he started walking towards the exit before he could regret his choice.

"Hang on there, young feller," came a country voice.

Michael turned and saw the man in the cowboy outfit. He stood a dozen feet from the doors, blocked by a table of old Chinese women, drinking gin and playing seven card stud.

"Why'rya leaving, friend?" he asked. "Don't tell me you don't like this place? I'm not exactly able to permit you to leave, as the item of my interest is right there on your wrist."

Michael glanced between the man and the door. He didn't trust the cowboy any longer. He realized he could see the fact that people in the saloon were dead—he saw their bodies and clothes waver like translucent, silvery ribbons, ciphering in a silent wind—and that their shadows weren't *their* shadows at all. They were the shadows of something else. He could feel the threads of a net in the air, cutting apart one world from the next. A sense of dread seized him by the throat. He had to leave. *Now.* But the cowboy had him frozen.

The cowboy rose his hands from his belt into the air, revealing twin pistols, polished bright as the moon.

"Now listen here, sonny. You've got what I'm looking for. So why don't you hand it over?"

"What are you talking about?"

"You know what I'm talking about, boy!" the cowboy said. "The bracelet! That brown leather, golden, glittering brilliant bracelet on your wrist. It belongs to me! Hand it over and I'll let you leave with your life!"

Michael covered it with his right hand. "What? Why? No, this is mine."

The cowboy bellowed in laughter. The laughter sharpened spike-studded, hot as sizzling coals, and went on for ages. His laughter smacked and stabbed the shadows and stopped abruptly. His voice pitched to a bloodthirsty shout before falling to a hiss. "It never belonged to you! Once upon a time, to be sure, it belonged to a man named Junipero Serra. The first to build white-man settlements in the state of California." The cowboy took a step towards Michael. "Did an impressive number on the land. Built missions, rounded up Indians to convert. A generous man—considered the death of an unconverted heathen a real tragedy, so he did his damned best to convert all the Indians in Californ-ai-ei. Course, plenty died along the way, raising the halls of white man's civilization, but not before they got Christianized. Hell, the man got sainted for it!"

"Let me leave," Michael gasped. He strained forward—the double-doors letting out into the desert were so close, but he couldn't move an inch.

"The point," the cowboy said, "the point, the point." He cackled. "The point is that Junipero Serra had himself a little bracelet made. The bracelet does not belong to *you*. It belongs to the lauded men willing to purify this earth. It's meant for killing and it's wasted in your shaking hands. Don't hide it now, boy, let the world see that holy gold glitterin' on your wrist."

Michael grasped the bracelet, squeezing so hard that he couldn't feel his fingers.

"It belongs to me."

And in a flash he had his twin pistols out and cocked, pointing at Michael. A flurry of cries rose up throughout the room. Women and men and those in-between gasped and backed away and angry shouts spiked to the ceiling and Michael froze in terror and the cowboy licked his lips.

"Please!" Michael cried, nails digging into his forearm as he tried to tear the bracelet off his wrist and throw it to the earth.

BANGBANG

Gunshots scarred the air and everyone was screaming, rushing towards the walls. Michael felt the crippling force of the bullet pierce his chest and hot blood spill as the man triumphantly twirled his pistols and slapped them into their holsters.

"I'll be taking what is mine," he said. He hopped over Michael's fallen body and yanked his wrist up in the air. With his other hand, he carefully slid the bracelet off of Michael's hand, and slipped it onto his own. Michael moaned in unbearable agony; pain surged as blood spurted in clumps and jerks and fountains from his breast.

"So you tell me, Michael," said the man, large and terrifying, looming like a God as he removed his flesh-made mask from his face to reveal his true face: not the cowboy but a wrinkled Russian gentleman, Michael's Uncle Rubin in a big black kippah and t'fillin, a monstrous horn for piercing human flesh, *"who does dis vorld belong to?"*

Life-force pumped in Michael's veins and the entire cosmos. With a burst of strength he never he knew he had and would never have again, and before his uncle could even reach for his guns, Michael Stern bounded to his feet and bolted for the door. Screaming and shouting filled his ears as he pushed through the frothing crowd and knocked open the swinging doors as blood poured through his shirt and hands and out into a winter night of endless, enormous pure white snowflakes that hovered in the air like a field of stars brought down to earth to sparkle and resound.

21

The Delaware Water Gap, Part Two

Phlebas the Phoenician, a fortnight dead,
  Forgot the cry of gulls, and the deep sea swell
  And the profit and loss.
  —*My 10th grade English teacher.*

הנני
  Behold!
  —*God, when shit needs to be beheld.*

This is gonna sound like a major tangent, especially at the moment of death and all. (Will our handsome hero survive the terrors of Hurricane Katrina, or will he perish in its awesome floods? *After this commercial break!*) Just bear with me.

I was never a huge music person. Becca had her lists; I mainly listened to whatever Will handed over. But I *did* have a pretty great ear in terms of memory, so I could play songs that I knew well in my head, whenever I wanted. Over the years, I collected a mini playlist of songs to listen to when I was bored. 'Last Nite' by the Strokes was one, Jeff Buckley's rendition of 'Hallelujah' was another, 'Let's Get It On' was a third. But whenever I got into a bad place, I played 'Tirándote Flores' by Eddie Palmieri. It's a classic Latin jazz tune, one that Grampa Andy used to play in the car. Grampa Andy loved jazz and Latin jazz most of all. The song bore no real relation to anything, but somehow it bore the most significant relationship out of anything to me drowning in the Delaware River. I've always dug Tirándote Flores because of the distinct rhythm. My mind can get into its groove. There's the rhythm of the drums intersecting with the cowbell, swaying horns, that dancing piano. Palmieri's voice fills with longing at the change-up. It's stuck with me, especially the accompanying image—'throwing you flowers.' I see a shower of flowers in my mind, thrown at someone, that someone depending on the situation. When I asked Paula Klein to the homecoming dance and she said no, flowers thrown at Paula. When we waited for the police after Becca got into a car crash, thrown at Becca. As I contemplated whether or not to try to kiss Christine, at Christine; when Mom told me Grampa Andy died, at Grampa Andy's crushed corpse. But never until drowning in the Delaware River had I seen those tirando flores coming at *me.*

That's all I saw. Thrown flowers, falling on me. Cowbell popping. Trumpets shouting. Piano dashing all about and Palmieri with his head bent in towards the mic, eyes sealed tight, lips that groan and sing.

Tirándote Flores has such a lust for life in it. But unlike a howling opera or agonized tango, it allows for dance. You've got the passion for life on the one hand, and the action that expresses the passion in the other. A balanced, tangible will to live. Grampa Andy taught me that there's nothing more like living than a good Latin jazz tune, and this was the one that I knew best.

Maybe that's how he went out. Dancing a chacha or mambo in his mind as the train exploded around him.

I swallowed water. *Baa'a.*

Turned up the Palmieri.

The thunder sounded like a city crumbling around us.

I swallowed water, turned up the Palmieri, tried to ignore the cataclysmic lightning and pelting rain. Becca grabbed my arm and kept both of us above the surface with strong kicks and shoves. I tried my best to tread but Becca was pulling us one way, so I pushed in the same direction. I felt compressed and stretched and twisted by all the different forces around me—the water, the wind, Becca, my own body, my own soul.

I lost track of time and space. The water had battered me beyond numb, and I couldn't tell if we were moving up the river or being sucked into it. The Palmieri started to fade. Rain, river, water, water, water.

The motion suddenly stopped but the world kept spinning.

Becca was screaming at me and I pulled on her with one hand and on a root with my other. The muddy ground smeared my arms and we shot out of the water, leaves and twigs swallowed up by the void left behind us. Water blasted and knife-sharp winds tore and we scrambled to our feet and sprinted into the woods, water pouring from our bodies like blood. We ran.

A sense of space and an awareness of my own body gradually returned, but time remained a restless blur. We were sprinting uphill. Becca lost a shoe in the mud, and we sloshed our way around to a stony cliff-face and slipped under it, elevated off the muddy ground and blocked from above by a heft of rock but only the very back wall was dry. We crawled there. Both of us were too exhausted and shocked to even speak.

My mouth was cold and gummy and I thought about the bracelet. Thoughts came and went like those wispy clouds that are so thin you're not really sure if they're clouds or just a trick of the light, with my limbs dragging heavy and then floating light, strangely warm and then frozen up. I curled into Becca and she didn't react. Feeling warmer, I think I fell asleep.

The night was terrifying. Thunder screamed at the mouth of a cave, suddenly deep and we lay in its blackest depths. White shadows leapt from the mouth and slithered towards our frozen bodies like the scorching tongues of flames. Flashes of lightning illuminated shadowed hulking trees and black hail cut through rings of dizzying rain. Cowboy Jim visited in the night. His boots sizzling on the marble. The cigarette-powdered glow of his beard and sparkling teeth in red. *You're too far gone*, he said. *You're in my world now.* Shadows danced across the stony walls in purple mud. One of the shadows was Kaori. One was Rubin Yakovlev, his flattened body stretched and squeezed into sickening shapes. Come back, Grampa Andy, where are you?—I miss you—I need you—Yakovlev white-star eyes tracked the course of the hidden moon, the mouth of the ever-deepening cavern became round and ringed with sunset mist. I was at the back of a cavern and the bottom of a well as I took the college kid to Becca, Jonathan Stein, that was his name, into the depths of a well of dandelions, and the paintings that he always left on our street corner were celestial cave paintings, river swirls and parted garnet lips, and Jonathan tripped over the edge and fell in a torrential downpour but rose in a blackwater spring, and clinked into the iced tea that Grampa Leo always drank. All the while stormwater roared and as I soared deeper underground it grew louder instead of softer. The top of the well, the road back home, rounded into a leather bracelet and the rising sun illuminated a floating golden coin. The shadow of the moon was the brim of the cowboy's hat that shut off the light and trapped me in darkness.

You're in not in America anymore, he said. *This world belongs to me.*

When I came to, I can't say that I was happy to be alive. Home. I wanted home. Pain stabbed at my stomach and my forehead. Home. My back was sore from the rocks we slept on. I remembered Cowboy Jim dancing, dancing, saying that he never sleeps, that he will never die, that he will kill us all. I was certain now that the dark secret of the bracelet that Uncle Michael mentioned, it could not be that Cowboy Jim existed. Because that was obvious. Since the beginning of this trip, I had begun to realize how much evil there is in this world. The secret must be something even worse.

The rain was falling lightly and Becca slept, arms thrown across my body, neck crooked and mouth ajar. I rearranged Becca's arms to be more of a blanket across my chest and fell asleep again.

The moment dawn came through the leaves, we climbed down from the rock.

The morning gloom of the woods reminded me that the Earth itself is dark. All the light in the world comes from the exploding sun, and then flows along the breadth of the sky like water filling a basin. I looked at the dull leafshine, the sunlight particles scampering across their flat stomachs. I can't go on, I realized. I'm in his world now.

Becca made a plan. Neither of us took even a sentence to remark on the calamity that had occurred. A car swept away by a flooding river? It felt easier for us so long as we didn't talk about it, so we didn't.

We found the highway by following its noise. We flagged down a trucker, Bucky-style, got dropped off at a gas station in Columbia, New Jersey, and called a taxi for the nearest hotel. We called Mom for her credit card number, told her nothing, and promised to call back. We didn't talk and I didn't think; we acted in determined silence. Becca told me what to do and I listened. We taxied to Walmart and bought new clothes and shoes and toiletries. We booked a bus to Newark. Finally, at the end of the longest day of my entire life, we called home from our hotel room. We put it on speaker phone and Becca explained to Mom what happened.

Mom cried. Loudly. She couldn't believe she let us go. She drilled us on how we made it to the hotel alive. She asked for the license plate of the truck driver that picked us up, the phone number and address of the hotel we're in. Becca told Mom the booking number and our scheduled arrival time in Newark.

"I'm coming out," Mom said.

"What do you mean?" Becca asked. I played with the bus tickets, turning and flicking them before Becca snatched them away from me.

"I'm booking a flight to Newark—I'll call back in a half-hour to let you know when I get there. I'll add two seats on the return trip. I should be able to get a red-eye tonight, so I can meet you in Newark when you get there on the bus tomorrow. Do you understand?"

"No," Becca said.

I could picture my mom's face. She doesn't really have a surprised expression—she goes straight from confusion to disgust. And right now, she was probably scrunching up her face like Becca just dropped the nastiest deuce the world has ever seen.

"Becca, do you understand what you're saying? You need to come home. The car *drowned* in the river, with all your luggage! You *need* to come home!"

Becca looked at me with wide eyes. I knew what they were saying. *Kaori.* We hadn't met her yet. *The bracelet.* We hadn't found it yet. She was asking me for help. Rubin Yakovlev and Grampa Andy had failed, Cowboy Jim was a murderous devil on the horizon, waiting for the first chance to shoot us in the streets, and we knew the bracelet had been in Newark, but we'd be better off not going anywhere. I knew that whatever was left for us to find was a horrific evil, an unimaginable horror, and that we would be better off turning back.

But Becca didn't stop looking back. She kept looking at me. She was begging me. But why? Why did the trip have to go on? Why couldn't we give up? Because Becca planned to meet Kaori in New York? Because of childish travel plans made when we were too young to understand? When we were too stupid to comprehend history, to comprehend death, to comprehend true evil? But her eyes, her eyes, they're my eyes like no one else's eyes have ever been. I'm afraid I will never refuse Becca anything as long as I live.

"Mom," I said, unsure if I was actually speaking aloud, "we can't come home right away. We came so far—we may as well spend a few days in New York City." Mom tried to interject but I cut her off as best I can. "Mom, stop, listen, please, please listen. I do want to see you, I do want to come home, especially after this whole mess, but it was nothing but terrible, awful, unimaginable bad luck. Both of us want to spend some time in New York. Kaori is coming all the way from Japan to meet us there. So let us at least go there before coming home."

"Matthew Rosen," my mom hissed, her voice scratchy through the line, "you and your sister are flying home from *Newark* as soon as you get there. You are *not* to go to New York City and get yourselves in more trouble. I'm flying to Newark, and we will all go back home together. Right. Away."

"We're meeting Kaori there," Becca said.

"For God's sake, it can't be worse than what the two of you have already gotten yourselves into—"

"WE'RE MEETING KAORI THERE!" Becca screamed.

Silence.

"I mentioned it, to you, Mom, I told you." Her voice cracked. "We've been planning to meet up for almost two years. Because we were delayed in Chicago, she's already there, in New York."

"Did you mention it to me?"

"I did."

"You must've said it very briefly."

"I did, but—"

"She's already there? In New York? I should come and meet her."

"She's staying at a hotel in Brooklyn," Becca said. "And no, don't. Please let us go to New York and then fly home. Like Matt suggested. Seven years Mom—we haven't met in seven years."

Kaori won the battle for us. Mom reconsidered flying out. We explained to her that we already have a bus booked one more time. When we promised to call from Newark and then hung up, the receiver told us the phone call had been an hour long.

Becca flopped on to the bed, stomach down.

"My lord," she groaned. "Thanks for that. You know how much I want this."

I sat next to her. "It's okay," I said. "But it's not just Kaori, right? It's your dreams, too, isn't it?" I paused. "Are you ever going to tell me about your dreams?"

"Soon enough, you'll know." She twisted around to look up at me. "Or maybe you already do. And the bracelet..."

I scratched my head. "We don't have the notebook. We're out of clues from Rubin Yakovlev and Grampa Andy." I scratched my eyebrows. "When we were in the woods, during the storm, something changed for me. I wish I could put my finger on it." All I had was Rubin Yakovlev's final note, miraculously, still in my pocket. I took it out and unfolded it: water-stained and barely legible, which seemed like a miracle in itself. It had the Yiddish, and my translation of the poetic but useless line: *I am at the bottom of the well. I am the gear in the clock. The sword of the angel. All dreams come true.*

At one point near the end of the notebook, Rubin Yakovlev had written about the Kabbalistic origin of the universe. The Zohar says that once upon a time, God was a pure giving force in an empty universe. Since there was nothing to receive his love, he made a vessel. God gave, the vessel received. But since the vessel was made out of God, it had some of God's attributes—namely, that the vessel was inspired to give as well. All it did was receive, but that vessel wanted so badly to give as well that it tried to give back to God and in the process, it shattered. That shattering was the Big Bang, and the vessel shattered into the atoms in our universe. With something like Hurricane Katrina, it was easy to remember how much we all get from the universe. We get, we receive, we take. But part of us—this tiny, fluttering part of our souls—wants more than anything to give. To this day, I believe that Becca and I survived the storm because our souls still had something to give.

"We have what matters," I said. "We know about Ricardo Diaz, a jeweler in Newark. That's all we ever needed to know."

Becca nodded. "You know, Matt. At first, I thought this trip was about getting to Kaori in New York, and that she would show me the bracelet, and my dreams would come true."

"And things have changed?"

She seemed to suck in an entire universe of air. She said: "I still think there's a chance that my dreams will come true. But I also think there's a chance we're already living in the dream. I mean, we almost drowned in a river." Something like a smile tugged at her lips. "I mean, when you think about it, a lot of crazy stuff happened. How about when you pulled over for Bucky? What were you thinking?"

I laughed. "I was lonely, Becca! I can't talk with you when you're thinking in Spanish." She laughed, and I laughed, but it wasn't true. I knew a little Spanish.

"So you really think Kaori knows where the bracelet is?" I said.

"If it's not in Newark, then she can take us to it."

"All the better. It sounds like she's got our backs. And if there's a God out there, probably him too."

And Becca said: "*Amen.*"

22

Newark

On the bus ride, Becca told me more about Kaori. They started off as pen pals after our Japan trip seven years ago, and never stopped writing. They could talk to each other about anything. "If you're my brother, she's my sister," Becca explained. "We tell each other everything." I wasn't about to complain about the arrangement. I didn't need to hear *everything* about Becca's life, and she didn't need to hear everything about mine.

"And how does she feel about the bracelet?" I asked.

"She's been thinking about it for a while," Becca said. The bus bumped and we jittered in our seats. "It sounds impossible, but she knew about the bracelet before we did. A long time before. You saw the letter. She has those dreams, and me too, but only sometimes. It's difficult to explain—they're dreams but they're *real,* and for Kaori, it's like she has another pair of eyes at night, that can go anywhere and see anything. She just has a way of knowing things, and she knows that New York is a place we need to go."

Revisiting the letter was making me nervous to meet Kaori. I tried to recall any mention of New York City in Rubin Yakovlev's notebook, which reminded me that the notebook drowned in the river.

"Ach!" I felt a pang. The loss of that notebook nearly tugged tears out of my eyes.

"What is it?" Becca asked.

"It's gone," I said, hand over my mouth. "All the notes. 75 years of history." It was as if I had witnessed the death of thousands. Those words, clothed in the dusty boots of Arizona, the polyester suits of New York, and everywhere in between—they were worth more than one life, and if I could've saved the notebook by sacrificing my own life, I should've.

It was as if in order to cross the Delaware River, the universe thought it necessary to erase the past: our belongings, our grandfather's gifts, the entire recorded history of the bracelet. Maybe it was the Cowboy Jim's doing. His toll upon us entering his murderous east coast wonderland. Hurricane Katrina did more than wipe the slate clean—it destroyed history. If Becca and I had also died in the flood, there would be nothing left to show for a hundred years of struggles all across America.

It made me realize how fragile history is. It's more of a liquid than a solid. You can barely hold it, and even if you construct special containers to keep it in place—books, recordings, movies—leaks can spring up. History is water. Earth has it in abundance. Oceans of unfathomable depths cover most of the known world. But we cannot own them, barely understand them, and rarely interact with them of our own will. I think hunter-gatherers telling tales of their ancestors is like how those same hunter-gatherers would search miles for springs or a stream. With a fragile source of water, there is a fragile source of history. Today we have reservoirs and irrigation, history books and the Internet. Yet even a minor change in climate can render all that technology worthless. Abrupt climate change and societal collapse, after all. Human existence is full of holes.

The bus exited the highway. We made it to Newark. All we had to do was find a jeweler named Ricardo Diaz.

Mom was so worried about us that she had insisted on paying for everything, which was great news considering that in a few years some lucky kid in Portugal will probably be finding my wallet and bank card. That meant we got to stay at a not-too-crusty hotel downtown. It was too early to check in, so we ate at a deli and walked to the library. It wasn't a nice walk, as they were doing construction on the riverfront (presumably to make it into a nice walk).

The library fronted a big marble atrium and speckled stone columns and arches. We went up a broad staircase and wandered till we found a community room. Becca used the phone to call Kaori at her hotel while I used a computer to look up Newark jewelers. I clicked through a dozen pages before seeing a mention of Fine Gold and Jewelry in west Newark, owned and operated by Mr. Ricardo Diaz. I wrote down the address.

We went to the nearest gas station (even without a car you still need 'em) to use the ATM and buy a new set of maps, and figured out how to get to Fine Gold and Jewelry. We boarded a local bus west-bound. Everyone else on board was Black. I've done the only white guy in a room of Asian people thing before, and certainly the only Jew in the room thing before, but this was a first for me.

The roads were bursting with cracks, and broken glass lined the edges of the sidewalk. A lot of buildings were boarded up. A few massive Victorian homes, like the ones where Grandmother lives in Oakland, peaked gables and wraparound porches and all, created an eerie variation between themselves and the low-lying sandy buildings around them. I wondered who on earth lives in them.

We reached a strip of shops: a wing joint, a Greek restaurant, a loan office, a shoe store with cracked windows, and Fine Gold and Jewelry, by far the nicest shop on the strip. The sign was polished, and the tinted glass prevented you from seeing in. We entered.

"Bienvenidos," called an older woman from the checkout in the center of the small store. The walls were covered with advertisements and the jewelry stood in proud glass cases underneath the checkout desk.

"Hola," Becca said. "¿Sabes si Señor Ricardo Díaz está hoy?" She spoke even quicker and more fluently than I thought she could. "Tenemos una pregunta pequeña que nos gustaría hacerle, aunque me gustaría poder comprar algunas joyas..."

"Sí, él está aquí, él es mi esposo. Soy Stefanie Diaz. No hay nada que te impida comprar, sabes. ¿Cuales son tus nombres?"

"Me llamo Rebeca." Becca looked at me and nodded.

They were speaking way way way too fast, and my face was bright red. "Me llamo..." I stuttered. "I'm sorry, I don't speak Spanish very well. No hablo..."

Stefanie Diaz opened her mouth. I couldn't tell if her smile was friendly or mocking. "So sorry about that—you speak great!" she added to Becca.

"I'm fine. We're from California." Becca raised an eyebrow at me. My blood was boiling.

"California!" Stefanie Diaz said. "Quite a journey, huh? Let me call my husband."

We waited for a moment before Ricardo Diaz came bustling out from a back room. He was old, short, and dark-haired, wearing neat black pants and a white shirt. Spectacles hanging low on his nose made him seem like he was peering up at you.

"What can I do for you today sir and miss?" he asked. "It is too soon for the engagement, I'm afraid."

I didn't understand at first because of his accent, but Becca laughed and told him that we're brother and sister.

"Good for you, less business for me," he said. "What can I do for you?"

Becca asked him if he'd ever seen a leather bracelet with a gold Spanish coin.

His reactions said it all: his thick eyebrows nearly shoot off his face. Mouth turned into a deep frown. Lowered chin, shook head.

"No good," he said. "What would you want with such a thing? Of course I know of it, it was here. It has been gone from my store at least three years."

A familiar feeling: my heart breaking into a sprint. Three years ago? Holy fuck. Three years ago! In bracelet-years, that's *yesterday!*

"What happened to it?" Becca asked.

He shook his head again. "I can't say."

Becca and I glanced at each other.

"I don't want to make you tell us anything you don't want to," I said, "but we're from California. We came all the way across the country to find the bracelet."

His head kept shaking. "I don't think I should tell you. Go back to California. California! So far. I would like to go there, maybe when I retire."

"Please," I implored him. "Just tell us what happened to it. That's all we want to know."

"I'll tell them," Stefanie Diaz said. We turned to her. Her head hung low, as if she could hardly bear the weight of her own thoughts.

"Stefanie, you don't have to. Some stories are better left untold." Ricardo Diaz jerked his head to the door. "Now you go."

"I'll tell them."

We faced her more earnestly. Behind us Ricardo's head was shaking *No* and his eyes were closed.

"There's a good reason my husband doesn't want to tell you what happened," she said. "And I will get there.

"We are from Cuba. We came when we were children, so we can barely remember our mother country. We haven't gone back, and it seems like we never will be. I haven't seen my brother or my cousins in almost fifty years. Ricardo and I met in Miami, forty years ago. We came to Newark and opened a jewelry store. All this time we had good fortune. We had children, and we all worked hard, even though we never made much money.

"Several things happened about five years ago. The first is that our son died in a terrible car accident. That meant his two sons came to live with us, but without their father, they were not good. We tried to take care of them, but they were reckless and got into all sorts of trouble. I don't know what they did, and I never wanted to know. We should've moved, sent them to different schools, but we were busy because our business was doing well. The surrounding neighborhoods were changing. It was a very exhausting time." Every once in a while Ricardo Diaz nodded along with his wife's story, but otherwise he stayed quiet.

"Around this time my husband bought the bracelet. This was fine. It was a nice piece of jewelry and easy to sell. But our oldest grandson saw it and took such a liking to it that we gave it to him, hoping to keep him out of trouble. It didn't work."

Stefanie Diaz sighed and clasped her hands together.

"Pare," Ricardo said sharply. "No sabemos lo que pasó."

"The bracelet is cursed," Stefanie declared. "After my grandson took it, within one year, he and his brother were murdered!"

"Be quiet, crazy woman!" Ricardo exclaimed. "That's not what happened. There was a fight between our grandsons and their friends and another group of boys, and those boys had guns, they were gangsters. That's all! Those boys had guns and our grandsons did not and so our grandsons died instead of being murderers. Who had guns and who did not was the difference. There was no murder, no curse. It was just a tragedy. A terrible, terrible, terrible tragedy."

Stefanie's face turned pale and she took my hand. I jerked away from her in surprise but her small hand latched on to mine. "My husband is lying to himself," she said. "There was a murder. I saw it with my own eyes, te lo juro. They were coming back towards the house and had a fight with the other boys, yes. There was a fight. But then a tall man in a cowboy hat came and shot both of my grandsons at the same time with his two guns—*shot* both of them, right in front of my eyes! I had already called the police but by the time they came the man was gone!"

"This is why I told them *no*," Ricardo said angrily to his wife. "You are raving. None of this happened. There was a fight, and the other boys had guns, and Ian and Leo did not, por supuesto que no los tenían, and they ended up dead. They got into too much trouble always—"

"Not that much trouble!" Stefanie cried, and let go of my hand. I backed into Becca. She was trembling. A film of sweat formed on my palms. It was like the man I had seen with my own two eyes. I glanced out the window and winced, half-expecting to see the smirking face of Cowboy Jim in the glass.

Husband and wife stared each another down. I could feel the sadness and anger in their gazes like electricity. Becca didn't stop trembling. Then a bell jingled, and a customer walked in, and it all dissolved.

"Bienvenido! Welcome!" Stefanie called to the customer, who responded in casual Spanish.

Ricardo looked at us. "That's all." He glanced at his watch. "I must get back to work." He started to walk away.

"Wait!" I called after him, and he stopped. "Please—do you know where he went when he took the bracelet? The cowboy?"

"I will never tell you," he said. "The truth died with my grandchildren."

Ricardo did not turn around and continued to the back room and the door swung closed behind him.

Stefanie and the customer were speaking rapid Spanish. I was angry. Breathing hard. For them to deny us the truth now! My fists were curled and my whole body was shaking when Becca put a hand on my shoulder and I realized I had been overcome by a foreign rage, the anger of another person. What was the feeling? Where had it come from? Where does Cowboy Jim come from? Why are we looking for the bracelet? And what will Kaori know? Full of more questions and feelings than ever before, Becca and I left the shop and got back to our hotel to pack as quickly as we could.

23

Brooklyn

We met Kaori at her hotel in Williamsburg. My heart was pounding in my throat. She was the same age as Becca, a shy, small girl with black, curly hair, and at first she didn't even make eye contact with me. Becca kept apologizing for being so late and Kaori kept saying it didn't matter. I introduced myself as if we'd never met. I felt like I was intruding on their reunion—the hotel room was suffocating.

"I'm going to get some fresh air," I said. "Take a little walk down the street."

"You shouldn't go alone," Kaori said. "Let's all go for a walk."

Becca agreed and we made our way outside and around the corner to a strip of boutiques and restaurants. Becca asked Kaori how she likes New York; if it's been difficult for her; if she's been okay. Kaori smiled and said that it's an amazing city, surprisingly easy to navigate compared to Tokyo.

"There is one thing," Kaori said. She had an accent, but it wasn't strong, just blunted 'th's and rolled 'r's, closer to British English than American. "Everyone looks at you on the street. At first, I thought I was a witch, but then I recognized—how do you say it? Eye contact—that everyone does eye contact."

I chuckled. "New Yorkers," I said. "They're probably sizing each other up."

"What does that mean?"

"Checking each other out. Seeing who would win in a fight."

Kaori laughed at this with a hand over her mouth. "Could that happen?"

I shrugged. "We're from the west coast."

We wandered around a bit before passing a Ben and Jerry's. Kaori insisted that we go even after Becca and I explained several times that we could probably find better ice cream, somewhere local. But Kaori had never had Ben and Jerry's before, and after a pretty dank scoop of Americone Dream I concluded that Ben and Jerry's is, in fact, above average. Kaori got very excited about Cheesecake Brownie and Becca watched her with a smile. Becca ordered nothing, then insisted on tasting both of ours.

"Not mine," Kaori said, holding her cone at arm's length when Becca reached over.

Becca turned to me and I shook my head with a grin, hiding the cup behind my back. Becca scowled and got back in line. She got two scoops of Chocolate Therapy.

Kaori and I waited for her by the window, watching tourists and locals. "There are so many men with beards," Kaori remarked. She was right. Some of them were hipsters with cashmere sweaters and stupidly large pants, and the rest were Orthodox Jews with sideburns, black hats, and tzitzit dangling out of their long coats. Rubin Yakovlev and his sister, my great-grandmother, lived here eighty years ago. I remembered the notebook, and as I recalled his words and the inscribed Hebrew letters, I could almost see the bracelet glinting on my great-grandmother's wrist as she schleps to and from the market and from shul.

Becca sat down. I could tell there was some sort of tension. Maybe Becca had expected her reunion with her cousin might have been different in some way. Personally, I was totally relieved. Kaori and me, we've got the same eyes. She has a Japanese face, and her eyelids are single-lidded or whatever you call it, but besides that, our eyes are the same. Exactly the same. And the famous Stern curls were out in full bloom.

"I'm sorry we've been out of touch," she said. "I have so many things I want to say to you, Matt, and I was going to tell you about the bracelet, too. At least we got to meet now, but... I wish we could spend more of this kind of time together."

What things? I wondered.

"That's why we're here, aren't we?" Becca said. "We can go to Manhattan tomorrow. Central Park, Times Square, the Met... there's so much to do! We need to eat in Koreatown and Little Italy. And I heard about this amazing cupcake place—"

Kaori was shaking her head. "There isn't time."

"What do you mean?"

"You met him, didn't you?"

"Who?" Becca asked.

"The cowboy."

Becca fell silent.

"Kinda," I said. "He's showing up everywhere. Do you know who he is?" When Kaori didn't respond I leaned over the table. "Kaori, the bracelet was in Newark only three years ago. What do you mean when you say there isn't time?"

"The cowboy moves quickly," Kaori said. "We have to stop him."

"What is he going to do?"

Kaori stared at the floor. "We have to stop him, I only know that."

"And how do you know this?"

"I saw a dream."

"About what?"

Kaori looked at Becca. "I'm worried that we don't have enough time." She looked at me. "I think I know where the bracelet is."

I nodded. Becca had prepared me for this—that Kaori might somehow know what Rubin Yakovlev never could.

Becca inhaled sharply and blinked rapidly. For a second, I swore I saw tears in her eyes. What on earth was she feeling? Why couldn't she express it to me now, of all times? We almost died together, hadn't we? But Becca kept silent and blinked the tears into oblivion.

I turned and watched Kaori. She was looking past us, out the window. What else did she know? What are the consequences of failing here, now that we've come so far? I needed to know everything she knew and again I jerked around to the window, suddenly terrified that the devil cowboy might be watching us on the other side of the too-thin glass.

"It isn't far," Kaori said.

I nodded. We'd gone all the way across the country—it better have been close.

"Everything is moving very quickly." Kaori touched Becca on the arm.

"And if we don't hurry?" I asked.

"If we don't get the bracelet before the cowboy," Kaori said, "someone will die."

"What? Who?" I couldn't believe it. "How?"

"I don't know," she said. "But someone. This I know."

I wish I could've hit pause on the whole damn train. I wish I could've. But I had to take Kaori's word. I had to, right? If I didn't, I'd run the risk of someone dying. It meant we would keep running the same old race, anyhow. I wondered if I even knew how to do anything anymore *besides* bracelet-chasing. Did Rubin Yakovlev really spend his whole life this way? To lose a life to this one thing... I couldn't let it happen. I lost Grampa Andy entirely and ended up following Rubin Yakovlev instead, a man I never knew and never will. It didn't feel like Grampa Andy's journey at all anymore, and that hurt. I did this for him, I did it all for him, but in the end, I suppose Grampa Andy only had a passing interest in the bracelet. Enough to encourage us to look for it, to look for it himself, but nothing more.

"A dream?" Becca asked.

Kaori shook her head. "More than that. Worse than that."

I looked up from my shaking hands. "We better hurry."

We left Ben & Jerry's and followed Kaori. She asked us to explain what we had found in Newark and nodded along as if she'd heard the story before. We headed some fifteen blocks east and south. The pedestrian traffic eased up as orange beams of light sparked between the occasional gaps in the buildings. The neighborhood became more residential, and the traffic lighter, and the beard ratio ticked up even more.

We arrived at a brownstone on a gray street. We paused on the stairs up to the front door.

"I saw this place in a dream," Kaori said. "I don't know who lives here. But I know that the bracelet was in this house."

It was an ordinary brownstone, the same as the rest. I have no idea how Kaori could tell it apart from the others. Barred basement windows on the street-level. Each of the three floors above had two tall, rectangular windows. I noticed that the front door had a gold mezuzah marked with an ornate ש.

Kaori glanced at us and skipped up the steps. She rang the bell. Becca and I slowly climbed behind her.

A moment passed before a child opened the door: a little boy dressed in a white shirt, black pants, with a yarmulke and curly sideburns that bounced as he watched us.

Kaori didn't seem like she had any more of a clue what we were doing than I did, and I couldn't bring myself to move, so Becca took over the conversation. She asked if his parents were around, and he called for Mama. Mama came to the front door, a woman with large dark eyes, upper-thirties at most, wearing a headscarf, black shirt, and long gray skirt.

There was neither time nor energy left for chitchat. Becca told her that we were sorry to bother her and that we were looking for a leather bracelet with a Spanish gold coin on it.

The reaction was familiar, and haunting. The woman's lips began to tremble, and then her hands. "How?" she whispered.

"We're looking for it," Kaori said, disguising her accent with carefully enunciated words. "Do you know it?"

I felt my stomach curling up. We were about to be in for some sort of gruesome, terrible story. The only question was what kind.

She shook her head. "We used to own a bracelet like that. We had it one year ago, before my son gave it to a friend."

"Who did your son give it to?" Kaori asked.

"His friend."

"Do they live in Brooklyn?" I asked.

The woman frowned. "Yes—but—no, they don't have it anymore."

"We really need to find it," Kaori said. "If your son's friend doesn't have any more, do you know who does?"

The woman sucked in air, looked at the doormat, and back up at us. "It's out of the city. My son gave it to his friend—but that friend—he's in the hospital. His family returned the bracelet to us, and I got rid of it again. I gave it to my cousin. He lives in Salem."

"Where is that?" Kaori asked.

"Massachusetts," I quickly told her, and she nodded. We got the cousin's name and address, and Kaori wrote it down on a stylish pink notepad. My heart was beating fast, and I wanted to get out of there before the woman told us how her son's friend ended up in the hospital. But everything was ruined. I was about to turn and run down the stairs, *run, run, RUN,* before Becca's words opened the door to the horror.

"I'm sorry to intrude," she said, "but if I may—how did your son's friend end up in the hospital?"

I wanted to cover my ears, even scream to drown her out, as the woman told us. The words came out swiftly, even eloquently, as if she has been preparing the words in her mind but only just now had let them leave her lips. I couldn't help but to hear every word. Her story—perhaps more than any other that I'd read in the notebook or would hear again—impressed itself on my mind like a brand. I focused on a wispy cloud way up in the too-blue sky to keep the tears inside of my face, as the agony of it all mounted pressure on my temple.

The story: three years ago, after much familial conflict and outrage, her thirteen-year-old son, Asher, enrolls in a summer program to create and facilitate dialogue between Jews and Muslims. 9/11 happens, and there are follow-up meetings in the program. Asher talks of Muslim friends in the program suffering verbal taunts or abuse after the attack, and many of his Jewish friends in the program are forbidden by their parents from attending. But Asher stays, and an instructor in the program gives him the bracelet as a personal gift for his hard work (no, the instructor did not wear a cowboy hat, what a strange question). Asher's good friend Ramiz, Yemeni and Palestinian, has to deal with a persistent school bully that keeps insisting Ramiz's parents are terrorists and pushes him around. Asher gets the idea to give Ramiz the bracelet as a present. The two families even have dinner together. Asher and

Ramiz spend more time as close friends and nothing happens until something does. A drunk group of older teenage boys throw copies of the Quran at Ramiz and Ramiz loses his temper and hurls back insults. He throws words, and the boys return them with punches. They pummel the shit out of him. They don't stop. They can stop, but they don't. Asher is watching. He watches it all and wants to help but can't. He's too scared to even move. Ramiz ends up in the hospital, a paraplegic. Ramiz gives back the bracelet to Asher. He doesn't want it anymore.

The bracelet is eventually given away to Cousin Adam in January 2004.

I listened to the story more and more closely as it went on and by the end, I found myself looking into Asher's mother's eyes, breathing deeply, breathing slowly.

"Is Asher here?" I asked. "I'd like to meet him. Just to say hi and thank him for doing something good with the bracelet. It seems to carry both good luck and bad luck, and it makes me so happy—it makes me feel proud, even, that he tried to do some good with it."

The woman was breathing as if she was in labor. Her closed eyes leaked tears as she told me that two years ago her son decided to end his own life.

I burst into myself, a silent chasm plunging inwards. Dying in sin. There is no connection. Maybe Asher was depressed and struggled in school, and it had nothing to do with this. Maybe Asher was gay and in love with Ramiz. Maybe he couldn't handle how the bracelet was returned by a broken child and the revelation of the unspeakable terror his love had brought on the world. The light and air around me, thin and pale, melting into dusk. Becca and Kaori pulled me away and down the stairs.

Ramiz... Asher...

"Thank you," Becca said, taking my hand.

She hadn't held my hand in forever. The last time might have been when Grampa Leo was still alive, and Becca and I would playact as a fairytale couple in his bedroom in the Los Angeles house. We would hold hands and pretend to cook dinner and argue over who has to do the laundry. Then Grampa Leo, pretending to be an ogre, would stampede in to "EAT THE PUNY HUMANS", pick us up and throw us on the bed. We'd scramble off and he'd send us bouncing back onto the pillows, hooting and scratching his gorilla belly. Becca and I would scream and hold each other. Now, Becca held my right hand, and, strangely, Kaori took my left. We started walking back.

It was many blocks back to Kaori's hotel, but I didn't feel them pass.

Becca's hand was so much bigger than Kaori's. It's funny. Becca had been using sunscreen and I hadn't, so I was at least three shades darker: we looked like some major hooligans, stretched across the whole sidewalk, a multiracial threesome, polyamorous teenagers trying to show Brooklyn what we're made of. But who gives a shit what Brooklyn thinks. Especially Brooklyn Orthodox Jews that probably don't fuck with gay people or dating goyim.

For a while I thought I was crying, but my sister and my cousin had both of my hands and my face was dry when we were only a few blocks from Kaori's hotel.

"Do you think they have rooms?" I asked, and Becca shrugged and simply said she'll ask the concierge. How does she do that? How could she simply do these things, these practical steps, as the earth shook and stormed and changed around us every day?

We crossed the street. On top of the New York humidity, the city had its own sizzling energy, rising off the sidewalks and stirred up by flocks of strangers passing. I felt uncomfortably warm and our hands came apart.

"I guess we'll sleep here tonight and head to Salem tomorrow?" Becca asked.

Kaori nodded thoughtfully. "I suppose there is a train to Salem from here."

"I would assume there's a bus," Becca said. "We'll have to go to the bus terminal, first thing in the morning."

"Do you think the bracelet is still in Salem?" I asked Kaori.

"It may be," Kaori said. "A lot can happen in a year."

"You'd think *someone* would hold on to the bracelet for more than a year," Becca said.

"They can't keep it," I said. "It's Cowboy Jim."

"Cowboy Jim," Becca muttered. "I get the point, but if the cowboy keeps on stealing the bracelet from everyone, how does anyone end up with it in the first place?"

I thought about it. There must be some force that's countering him. A light side to his dark one. An *anti*-Cowboy Jim must be out there somewhere, beating him back; a guardian angel that delivers the bracelet to those in need. But that can't be true because the bracelet only seems to bring pain and suffering. For the first time I wondered: did the bracelet save my great-grandparents from the pogroms of Ukraine, or did it *bring* the pogroms to their doorstep, a magnet of violence and terror?

After all, from Japanese internment to the polluted Pyramid Lake, from Mark Jones's solitary confinement to Asher's suicide, what was the one constant? What was Grampa Andy's history project all along? What was the reason the bracelet mattered in the first place?

We were about to walk into the hotel lobby when Kaori grabbed me and Becca by the wrists.

"Ouch! What is it?" Becca asked, and I saw.

He was waiting for us in the lobby.

We were standing just close enough. The automatic doors slid open. He was alone in a chic lobby, alone in the center of the tile floor. He raised his head and the brim of his hat tipped up just far enough to reveal smiling eyes, darkened by the hat's shadow. His large, tanned hands opened his jean jacket, revealing two leather holsters.

Cowboy Jim flashed his white teeth in a curling grin. Our eyes met and I instantly felt sick to my stomach. Here, before my eyes, stood the source of evil. His belt buckle painted red, white and blue.

"RUN!" Kaori screamed.

The doors slid closed behind us as we sprinted back up the street in the onslaught of dusk. We heard two gunshots go off in quick succession, forceful bangs that nearly tripped Kaori by sound alone and the shattering of glass and the mad cackling of laughter.

"Taxi!" Becca hollered, waving frantically at a yellow cab cruising down the street. It pulled over and we scrambled into it. "Port Authority! Take us to Port Authority!" Becca yelled at the cab driver. "And *hurry!*"

The driver didn't question us. He didn't even say a word, and immediately screeched through a red light towards the Williamsburg Bridge. He must've thought we were travelers in a hurry, and he wasn't wrong. I didn't dare look back.

24

Salem

The bus ride to Salem was terrifying. I couldn't breathe, now I could, my mouth full of words and I looked at Becca and Kaori and their faces looked the same, choked full of fearful words, but none of us could say them, turn them into sound, make them real. Faded brownstone, graffiti tunnels to the end of the world, bushes mangled with plastic bottles, the industrial Connecticut coast in sharp bands of steel, concrete slabs and American flags on porches facing dazzling rivers. We had Adam Gersbach's Salem address and the relentless horror of daytime shadows, the emissaries of the cowboy.

I think I fell asleep, and then we transferred at Boston. I ruminated endlessly over the bracelet, trying desperately to figure out what it all meant. One idea was white supremacy. African Americans in jail, poisonous lakes on Indian Reservations, incarcerated Japanese... Yes, for in America, white terror kills both the Muslim and the Jew. Yes, that must've been it, and I proposed the theory to Becca, and she responded, "If you think that Cowboy Jim is the Grand Whatchamacallit of the KKK, that means you've got a white-savior complex and that's about it." I didn't understand what she meant by that, but if white supremacy wasn't the one constant in the story, then what was?

We made it to Salem sooner than expected. It was fast. Five hours stuck on a single train of troubled thought.

It was Saturday. We took a stroll through downtown to further calm ourselves. Salem is 90% witchy trinket shops, 10% upscale restaurants and boutiques. Economics. Port smell. Chowder. Out on the street, breathing in the sea-breeze, I finally settled down. Becca, Kaori and I emerged from the rattling shell of the bus, into something closer to reality. Becca kept her composure and expertly led us via taxi towards the palace of Adam Gersbach.

The lush suburban neighborhood was steaming in late summer humidity. The house a colonial, enormous, gorgeous dark blue and brown house with a wraparound porch and a rose garden. Marble steps faced the front porch.

"This is like a paradise," Kaori said.

"No," I said. "We're in hell now."

Armed with nothing but the clothes on our backs, we knocked on the door, and met Adam Gersbach.

Gersbach was a nice guy. Maybe too nice. He brought us in for a cold drink. When we asked about the bracelet, he explained that he gave it to his wife, but she was away on vacation in France and wouldn't be back for two days. When we insisted that we needed to get the bracelet at all costs, he accepted our determination, and let us stay in a guest bedroom with two twin beds on the third floor. There was even a little kitchen we could use. We were so tired that we didn't question his generosity.

As soon as we went upstairs, Kaori passed out. Becca and I glanced at each other.

"Regroup tomorrow?" I asked.

Becca nodded. "We'll need to go downtown, buy some clothes. If Kaori and I are on the same page, neither of us think we should stay here very long."

I nodded, considering the plush beds, feather pillows, flatscreen TV, all instruments meant to delay and deceive us.

Adam Gersbach didn't bother us at all. We tried different ways of thanking him, but he shrugged them all off.

I slept soundly. We spent the next day walking around Salem, the site of America's original TV show. Handsome bearded men and curvy women in silky dresses, your doctor-prescribed dose of fantasy, detective-work, scandalous court trials, and sex. Meanwhile, Kaori enjoyed the more ordinary aspects of American culture. "It's nothing like the movies," she said, as we made the trek from Gersbach's house. "Why are there no buses or trains? How do you get anywhere?" At dinner: "The food is so creamy, I think I've gained two kilograms. Are those people speaking Portuguese? *Sugoi!*"

I changed the subject."I don't trust something about Adam Gersbach," I said.

"What?" Becca asks.

"He's a lawyer, right?"

"Yeah?"

"Then he's worse than dad! He's a hotshot east coast lawyer, and they're even lamer than west coast lawyers. Dad's as about as lame as a porcupine, but Gersbach, this dude is breaking new ground. Young, dresses in dapper suits, has loads of money—and get this—have you seen their family photos? His wife's Jayne Mansfield, and the kids are blonde too."

"So what?" Kaori asked, intrigued by my frustration.

"Think about it," I said. "Blonde wife with the maiden name Williams. Summers in Nantucket. Gersbach's not even a religious man, but the guy said his wife *converted to Judaism.* That shit breaks assimilation."

"Our grandfather married into old, Christian money too, if you've forgotten," Becca said.

"That's on the west coast," I said. "There aren't real Jews out there. No choice. There are so many *real* Jews here. And Grandmother never converted. You can't just *switch.* It seems so much more delusional."

"No more applying to schools on the East coast?"

"Hell no," I declared. "New England trees are for thorny, old-school fuckers who got here on the *Mayflower.*"

"Or at least 1875," Becca added.

"So you agree?'

"No, you're being ridiculous."

"I've never been to the west coast," Kaori said. "But it's full of *huge* deserts and mountains, isn't it?"

"Pretty much."

"The Jews came out of the desert," she said, "so maybe you're better suited for it, deep down in your bones."

"It's possible." I looked at her. "*Our* bones. You too."

"Me too," she said, putting her hand on her neck.

Becca and I bought a few pairs of clothes downtown. We added them to our backpack of necessities that we had gotten back in Newark. Kaori had two big suitcases in the Williamsburg hotel that she left behind, so she bought a nice handmade leather bag at a downtown stand. She dressed well, so she went for the best designer fashion in Salem—sky-blue heels, a beige romper with a hand-sewn shirt pocket, a sun hat. She said repeatedly, as if it were embarrassing, that at home she wore her school uniform pretty much all the time in Kyoto so she wanted to wear anything and everything while 'free of Japan.'

When we got back, Laura Williams Gersbach was home, but didn't know anything about the bracelet. Gersbach hit himself on the forehead and said he must've misremembered. An hour later, he knocked on our door.

What happened next was strange and disturbing. As if we were his close friends and confidants, he confessed to us that he had an affair with a different woman a year ago, and that he had in fact given the bracelet to *her*, not his wife. Okay, Gersbach, fucked up, but whatever. At this point it didn't matter to any of us what he did with the bracelet, so long as he could get it to us. He promised to look up the woman's whereabouts. We tried to help but he asked us to let him handle it; he'd find her tomorrow at latest. All the while a little demon in my gut was screaming, *YOU'RE GONNA DIE, MATT, YOU'RE GONNA DIE.*

Day three in Salem. We spent the day at home, discussing whether to stay or go, wandering around Gersbach's neighborhood, resting in the shade of trees that felt almost as big as California redwoods. I had never been so tormented by the simple passage of time.

Then, things got worse. Fast.

Bad Thing One: Gersbach, for some reason, had trouble finding this ex-lover of his, whoever and wherever she was, and told us that we could stick around his place, no problem; he would find her by tomorrow at the latest. Okay, Gersbach.

Bad Thing Two: Kaori, by accident or intuition, found several ounces of cocaine. She went to the bathroom downstairs and was compelled to look in the cabinet under the sink. Voila, a cigar box full of coke. Becca and I took trips to the bathroom to confirm. I'd never seen cocaine before, so I was tempted to touch it or give it a lick, but feeling superstitious of Cowboy Jim, I didn't.

We were already freaked out, and Gersbach's goodwill seemed freakier by the hour. We agreed that we should leave first thing the next morning: grill Gersbach one more time about this ex-lover, and if he didn't fess up, we'd have no choice but to rely on Kaori and a stroke of luck to get back on track. It had been three whole days, and every day wasted was a day that the bracelet got further away, or that Cowboy Jim could somehow find us. August was over, which meant Mom was about to get real pissed, put on some gloves, and come out and drag us back to Chestnut Creek.

At about eight the next morning, we packed our bags and went downstairs. Laura Williams was off somewhere, and Gersbach was making the kids bowls of Fruity Pebbles before he sent them off to play in the backyard, behind a deep blue pool and stone-tile patio.

"You're not heading out, are you?" Adam asked, pouring a glass of whole milk.

"I think so," Becca said. "Thank you so much for your hospitality, but we can't stay any longer. We'll look for the bracelet somewhere else—we can't impose on you anymore."

"Oh no," Adam says. "I don't think you understand. It's quite all right. You see—" he served the chattering kids their cereal "—she's coming over at lunch, today—the woman I told you about! She confirmed she had the bracelet, and said she wanted to meet you in person." He laughed. "A nice lady. Thank god my wife's not here. You can just put your bags by the door and hang out in the house. I think she'll be coming over around..." He checked his watch. "11:30? 12:00 at the latest."

It was just before 9:00. Becca and Kaori and I exchanged glances.

"Of course," I said. "She said she was coming here?'

"That's right," Adam said. "I need to go run an errand, then I'll pick her up and bring her over. 12:00 at the latest. She says she has it, so she can hand it over, and you can just get on your way."

Adam waved goodbye as a nanny arrived for the kids. She was an old white woman and she stared at us, wide-eyed. "Ir muzn geyn!" she whispered and hurried outside to watch the kids.

Becca and Kaori and I hung out in the sunlit family room. Becca flipped between *The Princess Bride* and MSNBC, where they were talking about the destruction in New Orleans and Angela Merkel. I stared at an enormous piece of modernist art on the opposite wall. The painting looked sexual to me, with one curved fold of color pierced by a flurry of darker lines like arrows or rain. As I watched it, the noise from the TV started to seep into the painting, infect it. FEMA ordered 20,000 body bags and it wasn't nearly enough. Clouds sparked and recessed into white noise. The shapes were nothing but shapes, the colors nothing but color, but I still saw all sorts of things in the painting: Hebrew letters, a scorched wasteland, and the dark brim of a cowboy hat...

"Matt," Kaori said.

I looked at her. She was staring out the window at a clump of fluttering leaves.

"Yeah?"

"When Becca visited me in Japan, do you remember?"

I shrugged. "Not well. I want to go back, maybe that would help me remember. All I remember is being upset with Becca because you two spent so much time off on your own together. I was bored, and definitely too young to appreciate being in another country."

She shook her head. "No—not that. A few weeks later, when she went down into the well in your backyard, and you helped her return home."

I snorted. "Well, it wasn't in *our* backyard. How do you know about that?"

"Matt, Becca really visited me that day. I was sick in the hospital. I had pneumonia. But Becca came and visited me. You were so close, Matt—I could hear your voice."

I stole a glance at Becca. She was watching TV.

"No," I said. "You guys were playing pretend, pretending she visited. She was pretending that she went, and you were imagining that she came."

Kaori raised her eyebrows, as if she had never considered the more realistic alternative before. "I must have imagined it so many times that it turned into a memory."

"I would like to come back some day," I said. "I'd like to see Kyoto, and your friends."

"My friends? Why would you like meeting my friends? They don't speak English, you know."

"I like meeting people." I chuckled. "I don't care about English or Japanese. What about a boyfriend?"

Kaori blushed and I felt bad. I saw Becca try to repress a grin.

"You don't need to say anything."

"No, no. You caught me by surprise, that's all. There's no boyfriend. There is a person who I like. In Japan we say *suki.*"

"You going skiing with your crush?"

"Sometimes you do," she laughed. "*Suki*—it means *like.* Or maybe love. Or maybe both."

"Matt and I tease each other about who we're dating," Becca explained. "Now he's brought you into it. But Matt—he's juggling the affections of not one but two lovely young women."

Now it was my turn to blush. "And Becca is trying to break up with this big hairy Jew but keeps hooking up with him anyways."

Becca laughed and she and Kaori exchanged a glance. Right, Kaori definitely already knew that. "*Two?*" She winked. "You're popular."

"It's closer to zero," I said. Truth was, I hadn't texted Christine or Chelsea in weeks. I certainly didn't care about Chelsea anymore. Time and space had narrowed it down to Christine, but I could barely remember her either. California was truly a different universe. Ever since we had crossed the Delaware Water Gap, things seemed different, the shadows darker, the sky lower.... I looked at Becca. "So you think both of them are interested in me?"

That proved way too much for Becca. Kaori was giggling, and Becca was laughing like a madwoman, and I started laughing at myself. The laughter cracked across the plastic family room.

But the laughter faded away. It was almost 11:00 and all three of started to remember. For a while we sat there, thinking. I had always doubted the ex-lover of Adam Gersbach would have the bracelet, but now the whole story seemed totally unbelievable. I could tell Kaori and Becca were thinking along similar lines, and eventually Kaori said:

"I get a bad feeling."

"What do you mean?" Becca asked.

Kaori shook her head. "Adam Gersbach is lying."

"I agree," I said.

"I would believe it," Becca said.

"Should we leave?"

Kaori nodded. "There's nothing for us here. Let's get our bags and go. Just a little, I need to use the bathroom."

I considered the possibility that this ex-lover was really coming over, and that she really did have the bracelet. But it made no sense. Adam Gersbach's story kept changing, and looking back, I was confident that he had been making it up as he went along. I had no idea *why* he would do that, but Becca and Kaori and I were finally on the same page: Adam Gersbach is one fishy goyish Jew, and we should exit stage right the fuck out of his house.

We grabbed our bags from the laundry room and headed out the front door. As soon as we stepped out of that house onto the marble doorstep, I felt enormously relieved. Becca remembered there was an old bookstore about a half-mile down the road, so we could call a cab from there. We started to walk away from the suburban temple. We had been trapped in there, and even if we were technically taking a step backwards in our search for the bracelet, at least we could regain our freedom. Freedom of movement and all.

As we made it to the bottom of the long driveway, a gently sloping hill, the growl of Gersbach's Jaguar came snarling up the street. He stopped abruptly at the bottom of the driveway, rolled the window down. I couldn't see the passenger seat.

"Couldn't even wait till 11:30?" Adam said, getting out of the car, but leaving the engine on. "What's the big rush?"

"I'm sorry, Mr. Gersbach," Becca said. "We can't wait anymore. We're sorry for treating you this way—"

Adam shrugged and laughed. "Look, I'm not offended. I'll drive you downtown if you like."

"We're fine to walk," Kaori said, inching away from him and nodding her head—*walk away.* And when we started to walk away in spite of Gersbach's protests, the passenger-side door opened.

My heart stopped as I heard the resounding echo of boots on marble.

And then a gentle, country-twang voice said:

"Why don't you stop right there?"

It's over.

I spun around to find in front of the Jaguar, tall, sun-weathered like a stalk of corn, with his twin pistols cocked, loaded, and pointed right at us, Cowboy Jim.

Time slowed down. Breath caught in my throat.

I looked to my right. Becca was a few yards away from me, near the car. Adam Gersbach stood a little farther down at the base of the driveway. I looked to my left. Kaori stood there—*impossible!*—holding a gun of her own.

My limbs shuddered and sweat gushed from every pore in my body. Kaori raised the handgun, pointing it at Cowboy Jim's big, sparkling smile.

"Hey!" Gersbach shouted. "Where'd you get that?"

"Where you keep it, in the bathroom," Kaori said, inclining the gun towards Gersbach, "and you shouldn't move, either."

Cowboy Jim chuckled. His shadow was massive, it covered the whole driveway, writhed under my shoes and I felt its chill on the soles of my feet. "Now put that nasty thing down, China Doll. You don't know how to use it."

Kaori shook her head. "I can use it on you."

Cowboy Jim kept smiling at Kaori. He opened his mouth wide and bellowed maniacally:

"*SHOOT IT, YA GODDAMN JAP!*"

The words echoed off the marble steps. Kaori trembled as she takes a step towards Cowboy Jim.

"Where is the bracelet?" she demanded. Her hands shook so much that it looked like she was going to drop the gun. "*Where is the bracelet?*"

Cowboy Jim stepped towards Kaori and she stepped back. A dance. Two guns at her. One at him. What is happening? Should I cry for help? No—he'll shoot. Charge him and knock him over? Risk getting shot? Risk Kaori? Do I have the courage? Am I willing to die today? What should I do what will I do? My mind started to freeze over and my thoughts drowned in a river and all I could do was watch and listen.

"I suppose this is the end of your little adventure," he said. "For that reason, I don't mind explaining myself." He looked at Adam Gersbach and back to Kaori. "I'll cover the bracelet first. You want to know where the bracelet is? A girl named Ellen Reed committed suicide today and drowned to death. She lived in Bar Harbor, Maine, with her grandmother. Even the boy that loved her couldn't save her. As for myself, after I dispose of you, I'll travel there and recover the bracelet, and deliver it to someone new."

"To kill them, too?" I shouted. "You're a monster!"

"You interfere with my process," hissed Cowboy Jim. "I have been operating for many years. I keep America pure and strong, purged of the mice and the vermin. Weaklings, non-Whites, alien immigrants, the broken poor. You should understand better. After all, you're the kin of the Rubin Yakovlev. He was a great co-conspirator of mine. The Stern family has been both a thorn and a rose to me, a precious, sweet-smelling spiny rose." He took a broad stance and raised the pistols from his waist up to shoulder-height. He looked like a Roman statue, a sculpted devil, a god of shadows as he swelled to superhuman size as his voice thundered and every hair on my body stood. "Which is why I must end your life. I will not—"

I saw Becca move in a flash, wrenching open the Jaguar's door.

Jim spun fired glass shattered.

Kaori pulled the trigger.

The car roared burst forward a smacking thud. I dove out of the way pulling Kaori with me Gersbach screaming.

My mouth was full of dirt my head pounded in a savage pulse. I got on my hands and knees saw Becca running towards me. Gersbach lay on blood-soaked pavement Kaori's bullet must have hit him I couldn't see Cowboy Jim. Becca's hands pulled me up and I instinctively pushed back, she's pulling me *back* towards the chaos not away from it, but Becca pulled harder Kaori and I smacked into the backseat of the Jaguar Becca yanked the gear into reverse blasted backwards turned sharply, screeched down the street and away from Gersbach's hellhouse, and I tried to gain control over my breath and stampeding heart. Looking back, I saw Cowboy Jim crumpled on the pavement.

"You ran him over," I gasped.

Becca said nothing and Kaori had fallen over in her seat, her head and hair against my arm. I could feel her body shaking.

"We stole his car," I said. "You ran him over! We're *criminals*, Becca!"

Becca shook her head and ran a stop sign. "We're not going to steal the car, idiot," she said. "We'll leave it at the bus stop. We're going to Bar Harbor."

The tall trees of Salem whipped past. The blackened beards of monstrous trunks watched us, crowned with the boiling gold of sun-cast leaves. I knew then that Salem's Puritan witches and Indian ghosts were real.

25

Mount Desert Island

Kaori slept for the entire ride to Portland, Maine. In Massachusetts, the trees were big with dancing leaves. In New Hampshire, wagging almond-shaped heads of cornstalk and gray grasses took their place. We arrived in Maine and its long needled pine trees. We transferred in Portland and waited two hours on a bench outside.

It wasn't too hot. Becca and Kaori wolfed down Subway sandwiches. I didn't get one. Somehow those girls beside me giggled as they devoured sandwiches, chattering about the superiority of cats over dogs with half-full mouths. Cowboy Jim was dead or incapacitated, but I didn't feel the least bit safe.

Once again, I was stuck in my thoughts, astounded by my sister and my cousin. *Who* were these girls that I was traveling with? *How* could they be so brave? So much braver than me? And again, I found myself in Kyoto, an outsider between them, watching them climb up the mossy boulders in Aunt Akari's garden.

There were seven of us on the bus from Portland to Bar Harbor: us, a bus driver whose facial hair suggested he was a good friend of Grover Cleveland's, and a family of four—a mother and three daughters, no more than seven years old. The girls poked at each other before they fell asleep on each other's shoulders.

On the ride, we quietly discussed, trying to piece together what had happened in Salem. When Kaori had gone to the bathroom before we left, she had checked the cabinet under the sink one more time—and found the gun. Or, she hadn't found the gun and had simply pulled it out of thin air when she needed it most. Regardless, Cowboy Jim and Gersbach clearly had some sort of relationship, maybe to do with the cocaine, and that's the only logical connection we could make out of any of it. If there was any logic left in the universe at all. I swear— this couldn't be reality, not anymore. We were living in a comedy, and the joke was on us—we were chasing a *piece of jewelry*, hounded by a comically evil demon dressed in a wild west costume.

And yet it was so much worse than even that.

A girl named Ellen Reed committed suicide today. Now I knew for sure that the bracelet wasn't a protective amulet. The bracelet was cursed. A cursed bracelet that Cowboy Jim spread around the country, bringing awful misfortune to whoever ended up with it. Mark Jones banging his head against the prison wall. The Diaz kids shot in the street. A girl named Ellen Reed. It sounded like a white name. So was she poor? Some other kind of vermin? We weren't bringing the bracelet home. Not anymore. We were gonna destroy that fucking thing. We were going to burn it like the devil's dictionary.

The bus stuck to the main highway for an hour or two before diving off on to a winding road with intermittent views of Maine's stony coast. Two-lane bridges crossed blue-gray inlets, the shore on all sides covered in evergreen. The sun set. The ensuing night was breathless, silent. Two people got on at Camden. The bus alone on the road. Alien lights blinded from the far side. Salt began to seep through the windows and we stepped out into Bar Harbor.

The air was saltier and fishier than California seaside air. The town was lively despite being the Wednesday after Labor Day. We passed multicolored galleries and restaurants, gorgeous B&Bs, and Maine-themed gift shops. The air smelled like grilled fish and candlestick. Becca followed a map to an inn a few blocks out of downtown and convinced the manager to give us a three-bed room even though none of us are 21, technically the requisite age. The room looked converted from a sailor's inn, with three beds arranged in a row towards a small window. The room had an old armoire and no TV. As soon as we settled down, I realized that I was starving. Becca and Kaori were already asleep.

I took the key and walked outside by myself.

It was 11:30. The shops were closed now, but the town shone with the mild yellow of streetlamps.

I wandered to the harbor. Silence swept over me like a blanket as I stared out across the rippling water. Reflections of lamps spread out from the dock all the way to the sleeping shadows of tree-covered islands. A cold breeze ruffled my hair.

For a moment, I was scared that Cowboy Jim might be lurking behind me, touching me with the fingertips of the wind. For a while, I thought about Christine.

I felt a persistent stabbing in my stomach, so I headed back into town and went into the first restaurant I saw, a pub called Hendrick's. There were two big bearded guys and a female bartender. I tell them I'm not 21 but hungry and will pay for food. The bartender calls into the kitchen and a knife-thin cook comes out and asks me in Spanish and English what I want. Scrambled eggs sound pretty damn good so I tell him huevos. I wait at the bar, listening to the bearded guys talk about seeing U2 live in 1999. The eggs come out poached, and with potatoes on the side. I definitely wasn't complaining about that.

I asked the bartender on a whim if she knew Ellen Reed. She said no. She made me a Shirley temple.

When I finally went back to the hotel, it was after 1:00 A.M. I left a twenty at the bar. Hopefully she gave some to the cook.

I hoped that Cowboy Jim was lying.

I hoped that somehow, Ellen Reed was still alive.

I crept into our room. The lights were out and the room was cold, but Kaori was awake, sitting at the edge of her bed. I didn't say anything and crawled under the covers. I took off my socks under the blankets. I heard the bed creak. I looked over and saw the dim outline of Kaori curled up, her knees to her chest.

"Is Ellen Reed really dead?" I whispered.

Kaori might've fallen asleep by then, but I thought I saw her shake her head. It could mean yes, or it could mean no, or that she has no idea.

When I woke up the room was empty. Were they taking showers? No, because I took a shower instead and got dressed to find Becca and Kaori back in the room, now with a telephone directory and maps. They showed me Valerie Reed's phone number and address in the thick yellow book—the name "Ellen" is listed below Valerie Reed, a dependent. The address was a few miles west.

"Should we call?" I asked.

Becca shrugged. "We may as well just go. It'll take a few hours, but how about walking there? After being holed up in the bus yesterday I could use the fresh air."

Kaori and I agreed. The three of us got a hearty breakfast at a diner. I had three pancakes and two eggs, Becca oatmeal with fresh berries, and Kaori a ham and cheese omelet. From there, we wandered west. Sometimes, to move forward, you have to take a few steps back.

It took us ten minutes to leave town center. Then for a while, we walked down the best-smelling road I've ever experienced. It was an ordinary concrete street, but lined with yellow wildflowers and bushes, plants heaving their scents over wooden fences and gray and blue houses. My sinuses cleared and my head swelled with honeysuckle, pine-needle, blueberry. The day started out crisp and sunny and cool, clouded over and got muggy.

I considered asking Becca and Kaori if they had any dreams last night, but I decided to enjoy the palpable world around me for the moment. I wasn't as concerned with keeping reality straight as I had used to be—I decided that a dream meaningful enough can be more important than anything real could ever be—but for now, reality felt like plenty. The taste of pollen, the buzzing of bees, the *swish* of flowers set in motion by the wind. We went under a stone bridge and made a turn onto a street lined with tall, thick-set evergreens. We continued for another half-hour before taking one of the dirt roads shooting off the side, named Dream Dust Road of all names. Perhaps I wasn't experiencing reality after all.

The tall pines crowded the dirt road and we passed by two smaller houses before arriving at a larger one at the end of the street, matching the address.

A nice house, white finishing, baby blue shingles, sharply angled roof and elevated deck out back. Did Ellen Reed hang herself from the deck? Did her father keep a handgun under the bathroom sink? Did Ellen find it by accident or intuition, hold it to her head, and pull the trigger? The gold coin of the cursed bracelet dangling from her wrist, flashing its glitter of malice?

The air tasted syrupy and purple flowers romped up a hill next to the driveway. We hiked the drive. I pulled open the screen door. Becca rang the doorbell.

Feeling hesitant, we didn't dare to ring it twice. Time longer than I could hold my breath passed, but the door, it opened.

It was an old woman with eyes as pale as water. Tall, imposingly tall. Her big bones made her look too lively for her wrinkles and straggly gray hair. She looked like she was caught between vigorous youth and the moment of death, turning back and forth between the worlds.

"Can I help you?"

I could tell Becca and Kaori were caught off guard by her massive size, as almost a full ten silent seconds pass before I managed to say anything at all.

"So sorry to bother you," I eventually said. "You see, we're not from around here. We were just passing through town, and... this is going to sound rude but—"

"Oh, I don't mind rude," she said.

My mouth hung open. My heart pumped faster. "Uh... we were looking for Ellen Reed."

"Friends of Ellen's are you?"

"That's right," Becca chimed in.

The old lady pulled on her ears and flicked at her earrings. "Well, you'd better come in. I'll make some tea."

I wanted the tea because my mouth was dry and my stomach queasy. Her response gave me a bad feeling. But without any other choice, the three of us took off our shoes and went into the house.

The high-ceilinged living room with a big skylight seemed like a northeastern theme. Rustic furniture: an unfinished wood coffee table topped with white flowers and quirky animal statuettes. The old couch was surprisingly soft.

The three of us waited in a patient line on the couch and didn't dare to meet each other's eyes.

After a seeming eternity, the old woman returned, holding a platter with a pot of tea and mugs. "I made Puerh," she said. "My favorite."

She poured and I accepted the ceramic mug with a weak smile.

"Call me Valerie," she said, settling down on the armchair on the other side of the coffee table. "So go ahead and tell me your names, and what I can do for you."

I accidentally met Kaori's gaze. I could tell she was trying to restrain a giggle. It must've been a strange sight for her—a disheveled old lady in a gorgeous house, and I realized that each of Valerie Reed's earrings formed the shape of a solar system of sun, earth, and moon.

"Well," Becca said, "like my brother was saying earlier, we're here for Ellen..."

"Well, she's asleep now," chirped Valerie Reed. "So you'll have to settle for me for the moment."

All three of us did double-takes and I had to bite my own tongue and press my feet down to prevent myself from leaping up shouting. The whole universe exhaled: the hummingbirds out the window, the clouds thinning in the sky, the wooden polar bear on the coffee table. She was alive. The devil hadn't won yesterday, after all.

"Sleeping..." Kaori muttered.

"Is she... ill?" Becca ventured.

Valerie Reed watched us quietly for a moment, sipping the tea. I raised the mug to my lips. It tasted earthy, pungent, filling my nose and mouth like hot, fragrant mud.

"I'm starting to get the sense that you three are of the magical sort," Valerie Reed said. "Maybe you're psychics, or fortune-tellers. Am I right? You must be!"

Becca stammered.

Valerie Reed giggled like a schoolgirl. "Don't take that the wrong way! But you seem to know more than you should. Ellen's not so bad, you can ask her yourself. But while we are waiting for her to wake up, what would you like to talk about?"

I was flabbergasted. What could I say?

"Why don't you ask me what I do, then, why don't you?"

Kaori was the only one who still had a nickel of composure. "What do you do, Mrs. Reed?"

The woman leaned forward, twinkling blue eyes full of ripples from the dark tea. "Thank you for asking, young lady. I'm a poet."

"A poet?"

"Oh yes. I have been since I was a girl. I've had my share of success. Now, I wasn't as famous as my husband—he was an architect, studied under Louis Kahn, the lucky man—I blame Sylvia Plath for not responding to my very nice letters—but yes, I did work hard. My book that did best was my Sappho translations. *Tima'dos a? De ko'nis, tan dh'rpo ga'moio oanousan.* People considered them very original, back then they did."

"Is that hard?" Kaori asked. "Translation."

Valerie Reed smiled. "What a lovely question. It's hard if you have a conscious! Translation is positively violent. You must rip apart a text word by word, letter by letter! Club it over the head! Slit its throat and pull forth the guts! Bloody consonants and vowels everywhere! Internal organs like great worms on the ground! A horrible scene. But, like a body in the soil, with proper funerary rites the human matter will recycle into the earth, into vegetative matter and vital-force... a veritable elegy. And yet, sometimes no matter how granular you get, words and letters can't be understood without looking at the whole, and words are no mere ligaments. They're constellations bound together by invisible fibers in the sky. Sometimes, you ought to surrender to a text like you do to the river of time in your most joyful days and intimate nights. Of course, such surrender is the same as giving yourself over to the black hands of death without a fight. Oh my, is that my Ellen? She takes such soft steps, but I do believe I can hear her now."

"Grandmother?" called a voice.

"We have guests, dear," Valerie Reed said. "They've been asking about you!"

I looked up and saw Ellen coming down the stairs. She was probably about my age, but had gray hair and bright, bright, dazzling bright green eyes, set strangely wide on her face, like someone had grabbed them with tongs and pulled each apart from the other. Seeing her here, walking down to us, filled a void in my heart. Finally, it became clear that yesterday we had defeated Cowboy Jim. All that remained was the bracelet—and there stood the girl who had touched it last. The sense of momentous tides hurtling around me channeled through my ears, hit me in the ribs and throat: *we've arrived.*

"Hi," she said. "I don't know you."

Ellen stood awkwardly at the edge of the coffee table, staring at the white flowers.

Meanwhile, Valerie Reed just sat there with a soft smile, pale eyes full of light. This was one of the weirdest situations I have ever been in. And you know that's no small feat.

"So..." Becca started, but couldn't finish. I supposed it was my time to shine.

"We're looking for something," I explained. "Something that used to belong to our family but that was lost long ago. It's a leather bracelet, with a gold coin attached. Have you ever seen a bracelet like that?"

Ellen turned to me, and I was met with the startling force of her green eyes. Forests, valleys—there were whole Earths in those eyes. I'd never seen anything like it. She looked amused.

"Yeah." A hand floated to her left wrist. "I used to have it. A friend and I found it a few months ago."

"Where did you find it?" Kaori asked.

"It's a long story," Ellen said. "Grandmother, do you remember Jim Hardin?"

"Oh, of course," Valerie Reed said. "What a tragic soul. He was halfway to Mars on methamphetamines and whatever else. You met him in the woods."

"Yes."

"A tremendous soul." Valerie Reed looked at the three of us. "Jim Hardin, the King of Dust and Tears, a King Lear of sorts, really, possessed this bracelet, and was lost wandering in the woods. Ellen met him and took him to the hospital. Is that right, dear?"

"Yeah." Ellen settled down on the far end of the couch and peered over at us. "He was... not in good shape. He had this gentle, country accent. He told us all terrible stories. How he does crack because his momma did, how his dad beat him like a dog. He said he was born out west, west Texas, but grew up in coal country and moved all the way to New York after the mines closed and his father passed away. He kept talking about cowboys and Indians, that his granddaddy was the best Indian killer the world has ever seen and won the west for President Jackson. But when we got to the hospital he said something terrible." She closed her eyes. "He said he dreamed his baby drowned in a river. 'You can stop bad dreams if you try hard enough,' he told me. 'My baby never died at all—it was just a dream.'" She ran a hand through her hair. "I think he's still in the hospital. But he gave me that bracelet when we got there. Leather, gold coin—just like you described."

I shivered. Was this the true identity of Cowboy Jim? The man whose soul had corrupted into a demon? Or had the violence of his grandfather distilled into a spirit that ravaged the country while the progeny wandered lost, lonely, suffering? Could this mean that the ghost of Rubin Yakovlev, always chased or chasing Cowboy Jim, might too, survive? Could it be Rubin's phantom that was moving the bracelet from place to place all along?

"And where is the bracelet now?" I asked.

Ellen shook her head. "I don't know."

"You don't know?"

"I lost it yesterday."

"You lost it?" I cried. "*Yesterday?*"

Ellen looked away from me. My words were harsh, I knew that, but I couldn't afford to come this far and fail.

"I—I don't have it anymore."

"It couldn't have just disappeared," I said. "You said you had it yesterday." I glared at Ellen, who did not meet my eyes. "What happened yesterday?"

"Matt, that's enough."

Kaori's words hit me like a snowball.

I looked despairingly towards Valerie Reed. The old creature looked delighted.

"This bracelet!" she exclaimed. "It must mean so much to you. Is it a sort of good-luck charm?"

"Just the opposite," I explained. "It travels across America left and right, leaving a trail of death everywhere it goes, and now it disappears without a trace? We're trying to find it. We *need* to find it. It was our great-grandparents' when they came to America, and they gave it away by mistake, but it's ours, and it's dangerous, so we *need* to find and destroy it. *We need to.*"

"A family artifact, is it?" asked Valerie Reed.

"Matt," Becca said. "It's okay. It's not the first time the bracelet has disappeared without a trace. But we've kept getting closer. Don't give up yet. We'll find a way." She looked at Kaori. "Won't we?"

Kaori nodded.

Breath came out of me like a hot-air balloon sinking. Falling, falling at dusk. Falling. I rubbed my pockets and took out the only piece of the notebook that remained, and it wasn't even the original words, it was my translation, my terrible translation scrapped together from online Yiddish dictionaries. *I am at the bottom of the well. I am the gear in the clock. The sword of the angel. All dreams come true.*

"Do you mind if I take a look?" Valerie Reed asked.

Surprised, I handed it over.

Her eyes swept over the scrap, and she smiled. "Delightful poetry. What do you think it means?"

I glanced at Becca.

"What do you mean?" Becca asked. "It's the last bit of the journal. After that, there's nothing else."

"Why would the writer say something like that?" Valerie Reed asked. "A well that goes deep underground is rather like a passageway to the world of the dead, symbolically speaking. And a gear in a clock represents one unthinking component of a greater, unified cosmos. The sword of the angel would mean a violent mission given by God. And 'all dreams come true?' That's the best of all. Surely it means something."

"It doesn't mean anything," I said. "They're just words. The trail went cold. It died. Maybe it was always dead. Uncle Rubin never found the bracelet."

"But," Valerie Reed said, smile never fading, bright eyes never dulling, "all dreams come true!"

Becca and I looked at Kaori. Kaori's utterly blank expression slapped into horror when she saw that both Becca and I had turned to her, and I laughed loudly. Not that the situation was funny in the slightest. But I had laughed, and the laughter felt like it shattered a glass screen we'd never even noticed.

"So he found it?" Ellen asked.

"Well, he must have," Valerie Reed said.

I wasn't laughing anymore. "That's impossible," I said. "Then it would be in our family."

"Do you know for certain that it's not in your family?"

"But—but..." I trailed off. This was insane. "Ellen, you just had it. Yesterday!" I looked between Becca and Kaori, trying to say with my raised eyebrows, *can we just get out of here?*

After a long silence, Becca swallowed. "Matt, it's true that we never *really* talked to Mom about the bracelet. This would actually explain her bizarre reaction when we first mentioned it."

"What, you want to call her and ask?" I felt blood rush to my face. "You think Grampa Andy sent us on a mad chase across the country for no reason at all? That's fucking impossible. Ellen had the bracelet *yesterday!* It's not in our family. Mom doesn't know shit about the bracelet. She doesn't care about our family history. She just wanted to marry a lawyer and keep the family peace."

"Matt, I don't want to believe it either, but it could be—"

"Ellen," I pleaded. "What happened to you yesterday?"

Ellen stood up.

She walked over. In front of me. Standing over me. All her forest, all her fog, stormed above.

"Matt," she said. "To be honest, it's not very nice to meet you. Yesterday I walked into the ocean hoping to drown, and the bracelet slipped off in the water, and why don't you call your mother?"

She walked away.

Walls crumbled around me. What is happening? What have I done? What am I doing? Ellen bolted an arrow to my soul and my mind began to sever. Across a fault line thunder sounded. I couldn't think now I couldn't do anything. To the sea to the sea the stormy sea that's where I should go. I should go do what Ellen couldn't and at least that would be something.

"I'll make blueberry pancakes," Valerie Reed was saying. "Maybe Ellen will come back down and help—she's a better chef than I am. Our neighbors just picked the blueberries this morning. And in the meantime, why don't you call your mother? Surely it can do no harm. She might know something!"

I heard Becca and Kaori stand up from the couch. Move over to Valerie Reed's telephone.

No harm?

No harm?

The harm was already done. All the harm, everywhere across this cursed cracked coldhearted country, it's all been done, already, tomorrow's traumas, tears, school-shootings and suicides. What Mom would say, what Mom wouldn't say. How could it matter in the face of all this?

Now Becca with trembling fingers dialed numbers on the phone; Kaori leaned over to listen; a beam of sunlight struck a line on Becca's white t-shirt, and I felt my heart collapse.

"Hi Mom."

...

"Yeah, it's me. Kaori and Matt are here. We're fine."

...

"Oh, yeah, we're fine, yeah. Look... I know you must be so mad at us, but there's something I need to ask you about."

...

26

Allison

A Well of Dandelions

September 1998, Chestnut Creek

September is the month for daydreams.

Full of gentle days free of storms and baking sun, whole Septembers can pass in a lazy Sunday afternoon. Allison Rosen was not the type of women prone to fancy, but for her it was not a typical September. Now that her kids were eleven and nine and good, sound kids, the type of kids that didn't require babysitting into their preteen years, she was back on the job market. She had spent all summer searching. It's not easy for a woman with an MS in Electrical Engineering, but who hasn't been employed in ten years, to find an appropriate job. Opportunities came up. She simply turned them down, holding out in hopes of something better. So when September came around, and she took a break from the search to take care of some 'spring' cleaning, she found herself inexplicably prone to the sorts of September daydreams that she always imagined plagued little boys and trapped housewives of a different social class.

What did she daydream about? Mainly travel. Gray mountains, deep river dales and lush valleys, sandy deserts—the sort of places her family would never go. She daydreamed about people, too: tall, shadowy men that served her in bars and cafes, European women with dirtied boots and designer bags.

She slowed down the dark SUV as she turned on to her street, thinking about smoky cafes and the murmur of foreign languages. Her daughter had been missing for twenty-four hours and her father was buried in the ground.

Before dying suddenly, her father had grown into a hard man. Her childhood memories of him were quite different: large hands tossing and catching her, a steady smile as he handed her a popsicle at the beach, tears in his eyes and a tremor in his flabby throat as he sent her off to college. But Leonard Stern had not aged well, and by the time he died he was a different person: cancer-ridden, angry, and religious. He had his heart set on making a pilgrimage to Israel.

"That's something Muslims do," she had told him, "not Jews. They go to Mecca."

"I don't give a damn what Muslims do," he had responded. "Fuck it. I'll *move* to Israel."

"Don't move to Israel."

"It's a place where Jewish life has meaning, Ally. I could plant trees. Beautiful pomegranate trees. Over here we're living in emptiness."

"Don't move to Israel. They're soldiers and psychopaths."

"At least they have something to fight for."

She couldn't think about it. She had to find her daughter.

She called school and the parents of Rebecca's friends. She called the cops. She should've called them a day ago. She called her husband and took three Benadryl and fell asleep on the living room couch.

Four hours later, her daughter was still missing. So when she spotted Jonathan Stein, a neighborhood college kid working shirtless on the deck of the house next door, she instinctively stopped her car. She had heard rumors that his mother died along with an adopted brother, and that he had been forced to withdraw from Santa Clara University.

She called out and asked him if he had seen a girl in the neighborhood. He pulled on a shirt and approached, saying he hadn't. They talked for a moment, and Allison mentioned that her father passed away. He had a listlessness in his dark eyes and Allison wanted to see if he would do her the favor.

"Can I do something to help?"

Allison smiled at him. "You have no idea how much that would help, Jonathan. I'm on my way to my brother's right now, but afterwards why don't you drop by our house. It's the one right next door—I'll need help searching the neighborhood, just for an hour, that's all."

"Okay, sure." He nodded and Allison lit a cigarette, a bad habit of her daydreaming weeks.

In the rearview mirror, Jonathan Stein tore off his shirt and went back to ripping up the rotting deck.

Allison wasn't going to the police, but rather to her younger brother's. First, she checked in with Matthew at home. He seemed content to eat Cheetos and watch cartoons. She told him to not make any trouble and that she'd been back in an hour.

In some ways, Allison preferred her brother Michael before his transformation. She thought about it as she exited the highway towards Marin. Of course, she didn't want him to overdose and die, but since he had gotten his life together, he had developed a frustrating sense of self-righteousness. She knew that however *he* was handling their father's death was the right way, and however *she* was handling it was wrong. But she had promised that she would come for a cup of coffee.

"Matt's fine at home?" he asked as he opened the door. He looked taller and tanner than ever. She hugged him and smiled at the welcome mat and potted plants. He lived in a small house with his girlfriend Tracey, a woman exactly his age and with a supreme moral upbringing.

"I'm not staying long," she said.

"Are you doing okay?"

"Tracey's out?"

"Still at work. Are you doing okay?"

He was making coffee at the stove. Allison sat down at the kitchen counter and watched his back, already fatigued. She was glad that he didn't have any art in the house, nothing tacky. There were only potted plants and a cornucopia of apples.

He turned and gave her a mug and raised an eyebrow. "Well?"

She shrugged and flicked the ceramic. "Are you going to deal with selling the house?" she asked.

"Tracey and I will deal with the house," he said. "I know you're occupied at the moment. Do you have any idea where she went?"

"Not for the life of me," Allison said. "It's because she's upset about Dad, she loved him so much. The kids love whoever gives them treats, and my father made them plenty over the years. S'mores, quesadillas, fluff and peanut butter sandwiches... He told them stories that made them laugh until they choked. Becca's upset and needed space to herself, and now she's lost. The only question is where."

Michael nodded, listening with great attention. He took a moment to sip his coffee.

"Children are volatile," he said. "There could be more than meets the eye. Is everything okay with her in school?"

Allison grimaced. "No, no, you don't get it. She's great in school. There's nothing else to it."

Michael said nothing, but Allison saw the movement in his eyes—a silent expression of mistrust. Sometimes the way Michael treated her made her feel like a lunatic. As if I were crazy! she thought. If I had the guts to show you crazy. How did it turn out this way? How am I so traumatized, while you made it out without a scratch? Because nowadays she couldn't stop thinking about it. All the deaths felt connected at once. Thinking about her father meant thinking about David. And Uncle Rubin and everyone else.

"Look, Michael, I don't want to be a burden. I should go home to check on Matthew—"

"Are you upset with me, Al?" he asked mildly.

"Michael, our father just died, and my daughter is missing. I'm upset in general."

"I wish I could make you feel better," he said.

"And I wish I derived more comfort from your presence."

His frown somehow widened. "Al, I don't mean to do this to you. Does this have something to do with Tracey?"

"Tracey, are you kidding me? It's not Tracey—" Allison paused and shook her head. Michael could wear her down, so quickly. She sighed. Of course, she didn't like Tracey—Tracey was too neat, too ordinary, a sweet Jewish girl from New Jersey who worked in real estate, more than happy to be a part of the family. "Michael, I haven't treated you well recently. Some day we can go travel together, like we always wanted to do with David, and we can relax and do what we want, and talk about old times and see new sights. For now, please just take care of the house and the funeral, and the cops will call any minute about Rebecca."

Michael nodded. "I understand." For a second Allison saw a flash of vulnerability as he took an extra swallow after a gulp of coffee. "To be honest, I can't stop thinking about Dad, either. You should be with Matt."

Allison watched his long nose and still-dark curls dip down towards the mug. She felt a pulse of warmth. Nothing gets me like a little male vulnerability, she thought. She put a hand on Michael's shoulder. "I think the problem," she said, "is that Dad wouldn't have wanted us to stop and think about him. He would've wanted us to move on, to say goodbye and get the hell on with our lives. But you and I aren't like that. Not even Lawrence. David is the only one who could've managed it, and he's twenty years dead. So I think Dad's corpse can get by with us grieving a little." She tried to smile and almost choked on tears that were breaking free. "After all, he managed to keep us together in California, didn't he? And without him being so goddamn stubborn, I wouldn't have someone to give me a cup of coffee while I wait to hear back from the cops about my daughter that's run away." She squeezed his shoulder, squeezed the tears back into her eyes, cleared their dishes, washed them, and departed with a wave.

She cried the whole way home. She had said the right things. It was good for her to remember that he was still her little brother, just a kid that built a fortress of faux maturity after nearly losing himself to drugs.

But nothing had changed. David was still dead, her father had never gone to Israel, nothing was forgotten, and nobody was redeemed.

She wondered about Jonathan Stein, who had promised to come help. What was that about? She couldn't help but to wonder about his life—his own losses. Maybe he was depressed. Maybe he was insane. It's not normal for a twenty-one-year-old kid to get forced out of school, to tear up suburban decks and wander around the neighborhood like a phantom. She had been seeing him all over her neighborhood, wandering like a monk, eyes narrowed like a spy's, often shirtless and muscled, hulking. When she arrived home and walked in the back door, she shrieked. Jonathan was there, this time wearing a shirt, but in front of him on the carpeted living room floor—Matthew and Rebecca.

"Rebecca! Becca, oh my! What—Jonathan, what? Oh, Rebecca, what have you done?" Allison sputtered and cried and hugged her daughter and shook her. Rebecca grumbled and pushed her mother away. Allison apologized to Jonathan and called the police and her husband and hugged and shook her daughter again. She told Jonathan not to leave, she had to thank him, at least let her make him dinner and a drink. So she brought her children and Jonathan into the kitchen to hear the story as she put a chicken in the oven and poured two glasses of wine.

Allison didn't register much. The details didn't matter, and the story didn't make much sense in the first place. Jonathan said he had come to her house and asked Matt to lend him a hand. Matt told Jonathan that Rebecca had gone down a secret well to a tunnel that led to Japan so she could meet her cousin Kaori, currently in the hospital with pneumonia. ("You told *him?*" shrieked Becca, giving her brother a whack on the head. "Hey, you've seen his paintings!" Matt protested. "He paints good! He's a good guy!") Matt led Jonathan to the well, an old, abandoned thing in the brush behind a neighbor's yard. They went down it and found Becca hiding at the bottom, who reluctantly agreed to come back home with them.

"One of their games," Allison said. "Becca's spent a lot of time in the neighborhood so I'm sure she's managed to find all sorts of things." She turned to Jonathan. "I really can't thank you enough. I know Becca's been upset ever since my father passed—"

"That's not it!" Becca roared from the corner. Her voice was strong and wrought with fury, trembling with resonance beyond her age. "*Kaori is dying!* What don't you understand?"

"She's in the hospital, Becca, and she'll be better soon." Allison deflated with exhaustion and glanced at Jonathan. "I'm sure you understand."

"I understand," he said quietly. "My mom died of cancer when I was about her age. So I understand."

Allison touched his hand. "I'm sorry, Jonathan."

The food was ready. As Jonathan ate the roasted chicken and some greens, Allison found herself telling him about her family. How she also painted from time to time. How her husband was a lawyer, and her older brother was in Japan, a script translator. "And my father, he was one of those Jews in the movie business," she said. "A big deal, and he married into an old-money California family. I used to want to travel Europe like my cousins on my mother's side. Dad never wanted me to, said the old world had nothing for us. But he's gone now." She paused. "I'm sorry about your mother, so young too. I lost my brother when I was about your age." Jonathan glanced up from the food. "He died of AIDS—this was back in the 80s, when it was brand new. It was terrifying, watching his body turn into a living skeleton drained of life and strength. He was the one who wanted to travel with me, even though Dad didn't want *me* going out there." She took a sip of wine. "What about you, Jonathan? Do you want to travel the world?"

"I've always wanted to go to Eastern Europe," he said. "Where my family comes from. I want to meet the woman who saved my grandfather during the Holocaust."

So, you're a ghost, Allison thought. We're all ghosts.

"I hear it's beautiful there," she said.

"And Australia," he added.

She watched him finish the food and a second glass of a wine. For a depressed and surly kid, he had sensitivity—he was full of love. She sensed that he had never really fit in. It allowed her to separate him from his age, and she shuddered as she realized that it was a pulse of attraction, almost erotic, fluttering in her throat. So what? she asked herself. He's young and beautiful, it's only natural. He's clearly dying for company, so why should she deny him it?

Evening had darkened into night. Allison offered him more wine and put the kids to bed. Jonathan stood with a wince, as if he couldn't bare to leave. Allison watched him stretch and start to turn.

"Allison," he said, "thanks for everything. Thank you."

She stepped across the kitchen towards him. "I just don't know how to thank you."

"You've done more than enough."

Jonathan was staring at her. Allison knew what he wanted. She saw his eyes trace her pupils and her irises, her lips, and down, and back up her body. *My body, at my age.* How did he know? How would a twenty-one-year-old know that a married woman would, in this instance alone and never before or after in her life, be mad and willing?

Allison took his hand.

They kissed. She shivered at his taste. He tasted like the red wine he had been drinking—nothing more. He was young and pure, as bare as the desert. That's how she knew he was too young. But there was no stopping it now.

The kissing quickened, deepened. First, she was kissing him, but soon it was him kissing her, her skin and her clothes and her jewelry. Jonathan pressed her head to his neck and their bodies together. His hands were strong and made her buckle against him, tremble against the pressure of hot, long kisses. Before long they were in bed and Allison above him in her underwear. And from that place above, aroused and yet distant, floating, as if a thin glass screen prevented their bodies from ever truly touching, she saw him start to tremble.

"I want to give you something," Jonathan said.

"What?" she whispered.

His pants were draped over the edge of the bed. He reached into the near pocket and pulled something out.

Allison fell off of Jonathan, off the bed.

Impossible!

"What's wrong?" Jonathan asked.

Allison tried to calm her breathing.

"Where did you get that?"

Jonathan looked up at her, unmoving, underwear a great bulge, legs under the covers and stomach, chest and head exposed. He held the bracelet in two hands above his mouth. The gold coin swayed gently, a faint darkness in the dark. She could almost make out its scorched letters in his throat, the forever engraved *CALIFORNIA.*

"I don't remember," he whispered.

"Why did you want to give it to me?" she asked. She raced away from him to the mirror, dressing, fixing her hair. She had to stay calm.

Jonathan's voice came out cracked. "I just—wanted to. You needed love. I wanted to love you."

SHUT THE FUCK UP she wanted to scream. His words nearly swept her legs out from under her.

"Get dressed and go to the kitchen," Allison said. "Make yourself coffee if you want."

She stood still. She breathed.

She waited for him to sit up and put on clothes. She breathed.

She sat on her bed while she heard his footsteps and the running sink.

She breathed.

And when she started to smell the coffee, she stood and went into the kitchen.

They sat at the kitchen table, as they had been sitting before. Allison made sure to not look at him too closely. She needed to make him a prop, something that she had used improperly and needed to put away with care. She had to pretend that he was nothing in particular, just some misspelled word, and that the bracelet was a dream.

When Allison glanced at him, he was looking at a small painting of a flower on the wall above the refrigerator, that she had done some ten years ago.

"Did you paint that?" he asked.

"A long time ago."

"Did you want to be an artist?"

She wanted to laugh. Did he like to imagine her as a trapped artist? Bitter tongs of self-hatred prodded her. She thought about David.

"Is it a dandelion?" he asked.

She didn't remember and had to look at the painting. "I'm not sure," she said.

"There were dandelions," he said. "Down by the well where I found Becca. There were dandelions inside the well, too, underground. But that wasn't all." He paused. "The ground had disappeared beneath my feet. I went diving down like heavy rain, and the sound of rushing water filled my ears. I was part of a waterfall. A waterfall of faces. A thousand, or a million or more. They were like ghosts, but they weren't. They were frozen and their bodies were made of frozen light, but they moved like water. I saw my mother."

Allison waited a while. When he didn't continue, she glanced at him. Don't you think it's strange? she wanted to say. Dandelions don't belong underground. What else could there have been? But he seemed to have closed into a shell, perhaps permanently.

Nervous, she began to speak.

"That bracelet did belong to me, you know. It belonged to my brother, I should say. So, thank you for bringing it back, but I don't want it anymore. Twenty years ago, after he died, my brothers went on a camping trip in the desert, and they lost it. Or maybe they left it on purpose. Either way, we knew we didn't want it anymore, so the three of us agreed to leave it there, missing in the desert. And now my crazy uncle, a historian, wants to go find it, so I've given him the old notebook, which I should've burned..." She stopped, realizing that Jonathan had no idea what she was talking about, but she had already stirred up her heart, her breath, shocked herself, stabbed herself, overwhelmed by the memory of truth, horrible, horrible truth, the horrible truth of what Uncle Rubin had done, how horrible that David had still worn it for three years! Uncle Rubin, the insane vigilante, who had gone traipsing across the country with the bracelet, who believed that he himself was the sword of God, and delivered the bracelet to those unto whom he would soon deliver the curse of death. Beads of sweat swam along her forehead and water droplets crawled into the corners of her eyes and she remembered tearing out pages from the old notebook and handing it over to Andy Wessel, a curious and enigmatic collector of all mysterious historical objects. Was he still searching for the poisoned apple? Why had she been too afraid to tell him what had happened? The truth would've been safer—why do we lie? Because the truth is violent? Because the truth is part of a story that is better off already over? Because the truth *is* the lie? How could she fear the bracelet? Just looking at it made her heart well with hatred. She wanted to seize Jonathan by the throat and drag him back into her bedroom—but no, no, no, no! Allison gasped and looked down at her open palms.

"How it possibly could have ended up in your hands..."

Jonathan said nothing. The sole yellow light from across the room deepened the creases in his shirt and muscled arms into vast shadows, condensed him into a shadowed cavern. He looked petrified in amber. She had succeeded. He no longer possessed volition. He was dead.

"Why don't you go home, Jonathan?" she said. "Take the bracelet and sell it, or even better, throw it away. It's getting really late and I'm so sorry for keeping you this long."

He stood up and left.

Allison never saw him again.

Seven years later, Allison Rosen will see the obituary of Jonathan Stein in the *Chestnut Creek Jewish Times.*

A few months after that, her daughter will call her on the phone.

She will not expect the call. Allison will have already resolved to fly to Boston and chase her children down. Warren will be in Santa Monica. She will have had this feeling twice before.

The first time, when her brothers came out of Joshua Tree, empty handed. The second time, when Jonathan Stein came out of a well of dandelions, pockets full.

Allison Rosen will open her mouth. She will tell her daughter a family story that comes out of her mouth and recolors all other stories, swallows them whole, reshapes stories, remakes stories, murders them, buries them, and gives them new life.

27

David

To Sam

I love you
I love you like a man
I love you like a brother
I love you like a flower
I love you like an egg
I want to give the world to you
I want to give my life to you
And if the world is yours then let me sleep in your bed
On the next page is a song we danced together
Charly wrote it
We may have died but Charly lives forever and in his lines we dance like eagles in the sky

Samba
The swallow makes a summer
Theme

28

La Lune

(The station wagon laid upon the northbound road, between the forest and the sea; Ellen steering its course; the dusty tail of twisted exhaust slowly unwinding from a large roll of it lodged in the bosom of the engine.)

Hineini. I took my voice to end of the world and offered it there for a burnt-offering: I didn't speak a word the whole way to Lunenberg Isle. We passed craggy seacoast pine trees and heavy clouds formed along the slick of a storm. We crossed the border and tidy Canadian highway towns, farmer's stands, soggy marsh, berry brush, orange grass, barns, flocks of geese and crows. Three loons over a river and the shadow of a moose's antlers in the gap between slanted trees. My eyes closed and I woke up on the bump of Becca's shoulder. Ellen was driving; the girl was tireless.

Becca and Kaori dreamed the same dream last night, a dream of the moon. According to Ellen, Lunenberg Island was a fishing island in Nova Scotia. Another dream, another clue, and I almost couldn't believe them or in any dreams at all. *Maybe the tide took the bracelet there. It's our duty to see this this through,* Becca had said. She was living as if she was in a poem, where things have symbolic meanings. Things like a bracelet, like a letter. Things have their meanings, and this is what she really believed in—a correspondence between people and things. She believed that things do not exist without people to perceive them, so every thing has a related person or experience.

This tendency explained why she wasn't upset when we lost the folder of Grampa Andy and Rubin Yakovlev's notes, because the mission they inspired would live on in me. That's why she wasn't upset when we lost Kaori's letters, because she would soon experience that relationship in the flesh. Human motives and objects dissolve into each other, objects survive in a state of becoming. But we're prisoners and slaves, voices of the dead and despairing. It's like there's thread connecting the stars, except there isn't. I disagree with Becca. A rock's a punk-ass, stony stern rock, and a tree's a tree. The work for life is to make that rock *more* of a rock, not less. I don't think anything will ever replace that folder, or those letters. When we close our eyes the world doesn't disappear. Even when we sleep, some fiber of our consciousness feels the earth murmuring on its track around the sun, and it jars us and makes us dream. And even when we die the world and all its voices echo, and its waves roll on.

It is not a story to pass on. I say this now because the neatness of our story, our journey—the quest for one object and one alone—had lulled us like a sea-born masthead into complacency and dependency, a dependence on symbols, metaphors, and meaning, and of course omens. These were the things that drove us to the island of the moon. These were the things that destroyed our identity. They took a leather bracelet in our hands for a perfect representation of the Star of David, or the myriad stars of the American flag. But there is no life, no personhood in you, you bracelet, most evil object in the entire world—why couldn't Becca see?

I couldn't shake it. It rattled me every waking and dreaming moment: what our whole family knew about the bracelet. About Uncle Rubin. How Rubin Yakovlev found it, gave it away, stole it, lost, bargained for it, killed for it. Again. And again. Again. And again.

How Uncle Rubin died and David wore it, how it disappeared in the desert never to be seen again. How somehow after 1982, it must have reanimated itself from the lifeless sands, found and taken to Ricardo Diaz, Asher, Ramiz, Adam Gersbach, Jim Castle, Ellen Reed, and finally the sea, floating towards the *La Lune*.

Who then is Cowboy Jim? Why then, did our uncle never get arrested? How then, did this secret survive despite the trail of blood it left behind? That dripping trail, the brim of the hat we thought belonged to a cowboy belonged to a Jew, a man in our family, the reaper of death entwined in our blood. None of it could be real, perhaps she had not told us all the story, the car AC chilled my shoulders and one by one the world became shadows and in the partial darkness I saw the form of Rubin tall and in a yarmulke under a dripping tree, other forms were near, the hosts of the dead, those that him of our blood had destroyed, gray and impalpable and dwindling like the bracelet in the sea. The object of our family's savior was mired in senseless violence. We are unmasked and unhooded. It is not a story to pass on. We will perish under its weight. No wonder it killed Rubin and David and disappeared in the dead dead desert where dandelions will never bloom. But what if it was a lie? All we had to rely on were her words, not even written down in Hebrew in a notebook with some semblance of concreteness and historicism, they were just words in the wind, air in Hua-Jin's *xun* blown in the attic, air in Will's mic screamed in the basement. Remember, Matt, this is nothing but a story! It does not live—not even on a page! Only in my heart! Her words were nothing and yet everything, and my life is made out of floating words, my thoughts had to move past them. Becca said, *It's our duty to see this through.* Did Becca think we could somehow right the wrong by finding it? It made me want to laugh, I wanted to laugh and laugh and laugh. This is not a story to pass on. Grampa Andy, the fool, collected Rubin Yakovlev's notes and traipsed around the country in search of clues, unaware that Mom had held the bracelet in her own two hands, and that even if he were to bring it back it would be a horrible curse. A man on a pointless quest, and he died on a ski trip—it's hysterical, really it's hysterical!

So I said nothing for seven hours all the way to Lunenberg Isle, the moon high over the grizzled pines even in brightness of afternoon. Ellen was a wild driver, twenty over the limit and hugging the road's curves like elastic. Ellen asked Kaori about Japan, and Becca about the bracelet. They talked forever, they kept talking. Ellen let them choose the songs back and forth, and Becca put on 90s pop and Kaori a CD of Japanese ballads she found in a record store in Salem and hardcore rock and big-band jazz. And eventually Ellen told us what happened to her on the day she lost the bracelet:

(The curtain opens to reveal a desolate beach. Winds knock the dune grass left and right. Ellen removes her shoes.)

ELLEN REED

(Tragically, deeply sad.) ... *(Removes her shoes.)*

THE ATLANTIC OCEAN

(In all its churning, restless majesty.) Come to me, darling. Forget your grandfather, playing old Beatles records on a loop even though he can't stand John Lennon. Forget Evan, the boy who loves you for no reason and whose older brother fucked you from behind.

ELLEN REED

(Diagnosed with Waardenburg Syndrome, hearing loss, and clinical depression.) .... *(Walks into the ocean. The waves cherish her and saltwater pours into her body.)*

THE BRACELET

(Falls off Ellen's wrist.).................. *(Ellen, floating like a balloon, unable to drown, falls back onto the shore.)*

ELLEN REED

(Still depressed, but now, also, angry.) Fuck! *(Digs a hole in the sand and sits in it. Later, Evan, the boy who loves her, arrives in a putt-putt-putting Jeep and takes her home.)*

I could see them on the beach, Ellen and Evan-the-boy-who-loves-her, one comforting another. I felt a surge of envy for this boy, that he was able to be there for her. It's not that he was there for *her*, it's that he was able to be there for anyone because I still hadn't done anything for anyone, although others did plenty for me. *Becca,* I wanted to say, *I just realized something. What is it,* she would say. *Out of all the stories of the bracelet we've seen, not a single one of them has been about love.* And Becca would look at me: *You're wrong,* she would say, *All of them. Every single one,* she would say, but I didn't, and she didn't. How wonderful it would be to love someone, to comfort someone, to lick their wounds, to taste their blood, to do anything without ambition, without murder, without a hundred years of history. I wanted to love! I wanted to love, to love, to know the answer but never say it because putting it into words destroys the meaning.

But instead, I could only hate. I hated it all and I've destroyed it all by saying it all—persistent Becca, my lying mom, my idiot dad, murderous Uncle Rubin, pointless Grampa Andy, even Kaori who gets to have dreams, why are my dreams as dull as charcoal?—faint as mist?—I don't think I've ever had a real dream in my life except for this whole journey that I just need to wake up from...

The vegetation shrunk, got shrubby. The rain picked up, relaxed. Sunset and dusk came on, blinding glare on the street signs and copper-tipped pine needles. After we got off the highway, Ellen rolled all the windows down and played music I'd never heard before, a high-pitched male voice agonizing over lost loves and broken dreams, punching guitars and a wandering bass. I hated him too. He sounded like Will if he was better and made it big. Ellen sang softly, hitting every note, but I didn't hate her—wet wind filled my ears and nose and I watched the curve of her neck and her gray hair flutter and Chelsea's dark hair in math class—could that really have been in this lifetime?

(Creeak——shh.)

"There's a ferry here." Ellen parked the car.

(Thud. Thud. Thud. Thud. And the rain got heavier and the dusk
grew and a frosty light within held four small figures
slanted through a town with no buildings, pebble-paved,
dune-guttered, crossed by a red lighthouse
and a pier with the ferry—Sh, sh.)

"This is Quoddy. It's just a layover. Lunenberg Isle... well, let's just see when we get there. We need to wait for the ferry." We stood looking out at the harbor.

(Wshhhhhh! S-s-s-s-.

And on the final 8:00 ferry, the only passengers, they crossed

over to La Lune as rain leapt up on the greenish-gray

surface of the ocean like millions of flying fish.)

"Are you okay? You're pale as a ghost!"

"No, I can barely breathe..."

"Hey, it's raining."

(Khi-r-r-r-rf! S-s-s-s-.

Becca held seasick Kaori's hand while Ellen stood on the edge

of the small boat, overlooking the water.

Shadows in the waves stirred,

and a golden cloud of birds filled the sky.)

Ellen in the water...

She should've drowned and died, but she didn't.

I realized that this was the most significant fact in the entire universe. That when one girl should've died, the waves wouldn't let her.

Yet these things must happen every day... every day people who should die don't... yes, they must they must..........

And the ferry pulled into a dock as the storm picked up. Lunenberg Isle was small, a round basket in an ocean glimmering with greenish foam, refusing to reflect the steel sky; instead the ocean was up above, its ripples in the clouds, its tides in waves of rain. Just weather, *just weather?*—but so much more than that.

Is that me up there? Matthew Rosen, sixteen year-old resident of Chestnut Creek and Pine Woods High, future cross-country superstar and Stanford recruit? Who crossed the country, sought a historic prize, and went head-to-head with the devil?

Or future suicidal Santa Clara dropout who left nothing behind but a few nice paintings?

And we arrived on the southeast corner, a half-dozen barns with gardens and grazing fields for skinny cattle, and a dozen other buildings: houses, warehouses, a general store, a sailor's inn. Ellen mentioned that the island was a port of landing for Danes, and then the British, but that the population of permanent residents nowadays was no higher than sixty-five and almost entirely Sikh. The streets were dirt turning quickly into mud. After getting off the ferry, we ran to hide beneath the tin awning of the nearest warehouse.

Is that me up there? Matthew Rosen? *Am I mine?*

I spoke my own words for the first time since we started driving, feeling my voice like a bird in my throat:

"Now what?"

"The only people here are sailors," Ellen said. "And they'll all be at the inn."

"Then let's go there," Becca said.

"We can ask if anyone has come across the bracelet," Kaori said.

"We'll have to try," Becca said.

I followed the girls to the inn and we ate dinner at dirty table in a dim room. A dozen sailors drank at the bar, and another dozen at other tables. We were served by a young, brown-skinned man in a turban. He was friendly and brought us fried fish and potatoes. I watched him hurry to the kitchen. How did he get here? Was it him? His parents? His grandparents, or his great-grandparents, like me? And why? Why *here*? Why Brooklyn for Ariana Fuchs? California for Grampa Leo? Grampa Leo must've seen some appeal in California, the Golden State, even though the gold was long dug up. The sun rises over Lunenberg Isle, island of the moon, home to black swans, beavers, and sailors, and sets over groovy Cali, home to hippies, homeless surfers, and Google HQ.

"This is it," Becca said, digging into her fish. "We can't go further east than this."

Kaori smiled. "I never thought I'd end up in Canada. That's two countries in one trip. Not bad, right?"

The crisp, golden fry melted in my mouth.

"These sailors could take us farther, you know," Ellen said.

What a joke. My laughter tasted like fried fish. "No, they wouldn't really do that."

Ellen shrugged. "It's rural Canada. People are friendly."

After we ate, Becca called over a sailor, a tall, red-bearded guy with blue eyes. She apologized, and asked the one and only thing that was ever left to ask:

"I know this is a strange question, but does anyone around here have a leather bracelet with a gold coin attached? Or did you see a bracelet like that at all?"

"Leather bracelet, huh?" He chuckled. "Matter of fact, yes. Some ass bragging about his luck at the horse races boarded a big transport vessel headed cross the Atlantic. He had a bracelet with a gold coin that he claimed was sure as hell a lucky charm. Even the older crew were pleased, seeing they hadn't seen a good luck coin in ages. Not that anyone puts stock in old sailor's superstitions—they used to not even look redheads like myself in the eye before setting sail, but I'm on board without complaints."

To the end, Roger Emersen's universal spirit was on our side. Hearing the words from the sailor's mouth filled me with a sort of strength. Good words, plain words, true words. In the past, I would've cast a judgment on his little story, brief as it was—I would've considered the braggart and his bracelet a blessing or a curse, perhaps the devious work of Cowboy Jim, likely to sink the ship or worse. But now I felt neutral. It was just another event in a long, heavy history. A history that I could end.

I could get the bracelet now. I could wrest it from the sailor *now*, rip it apart with a knife and throw it into the sea *now*. My life had conspired towards this moment. No one would know, but silent shining ripples would cross a country and planet cured of the bracelet's curse. My runner's legs were twitching.

"We need to go," I said to Becca. I looked at the sailor. "Is the ship still here?"

"It was supposed to leave before, but they were waiting for the storm to pass. They were heading out from east harbor, just up the street to the left—"

It was all I needed to know. It was my chance to end it all.

"Where—"

"Matt!"

"*Matthew!*"

I bolted out of the inn into a roaring downpour, soaking me completely as I raced to the pier. My socks weighed down and my shoes filled with water. Rain matted my hair and turned me to a sopping slug squishing down the muddy streets. Thick white fog obscured the harbor and I couldn't see if there were any ships so I ran out onto the dock, I had to catch the ship but I also had to slow down in the heavy mist so I didn't go flying off the edge into the water and drown in Ellen's place.

Step by step the fog unfurled, revealing strips of weathered wood, barnacled dock legs, spats of dark sea and grimy foam and little white bubbles. I passed through layers of mist like digging through muck, crossing border after border until I was no longer on this earth. I wasn't afraid. Cowboy Jim, dead. Rubin Yakovlev and Grampa Andy, dead. Christine, Chelsea, Will, Grandmother, Mom, Dad, Uncle Michael—thousands of miles away. Even Becca and Kaori weren't close to where I stood, on the verge of the world. When I reached the edge of the dock and saw nothing but thick swaths of white like strokes from a painter's brush, and dragons of gray waves arching their backs and washing away, I understood that I had failed.

There was no ship in the harbor. The bracelet had set sail.

I scratched my head and caught my breath.

Just my luck. The bracelet was out to sea, headed all the way across the Atlantic. Now the bracelet would live on, causing suffering and joy for poor Irishmen in hats and German girls that go clubbing six nights a week. But even Irishmen in hats and German party chicks die no matter what, so if there could be one Ellen—one person who should've died but doesn't—then it might be worth it—wouldn't it?

I was at the edge of the dock and could go no further. I had to accept that I lost. I had to accept that I was powerless.

At first, throbbing anxiety filled me. But after a minute, I began to wonder: what if I could go farther? What if I *could* have a dream?

If I had a dream, this is what it would look like.

One step into the sea: I shake the hands, one by one, of everyone I met on the road trip, and thank them for their help. Maybe Ellen would smile at me, and I sock that muscly baseball kid in the mouth because he creeped on my sister. Oh, and I take the surly kid from Pyramid Lake that was fucking with his scabs to a punk show in San Fran and eat like a hundred tacos, because I feel like he would dig that, and so would I. Ankle-deep in the sea.

Two steps—I hug Kaori tight. Knowing her, however briefly, has been a wonderful thing. In my dream I go to Japan to visit her and win a spicy ramen eating contest and climb Mt. Fuji. We speak Japanese for hours, and English sometimes, when I'm tired. Thigh-deep.

Three—I hug Becca even tighter. In my dream she plays "You've Got A Friend In Me" on the ukulele and I cry. In a way, we have failed, but in this way we have succeeded: the bracelet is at the least gone from the American continent, away from our family and friends. We chased it away. When I'm a lawyer like Dad but one that actually helps people and have three kids and Becca has two we take them all skiing in Tahoe and force Mom and Dad to learn how to ski and we misremember everything about the road trip. Becca thinks that Kaori was with us when we almost drowned in the Delaware River and I'm convinced that Mark Jones had a box of jumbo dildos that he showed us. Belly-button-deep.

Four, five, six—I move across the ocean, in the growing storm and slashing winds. In my dream I pass Grampa Leo and Rubin Yakovlev, and Grampa Andy hollers out the window of his trans-Siberian train, moments before its implosion. Grampa Andy can't stop laughing when we tell him that our family had the bracelet all along, and he admits that he knew it too—he was just trying to get us out of the house and off those darn screens! And in my dream Rubin Yakovlev isn't sorry for the murders he committed, claiming that he's just an unhappy man in the grips of a violent history, and that many more were killed in the founding of the State of Israel. I won't ever forgive him, but I can't pretend like he's not a part of my family. Shoulder deep.

Seven, eight, nine, ten, and eleven—as I rush across the gray-green waves I meet and have pleasant, leisurely conversations with everyone I have never met who has been touched by the bracelet and all their souls resting among the scuttling crabs and gargling flounder and we all drink and play cards and dance in a desert saloon, presided over by the American kings of jazz, because in America we love music and we dance. Water and wind opens up my ribcage and bears my heart to a mouthful of salt, a handful of dust, and I swallow it all. The whole earth loves me in my dream. I live with cats and dogs and lizards and squirrels and a big beautiful garden with red tomatoes and lumpy autumn gourds in my dream. I pick flowers in my dream. Picking flowers? Neck-deep. Breathe deep and close mouth, close eyes.

From there, things are easy. I withdraw into the vastness of the sea, and long blue fingers take me. I leave America behind and follow the sailor's ship and a glittering spire of whale spout all the way to Europe, where there are a thousand leather bracelets with Spanish coins in Iberia alone. Even after Europe I keep going and one day I arrive in Japan, where people still have dreams about it all.

And that's where the dream ends. It ends with other people having dreams. So the dream goes on and on, it never ends. Do you get it? It's kinda kitschy, but a cynical Jew with taste like myself will call pretty much anything kitschy.

"We were too late, huh?"

I turned around. Becca and Kaori came out of the mist and walked to the edge of the dock. Becca came next to me. Droplets of water spiked her cheeks and nose.

"Yeah," I said. "Of course we were."

She put a hand on my arm and turned to face the mist. "Well, we can't do anything else about it at this point. The sailor said that ship's going all the way to Ireland."

"Next summer," I said automatically. "Let's go to Ireland."

"Ooh, how lovely!" exclaimed Kaori.

But Becca stared at me with her mouth agape. Her eyes boiled with a catastrophically volcanic hell glance. No, *worse* than a hell glance—that shit burnt a hole in my fucking forehead, it's the fiercest and most molten magma mashing glower I ever had the misfortune to bear witness to, as if God's judgment of the idol-worshiping Israelites condensed into a flash of boiling light, rending the earth to shredded beef.

"Are you joking? *Ireland!*" She looked away and laughed. "No *fucking* way am I going to Ireland with you next summer. *Hell fucking no.* Fuck that. Fuck that times fifty."

She smiled and shook her head. The weight of the rain stretched her curly hair into thin, dark wires. Beside her, Kaori looked over at me and smiled, her lips communicating something like *you Americans sure do love that word.*

"No," Becca said. "Next summer, we're going rafting in the Cascades, or camping at Joshua Tree, and that is the farthest we are going. Believe me."

I believed her. After that summer, I never saw anything like the bracelet again, not in my lifetime. Maybe you have in yours. Maybe not. I believe you, either way.

Matthew Rosen
California
2005

Three Sterns

A's

The Golden State

THE GOLDEN STATE

BY E. DION MARGOLIS AMERICAN JEW B. 1996 OAKLAND CALIFORNIA

THE GOLDEN
STATE
MATT AND BECCA'S SUMMER
ROAD TRIP THROUGH HELL

Acknowledgments

Gersham Johnson

Mom & Dad

Saho Yushita

Amy Hungerford

Susan Choi

Calvin Baker

Caryl Phillips

Peter Cole

Marci Shore

Joseph Bondi

Amanda Yang

Richard U. Light

William and Miriam Horowitz

David and Iris Fischer

The Zolot family

Ariel Losar - illustrations

Shinya Kondo - *The swallow makes a summer*

of course, Daniel & Benji

& Lucy

Sources

Aarons, Victoria. *A Measure of Memory*

Alter, Robert. *Defenses of the Imagination*

American Race Riots 1919 Collection (Yale University Archive)

The Arcosanti Project

The Elizabeth Harris Papers (Yale University Archive)

Emerson, Ralph Waldo. "Nature"

Freedman, Jonathan. *Klezmer America*

Freedman, Jonathan. *The Temple of Culture*

Hungerford, Amy. *The Holocaust of Texts*

Kehillat Israel Glossary of Yiddish Words and Phrases

Morrison, Toni. *Beloved*

McWhirter, Cameron. *Red Summer: The Awakening of Black America*

"No Spectators": Burning Man at the Smithsonian

North, Michael. *Dialect of Modernism*

Northern Paiute Language Project

Roth, Henry. *Call It Sleep*

Rothberg, Michael. *Multidirectional Memory*

Wirth-Nesher, Hana. *Call It English*

US Arizona Relocation War Authority (Yale University Archive)

Dreams - An Essay

I don't think we talk enough about dreams.

Each one of us has a different relationship with our dreams. Lately, my dreams fall into one of two categories: high fantasy, and high banality. A few nights ago, I had this vivid dream where me and my two brothers were trapped underground in a vast crystal cavern and each of us were assigned to slaughter a sacred ox. Uncomfortable with slaughtering my ox, I attempted to trick the examiner with a combination of a slippery tongue and rudimentary hypnotism, which failed, because (as it turned out), the examiner was Anubis in disguise, and turned to make the ox to slaughter me instead, by which point my brothers, who had successfully slaughtered their respective oxen, grabbed me under my arms and pulled me on a motorbike into the Martian desert where the oxen are raised and roam—and I woke up.

The following night, I dreamed that my high school friends and I were sitting in math class. And I woke up.

So for me nowadays, dreams have more to do with amusement than reality or the future or the subconscious or the waking connection or anything else. This is not the case for my girlfriend, who tends to have more relevant dreams that affect her day-to-day.

"I'm so mad at you," she told me. "I dreamed that you cheated on me again. It was terrible."

"Who did I cheat on you with this time?" I asked.

"It was some random girl. You ran away with her to Russia. I couldn't believe it I was so mad. I'm still mad."

"That's not fair," I said.

"Maybe you shouldn't have cheated on me, then."

"But I didn't!"

"Yeah, but you did in my dream."

For better or worse, dreams, like fiction, affect our reality. I've consumed a lot of fiction. Reading *On The Road* and experiencing the god is Poo Bear dancing fireworks over the Mexican desert and the Frisco fog when I was fifteen years old made me understand that I didn't have to follow the path in life that I felt like the world had set out for me—a reliable hike through college, on to law school, adulthood, horrible things, probably divorce, misery and pain, death, etcetera. Playing *The Legend of Zelda: Breath of the Wild* was such a genuinely euphoric experience that I remember the cold February days I spent on a couch, eyes glued to a television screen, navigating a green-hooded hero through high mountains and treacherous shrines as some of the most profound and thrilling of my twenty-five years. (Don't ask if I'm proud of this.) Reading Henry Roth's *Call It Sleep* in college illuminated the unbelievable and yet obvious reality that different languages pose different modes of being, and that the form of objects and ideas can accordingly construct different constitutions of thought—"so art *does* have meaning!" I realized loudly in front of all of my classmates and friends and people I would have liked to impress.

I have been quite sure of the reality of fantasy for some time. I attempted to write a novel, *The Lady of the Fountain*, at age eighteen, that proved this. The story was about a widowed seamstress in eighteenth century Wales who became a (metaphorical) goddess and saved her town from a (possibly metaphorical) drought when she encountered ancient Druidic legends that came to life (probably metaphorically). Not to brag, but I remember my creative writing teacher being confused *and* impressed.

In fact, recent research suggests that fiction may be the essential human quality that allowed the prehistoric *homo sapiens* to evolve into, well, us. In order to organize on the level of a town, city, ethnic group, nation, or globe, humans need to understand and believe in fictions such as mythology, religion, identity, history, economics, law, ethics, and so on. Thus in a sense, human reality in itself is fictive.

But all I need to be sure of to feel gratified in my 18-year old self's literary hypothesis is that fiction and fantasy are a part of reality because they affect the way we behave. This isn't about deeply ingrained fictions, like the concept of economics, or morality, but simply about stories. Like *Call It Sleep.* Like dreams.

Since I could remember anything—the taste of crisp autumn leaves in my first few months on the east coast at three years old—I've had three dreams that have not just become my reality, but have formed an essential part of it.

The first dream happened when I was very young. Maybe four years old. It's one of my earliest memories. My younger brother had been born recently. We were at the pool, and he had fallen in. He was drowning. He was a baby, still in a diaper. But he was in the pool, and drowning, and no one was helping, and I couldn't do anything. I was standing right there, next to the pool. But nothing was happening. I woke up when he hit the bottom.

My brother drowning was the first dream that scarred me.

The second dream happened when I was five or six. I stood in my grandparents' house—but not my grandparents' real house. In the dream, I knew that the house was Mom-mom and Pop-pop's house, but when I woke up, I realized that the houses were different. There were similarities: my mom's parents live in a large, stone house with corridors and dens and offices, and the house in the dream was an exaggerated version of this. There was a parlor straight out of *Twin Peaks* with a scorching-crimson velvet carpet. A long, stone stairwell hung over a spacious entryway. I crept through the house, in search of someone, maybe Pop-pop, or my mom. I came across a garden, through the kitchens, into a furtive office. I woke up somewhere along the way of realizing that I could not escape from this fictive trap house.

I felt curious and confused when I woke up. It was a fantastic, fabulous house. I remembered some of exquisite treats, not unlike those I actually did experience at Mom-mom and Pop-pop's: candy in the cabinets, closets full of puffy coats, sculptures in the corners, long corridors to explore. But everything in the dream was *fake.* No specific detail matched anything in my grandparents' actual house.

This was the first dream I had that conflicted with my concept of reality in a genuine way. It was a 100% real experience...but of course, it was not by any means real. I often remember that time when I got lost in my grandparents' house, only to have to remind myself a few minutes later that, of course, that was all a dream. It was the first dream in which I had to grapple with its meaning. When the outcome was not a simple emotion—fear, or longing, or happiness—but the urge to interrogate my own consciousness and understand the world and myself.

The third dream was by far the most thrilling dream I've ever had. I was seventeen. The dream was *Harry Potter*, *The Lord of the Rings*, and *The Wizard of Oz* combined and given a heavy dose of Adderall. In a single night, I soared through an entire fantasy plot. A cohort of evil witches oppressed my clan. We gathered clues, enhanced our abilities. We traveled across a desolate wasteland of crags and chasms. We sought the power of flight. We negotiated with the evil witches, and then we fought them. At first, we failed. But we lifted each other up. We taught each other special powers, deep, native powers of water, fire, and earth, and cast new spells that shocked each other with our own growth and capabilities. Sometime before I woke up, the witches unveiled a shocking devious trap that could devastate us all, but I never witnessed the conclusion. I was already awake.

It's not surprising that I would have a dream like this. I love fantasy. I read most of the notable kids' and adult fantasy series you could list, and loved them all. The schematic worlds of *Pendragon*. The scheming characters of *Game of Thrones*. I wrote many incomplete fantasy books all throughout my childhood and I continue to do so today. But what is surprising is that I would remember this dream so well. Not just that I had it, but that I can still see the greenish wasteland and recall the nervous thrill of flight, the pressure mounting and the dire stakes. The unity of my clan against all odds. This experience stuck with me. I lived through the dream as a genuine experience, and the emotions continued to ripple in my heart and mind after I awoke. It was a dream of triumph. Even if the witches possessed powers that we never would, it was a triumph of my own imagination, and final proof to me that fiction mattered. My whizzing seventeen-year-old brain fully constructed the world I had always longed for.

This was the first dream that I accepted as a genuine experience.

Three dreams that I'll never forget. A dream that made me feel real emotion.

A dream that made me interrogate my behavior in the "real" world. And a dream that, finally, totally, was real.

Of course, we don't talk to other people about our real dreams.

It would make us sound crazy. I think my girlfriend is crazy when she's mad at me for cheating on her in a dream. As necessary as it is for us to quarantine our dreams and live as if they never happen, it's a disappointing flaw in the ability of humans to connect with one another.

This isn't always the case. I've always embraced the dreams of one of my best college friends, mostly because they're so hilarious. Nothing made me happier than receiving a text mid-way through an economics lecture: "i had a strange dream with Frank from Everybody Loves Raymond, an Aretha Franklin/The Police duet, and Wobi Han: Queen of Handjobs."

I texted him back immediately: "Were there events in this dream??"

"there were a few events that i can't fully remember, but there was a scandal because they found a cellphone video of someone getting a handjob from Wobi; i think it was a politician."

Another time: "the sting/aretha duet was pretty lit. it was like super soulful vocals but over an Every Breath You Take sort of track. plus some groovy bass playing."

A third: "people dressed in red on a train going through a forest filled with The Unhappy. The only way to drive away The Unhappy was to play music."

I'm quite sure that music is for my friend is what fantasy is for me. I'm grateful that I can accept his dreams as a part of the reality of our friendship. Most of our friendship consists of conversations, anyhow, the greatest of human fictions. Fluffy as air, conversations never touch the ground, stir even a pebble. But they remain in hearts. We talked about which Beatle is best. Foucault and Adorno. The strange behavior of a friend that suddenly seemed determined to ignore us. How our suitemates changed and didn't over the years. Why certain times of years move faster than others. The dreams we had were no different from any of these other topics. They were truly, wonderfully real.

Does my dream of battling witches, or my experiences living out on the road with Jack Kerouac compare to the gut-punching force of reality? For example, the way I felt when I stepped out on to the coast of Yokosuka this spring, witness to the enormous cargo ships heaving on the pure blue waves, dozens of hawks whirling and screeching in the heavy winds overhead, with the greenest tangle and romp trees that I had ever seen in a horah behind me, and a sparkling sun, and a sprinkle of salt in the air, and the purest sense of discovery that one of the verges of the world was in fact this wondrous and glorious and mighty and true? Or the times I fell in love, in the misty rain in a park, rushing through a floating ocean to unload my feelings, and outside a car by a lake, cold autumn winds whipping around the dusk, gripped by disbelief at the discovery that my heart could once more ache and throb the way it did?

Maybe not. But even these 'real' experiences have fictions that are integral to them, and should we really grade experiences based on their relative significance in the first place? Classification and grading is yet another real human fiction, after all. But maybe all of the real and fictive things only become *really* real when they surpass the ability to be contained within the limits of our fictive terms.

It was a fiction that helped me overcome my fear of death.

Whenever I start to remember the overwhelming brutality and absolute nature of death, the thought that calms me is one that I learned from *Avatar the Last Airbender.* Well, a combination of Walt Whitman and *Avatar the Last Airbender:* That each action we take has an effect on the world, and therefore, we are immortal:

"And what I assume you shall assume / For every atom belonging to me as good belongs to you."

The world would not have turned out the way it did if we hadn't passed through it. Even stepping on a spear of grass in the summertime has such an irrevocable, spectacular series of ripple effects on the totality of the universe that I could still convince myself that I was immortal if it were the only thing I ever did. Much less talk to thousands of people, speak millions of words, try and fail several hundred times, go many places, leave dozens of objects behind, clean several places up, make a few friends. The human propensity to ravage the environment and heat up the earth is scientific proof of this fact.

Dreams and reality are one and the same. I love people who don't hide their dreams. Who embrace them. Who talk about them. Because dreams do matter. Not because they unveil our inner psyches, or display of Freudian urges for all to see. But because they are real in themselves.

Dreams are like human beings. Vanishing, always. But simply by passing through our minds—just as we pass through this Earth—they leave a footprint that can never be erased.

My dreams are to me as I am to the world: fantastically, irrevocably real, whether or not I, or the world, acknowledges them.

My dreams therefore prove my own immortality, as foolish of a fiction the notion may be.

Eric Dion Margolis

Nagoya, 2022

About the Author

Eric Dion Margolis was born in Oakland, California in 1996 and grew up outside of Philadelphia. He graduated from Yale after majoring in English and studying in Japan. He is a writer, journalist, and translator from Japanese currently living in Nagoya. Some matters of interest: piano, snowboarding, sea breeze, Pokémon, the times of year when you switch from hot coffee to iced and vice versa, and not dying in the climate apocalypse. He will write another novel some day, and until then you should follow him on Twitter.

You can connect with me on:

- https://twitter.com/ericdmargolis

Made in United States
North Haven, CT
30 March 2022